Rich Relatives

by Compton MacKenzie

ISBN-13: 978-1518604768

Table of Contents

CHAPTER ONE 3

CHAPTER TWO 12

CHAPTER THREE 18

CHAPTER FOUR 27

CHAPTER FIVE 37

CHAPTER SIX 46

CHAPTER SEVEN 54

CHAPTER EIGHT 62

CHAPTER NINE 68

CHAPTER TEN 73

CHAPTER ELEVEN 80

CHAPTER TWELVE 84

Chapter One

IT may have been that the porter at York railway station was irritated by Sunday duty, or it may have been that the outward signs of wealth in his client were not conspicuous; whatever the cause, he spoke rudely to her.

Yet Jasmine Grant was not a figure that ought to have aroused the insolence of a porter, even if he *was* on Sunday duty. To be sure, her black clothes were not fashionable; and a journey from the South of Italy to the North of England, having obliterated what slight pretensions to cut they might once have possessed, had left her definitely draggled. Although the news of having to wait nearly five hours for the train to Spaborough had brought tears of disappointment into her eyes, and although the appeal of tears had been spoilt by their being rubbed off with the back of a dusty glove, Jasmine's beauty was there all the time—a dark, Southern beauty of jetty lashes curling away from brown eyes starry-hearted; a slim Southern charm of sunburnt, boyish hands. Something she had of a young cypress in moonlight, something of a violoncello, with that voice as deep as her eyes. But for the porter she was only something of a nuisance, and when she began to lament again the long wait he broke in as rudely as before:

"Now it's not a bit of good you nagging at me, miss. If the 4.42 goes at 4.42, I can't make it go before 4.42, can I?"

Then perhaps the thought of his own daughters at home, or perhaps the comforting intuition that there would be shrimps for tea at the close of this weary day, stirred his better nature.

"Why don't you take a little mouch round the walls? That's what people mostly does who get stuck in York. They mouch round the walls if it's fine, like it is, and if it's raining they mouch round the Minster. And I've known people, I have, who've actually come to York to mouch round the walls, so you needn't be so aggravated at having to see them whether you like it or not, as you might say. And now," he concluded, "I suppose the next thing is you'll want to put your luggage in the cloak-room!"

He spoke with a sense of sacrilege, as if Jasmine had suggested laying her luggage on the high altar of the Minster.

"Well, that means me having to go and get a truck," he grumbled, "because the cloak-room's at the other end of the station from what we are here."

The poor girl was already well aware of the vastness of York railway station, a vastness that was accentuated by its emptiness on this fine Sunday afternoon. Fresh tears brimmed over her lids; and as in mighty limestone caverns stalagmites drop upon the explorer, so now from the remote roof of glass and iron a smutty drop descended upon Jasmine's nose.

"Come far, have you?" asked the porter, with this display of kindly interest apologizing as it were for the behaviour of the station's roof.

"Italy."

"Organland, eh?"

The thought of Italy turned his mind toward music, and he went whistling off to fetch a truck, leaving his client beside a heap of luggage that seemed an intrusion on the Sabbath peace of the railway station.

From anyone except porters or touring actors accustomed all their lives to the infinite variations of human luggage, Jasmine's collection, which alternately in the eyes of its owner appeared much too large and much too small, too pretentious and too insignificant, too defiant and too pathetic, might have won more than a passing regard. But since the sparse frequenters of the station were all either porters or actors, nobody looked twice at the leather portmanteau stamped SHOLTO GRANT, at the hold-all of carpet-bagging worked in a design of the Paschal Lamb, at the two narrow wooden crates labelled with permits to export modern works of art from Italy, or at a decrepit basket of fruit covered with vine leaves and tied up with bunches of tricoloured ribbon; and as for the owner, she was by this time so hopelessly bedraggled by the effort of bringing this luggage from the island of Sirene to the city of York only to find that there was no train on to Spaborough for five hours that nobody looked twice at her.

Somewhere outside in the sheepish sunlight of England an engine screamed with delight at having escaped from the station; somewhere deep in the dust-eclipsed station a retriever howled each time he managed to wind his chain round the pillar to which it was attached. Then a luggage train ran down a dulcimer scale of jolts until it finally rumbled away into silence like the inside of a hungry giant before he falls asleep; after which there was no sound of anything except the dripping of condensed steam from the roof to the platform. Jasmine began to wonder if there would ever be another train to anywhere this Sunday, and if the porter intended to leave her alone with her luggage on the platform until to-morrow morning. Everything in England was so different from what she had been accustomed to all her life; people behaved here with such rudeness and such evident dislike of being troubled that perhaps ... but her apprehensions were interrupted by the whining of the porter's truck, which he pushed before him like a truant child being thumped homeward by its mother. The luggage was put on the truck, and the porter, cheered by the noise he was making, broke into a vivacious narrative, of which Jasmine did not understand a single word until he stopped before the door of the cloak-room and was able to enunciate this last sentence without the accompaniment of unoiled wheels:

"...and which, of course, made it very uncomfortable for her through her being related to them."

At the moment the difficulty of persuading a surly cloak-room clerk, even more indignant than the porter at being made to work on Sunday afternoon, that the two crates were lawful luggage for passengers, prevented Jasmine's attempting to trace the origin of the porter's last remark; but when she was blinking in the sunlight outside the station preparatory to her promenade of the walls of York, it recurred to her, and its appropriateness to her own situation made her regret that she had not heard more about *Her* and *Them*. Was not she herself feeling so uncomfortable on account of her relationship to *Them*, so miserable rather that if another obstacle arose in her path she would turn back and ... yes, wicked though the thought undoubtedly was, and imperil though it might her soul should she die before it was absolved ... yes, indeed she really would turn back and drown herself in that *puzzo nero* they called the English Channel. Here she was searching for a wall in a city that looked as large as Naples. Well, if she did not find it, she would accept her failure as an omen that fate desired her withdrawal from life. But no sooner had Jasmine walked a short way from the station than she found that the wall was ubiquitous, and that she would apparently be unable to proceed anywhere in York without walking on it; so she turned aside down a narrow passage, climbed a short flight of steps, and without thinking any more of suicide she achieved that prospect of the city which had been so highly recommended by the porter.

It was the midday Sabbath hour, when the bells at last were silent; and since it was fine August weather, the sky had achieved a watery and pious blue like a nun's eyes. Before her and behind her the river of the wall flowed through a champaign of roofs from which towers and spires rose like trees; but more interesting to Jasmine's lonely mood were the small back gardens immediately below the parapet on either side, from which the faintly acrid perfume of late summer flowers came up mingled with beefy smells from the various windows of the small houses beyond, where the shadowy inmates were eating their Sunday dinners. She felt that if this were Italy a friendly hand would be beckoning to her from one of those windows an invitation to join the party, and it was with another grudge against England that she sat down alone on a municipal bench to eat from a triangular cardboard box six triangular ham sandwiches. The restless alchemy of nature had set to work to change the essences of the container and the contents, so that the sandwiches tasted more like cardboard and the cardboard felt more like sandwiches; no doubt it would even have tasted more like sandwiches if Jasmine had eaten the box, which she might easily have done, for her taste had been blunted by the long journey, and she would have chewed ambrosia as mechanically had ambrosia been offered to her. The sandwiches finished, she ate half a dozen plums, the stones of which dropped on the path and joined the stones of other plums eaten by other people on the same bench that morning. Jasmine's mind went swooping back over the journey, past the bright azure lakes of Savoy, past the stiff and splendid *carabinieri* at the frontier, pausing for a moment to play hide-and-seek with olives and sea through the tunnels of the *riviera di levante* ... and then swooped down, down more swiftly until it reached the island of Sirene, from which it had been torn not yet four full days ago; the while Jasmine's foot was arranging the plum stones and a few loose pebbles into first an S and then an I and then a decrepit R, until they exhausted themselves over an absurdly elongated E.

The weathercock of the nearest church steeple found enough wind on this hot afternoon to indicate waveringly that what wind there was blew from the South. Some lines of Christina Rossetti often quoted by her father expressed, as only remembered poetry and remembered scents can, the inexpressible:

To see no more the country half my own,
Nor hear the half-familiar speech,
Amen, I say; I turn to that bleak North
Whence I came forth—
The South lies out of reach.
But when our swallows fly back to the South,
To the sweet South, to the sweet South,
The tears may come again into my eyes,
On the old wise,
And the sweet name to my mouth.

She evoked the last occasion at which she had heard her father murmur these lines. They had been dining on the terrace until the last rays of a crimson sunset had faded into a deep starry dusk. Mr. Cazenove had been dining with them, and from the street below a mandolin had decorated with some simple tune memories of bygone years. The two old friends had talked of the lovely peasant girls that haunted the Sirene of their youth, a Sirene not yet spoiled by tourists; an island that in such reminiscence became fabulous like the island of Prospero.

"But the loveliest of them all was Gelsomina," Mr. Cazenove had declared. Jasmine was thrilled when she could listen to such tales about her mother's beauty, that mother who lived for herself only as a figure in one of her father's landscapes, whose image for herself was merged in a bunch of red roses, so that even to this day, by dwelling on that elusive recollection of childhood, the touch of a red rose was the touch of a human cheek, and she could never see one without a thought of kisses.

"Yes, indeed she was! The loveliest of them all," Mr. Cazenove had repeated.

Her father had responded with these lines of Christina Rossetti, and she knew that he was thinking of a fatal journey to England, when the unparagoned Gelsomina had caught cold and died in Paris of pneumonia on the way North to attend the death of Grandfather Grant.

And now her father was dead too.

In a flood of woeful recollections the incidents of that fatal day last month overwhelmed her. She felt her heart quicken again with terror; she saw again the countenance of the fisherman who came with Mr. Cazenove to tell her that a squall had capsized the little cutter in the Bay of Salerno, and that the only one drowned was her father. Everybody in Sirene had been sympathetic, and everybody had bewailed her being alone in the world until letters had arrived from uncles and aunts in England to assure her that she should be looked after by them; and then nearly everybody had insisted that she must leave the island as soon as possible and take advantage of their offers. Yet here she was, more utterly alone than ever in this remote city of the North, with only a few letters from people whom she had never seen and for whom she felt that she should never have the least affection. She was penitent as soon as this confession had been wrung from her soul, and penitently she felt in her bag for the letters from the various relatives who had written to assure her that she was not as much alone in the world as this Sunday in York was making her believe.

Among these envelopes there was one that by its size and stiffness and sharp edges always insisted on being read first. There was a crest on the flap and a crest above the address on the blue notepaper.

317 Harley Street, W.,
July 29th.

My dear Jasmine,

Your Uncle Hector and I have decided that it would be best for you to leave Italy at once. Even if your father's finances had left you independent, we should never have consented to your staying on by yourself in such a place as Sirene. Your uncle was astonished that you should even contemplate such a course of action, but as it is, without a penny, you yourself must surely see the impossibility of remaining there. Your plan of teaching English to the natives sounds to me ridiculous, and your plan of teaching Italian to English visitors equally ridiculous. I once had an Italian woman of excellent family to read Dante with Lettice and Pamela during some Easter holidays we once spent in Florence, and I distinctly remember that her bill after three weeks was something under a sovereign. At the time I remember it struck me as extremely moderate, but I did not then suppose that a niece of mine would one day seriously contemplate earning a living by such teaching. No, the proper course for you is to come to England at once. Your uncle has received a letter from the lawyer (written, by the way, in most excellent English, a proof that if the local residents wish to learn English they can do so already) to say that when the furniture, books, and clothes belonging to your father have been sold, there will probably be enough to pay his debts, and I know it will be a great satisfaction to you to feel that. The cost of your journey to England your Uncle Hector is anxious to pay himself, and the lawyer has been instructed to make the necessary arrangement about your ticket. You will travel second class as far as London, and from London to Spaborough, where we shall be spending August, you had better travel third. The lawyer will be sent enough money to telegraph what day we may expect you. Grant, Strathspey House, Spaborough, is sufficient address. We have had a great family council about your future, and I know you will be touched to hear how anxious all your uncles and aunts have been to help you. But your Uncle Hector has decided that for the present at any rate you had better remain with us. How lucky it is that you should be arriving just when we shall be in a bracing seaside place like Spaborough, for after all these years in the South you must be sadly in need of a little really good air. Besides, you will find us all in holiday mood, just what you require after the sad times through which you have passed. Later on, when we go back to town, I daresay I shall be able to find many little ways in which you can be useful to me, for naturally we do not wish you to feel that we are encouraging you to be lazy, merely because we do not happen to approve of your setting up for yourself as a teacher of languages. By the way, your uncle is not Dr. Grant any longer. Indeed he hasn't been Dr. Grant for a long time. Didn't your father tell you even when he was knighted? But he is now a baronet, and you should write to him as Sir Hector Grant, Bt. Not Bart. Your uncle dislikes the abbreviation Bart. And to me, of course, as Lady Grant, not Mrs. Grant.

Love from us all,
Your affectionate
Aunt May.

The few tears that Jasmine let fall upon the blue notepaper were swallowed up in the rivulets of the watermark. Although she was on her way to meet this uncle and aunt and to be received by them as one of the family, she felt more lonely than ever, and hurriedly laying the envelope beside her on the bench, she dipped into the bag for another letter.

The Cedars,
North End Road,
Hampstead,
July 22nd.

Dear Jasmine,

I had intended to write you before on the part of Uncle Eneas and myself to say how shocked we were at the thought of your being left all alone in the world. Your Aunt May writes to me that for the present at any rate you will be with her, which will be very nice for you, because the honour which has just been paid to the family by making your Uncle Hector a baronet will naturally entail a certain amount of extra entertaining. I am only afraid that after such a merry household The Cedars will seem very dull, but Uncle Eneas has a lot of interesting stories about the Near East, and if you are fond of cats you will have plenty to do. We are great cat people, and I shall be glad to have someone with me who is really fond of them, as I hope you are. It is quite the country where we live in Hampstead, and the air is most bracing, as no doubt you know. I wonder if you ever studied massage?

Love from us both,
Your affectionate
Aunt Cuckoo.

Jasmine tried to remember what her father had said at different times about his second brother, but she could only recall that once in the middle of a conversation about Persian rugs he had said to Mr. Cazenove, "I have a brother in the East, poor chap," and that when Mr. Cazenove had asked him where, he had replied, "Constantinople or Jerusalem—some well-known place. He's in the consular service. Or he was." He had not seemed to be much interested in his brother's whereabouts or career. And then he had added meditatively, "He married a woman with a ridiculous name, poor creature. She was the daughter of somebody or other somewhere in the East." But her father was always vague like that about everything, and he always said "poor chap" about every man and "poor creature" about every woman. He had a kind and generous disposition, and therefore he felt everybody was to be pitied. Jasmine wished now that she had asked more about Uncle Eneas and Aunt Cuckoo. Cuckoo! Yes, it was a ridiculous name. Such a ridiculous name that it sounded as remote from reality as Rumplestiltzkin. No girl, however large the quantity of flax she must spin into gold before sunrise, could have guessed Aunt Cuckoo.

To-day I brew, to-morrow I bake,
And to-morrow the King's daughter I shall take,
For no one from wheresoever she came
Could guess that Aunt Cuckoo was my name.

Jasmine was feeling that she ought not to be laughing at her father's relatives like this so soon after he had died, when suddenly she woke up to the fact that they were just as much, even more, her relatives too. It was like waking up on Monday morning during the year in which she was sent to school with the Sisters of the Seven Dolours in Naples and could only come back to Sirene for the week-ends. With a shudder she placed Aunt Cuckoo on the bench and picked up Aunt Mildred.

23 The Crescent,
Curtain Wells,
July 20th.

My dear Jasmine,

Uncle Alec and I were terribly shocked to hear of your father's accident. Only a few weeks before I was suggesting a little visit to Rome, a place which Uncle Alec knows very well indeed, for he was military attaché there for six months in 1904, and was rather surprised that your father never took the trouble to come and visit him. Unfortunately, however, His Serene Highness was not well enough to make the journey this spring. Of course you know that for some time now Prince Adalbert of Pomerania has been living with us. You will like him so much when you pay us your visit. He is as simple as a child. We thought at first that he might be difficult to manage, but he has been no trouble and when the Grand Duke graciously entrusted his son to our keeping without an A.D.C., it was quite easy, because it left us a spare room. Baron Miltzen, the Chamberlain, runs over occasionally to see how the Prince is getting on, but the Grand Duchess, who never forgets that she was an English princess, prefers to make her younger son as English as possible, and will not allow any German doctors to interfere with the treatment prescribed by your Uncle Hector. Of course the poor boy will never be well enough to take an active part in the affairs of his country, and as he is not the heir, there is not much opposition in Pomerania to his being educated abroad. Indeed Baron Miltzen said to me only the last time he ran over that he thought an English education was probably the best in the world for anyone as simple as the dear Prince. If we cannot get away to the Riviera this winter you will have to pay us a visit and help to keep the Prince amused. We have dispensed with ceremony almost entirely, because we found that it excited the Prince too much. In fact it was finally decided to entrust him to us, because after the first levee he attended the poor fellow always wanted to walk backwards, and it took us quite a little time to cure him of this habit.

Love from us both,
Your affectionate
Aunt Mildred.

Indeed Jasmine had heard about the Prince, because her father always told everybody he met that one of his brothers had been fool enough to take charge of a royal lunatic. She remembered thinking that he seemed proud of the fact, and she could never understand why, particularly as he spoke so contemptuously of his brother's part in the association. "Here's pleasant news," her father used to say, "my brother the Colonel has turned himself into a court flunkey. That's a pretty position for a Grant! Yes, yes.... He's taken charge of Prince Adalbert of Pomerania, the second son of the Grand Duke of Pomerania. You remember, who married Princess Caroline, the Duke of Gloucester's third daughter? I'm ashamed of my brother. I suppose he had to accept, though; I know it's hard to get out of these things when you mix yourself up with royalty. I really believe that I'm the only independent member of the family—the only one who can call his life his own."

Jasmine quickly took out Aunt Ellen's letter, lest she should seem to be criticizing her dead father by thinking any more about Prince Adalbert.

The Deanery,
Silchester,
July 21st.

My dear Jasmine,

When your Uncle Arnold, wrote to you about your father's sad death, he forgot to add an invitation to come and stay with us later on. Now your Aunt May writes to me that it is definitely decided that you should come to England, and your six boy cousins are most eager to make your acquaintance. I say "boy" cousins, but alas! some of them are very much young men these days. I fear we are all growing old, though your poor father might have expected to live many more years if he had not been so imprudent. But even as a boy he was always catching cold through standing about sailing boats in the Round Pond when your grandfather was Vicar of St. Mary's, Kensington. However, we must not repine. God's wisdom is often hidden from us, and we must trust in His fatherly love. I wonder if you have learnt any typewriting? Uncle Arnold so dislikes continuous changes in his secretaries, and his work seems to increase every year. He only intended to do a short history of England before the Norman Conquest, but the more he goes on, the further he goes back, and if you were at all interested in Saxon life I do think it would be worth your while to see if you liked typewriting. Ethelred has been learning it in the morning instead of practising the piano, but he does not seem to want to make a great deal of progress. It's so difficult to understand what children want sometimes. I suppose our Heavenly Father feels the same about all of us. When I am tempted to blame Ethelred I remember this. Of course as a Roman Catholic you have not been taught a very great deal about God, but we are all His children, and you must not grieve too much over your loss. "Not lost but gone before," you must say to yourself. I remember you every night in my prayers.

Your loving
Aunt Ellen.

Jasmine was asking herself how to set about learning to typewrite, and making resolutions to check a faint inclination to regret that she had so many rich relatives anxious to help her, when the languid puffs of air from the South swelled suddenly into a real wind and blew all the paper on the bench up into the air and down again into one of the little back gardens below the parapet—all the paper, that is, except Lady Grant's blue envelope, which even a gale could scarcely have disturbed.

Jasmine, brought up in Sirene, was not accustomed to conceal her feelings in the way that a well-educated English girl would have known how to conceal them. The loss of the letters dismayed her, and she showed as much by climbing on the parapet of the wall and gazing down into the garden below.

At that moment a much freckled young man with what is called sandy hair came along, and without looking to see if he was observed immediately scrambled up beside her. Even a Sunday school teacher on his way to class might have been forgiven for doing as much; but this young man was evidently nothing of the kind. Indeed, with his grey flannel trousers and Norfolk jacket, he imparted to the atmosphere of Sunday a distinct whiff of the previous afternoon; standing up there beside Jasmine, he looked like a golfer who had lost his ball.

"What have you dropped? A hairpin?" he asked.

Jasmine could not help laughing at the notion of bothering about a hairpin, and she pointed to Mrs. Eneas Grant's letter nestling among the branches of a sunflower; to where Mrs. Alexander Grant's invitation to amuse Prince Adalbert of Pomerania twitched nervously on the neat gravel path; and to where Mrs. Lightbody's suggestions, ghostly and practical, clung for a moment to a drain-pipe, before they collapsed into what was left on a broken plate of the cat's dinner.

The twelve-foot drop into the garden below was nothing: the young man accomplished it with an enthusiastic absence of hesitation. To gather up the letters was the labour of a minute. But to get back again was impossible, because the owner of the house, disgusted by the untidiness of Roman and mediæval masonry, had repaired and pointed that portion of the wall which bounded his garden.

"There isn't one niche for your foot," murmured Jasmine, almost tenderly solicitous.

"I must ring the bell and borrow a ladder," said the stranger. After a moment's search he announced in an indignant voice that the house apparently did not possess a bell.

A man in shirt sleeves, interrupted at the second or third of his forty Sabbath winks, leaned out of an upper window and asked Jasmine what she thought she was doing jibbering and jabbering on his garden wall; before she had time to explain, he perceived the young man in the garden, and asked him what he thought he was doing havering and hovering about among his flowers.

"I was looking for the bell."

"Bell! You long-legged fool! What d'you think I should keep a bell in my back garden for, when the children won't let the bells in front have a moment's peace?" Then he made a noise like a dog shut in a door. "Ough! Take your great feet out of my petunias, can't you! If I want my flowers trampled on, I can get a steam-roller to do it. I don't want your help."

"This lady dropped something in your garden," the young man explained, and the owner smiled bitterly.

"Aye," he went on, "that's what they all say. Please, mister, our Amy's dropped her damned doll in your garden, can she come round and fetch it back? It's like living in a dustbin. A scandal, that's what I say it is. A public scandal."

Then began one of those long arguments in which people roused from sleep seem to delight, provided always that they have been sufficiently roused to feel that it is not worth while going to sleep again. What occurred to lead up to the trespass was swept away as having occurred while the owner was still asleep; no amount of explanation as to why the young man was in his back garden was of any avail; no suggestions as to how he was to get out of it had any effect; and the argument might have continued until the 4.42 train from York to Spaborough had left the station, if in some inner room a child's voice had not begun to sing to the accompaniment of a harmonium:

There is a green hill far away
Without a city wall

"Aye, you silly little fool, that's right! Sing that now! It's a pity your dad doesn't live on a green hill without a city wall, and not in York."

The young man, who by this time had been rendered as argumentative as the owner, remarked that 'without' meant 'outside.'

"What's it matter what it means, if there wasn't a city wall?" retorted the owner, and vanished from the window before the young man could reply. From inside one of the rooms there was a fresh murmur of argument, which lasted until a noise between a moan and a thud was followed by a silence faintly broken by sobs. The slamming down of the lid of the harmonium had evidently relieved the feelings of the man in shirt sleeves, for when presently he came out into the garden and found himself at close quarters with the intruder, he became genial and talkative, and began to point out the superiority of his dahlias.

"I reckon they're grand, I do," he said. "Like cauliflowers. Only, of course, cauliflowers wouldn't have the colour, would they?"

"Not if they were fresh," the young man agreed.

And then he began flatteringly to smell one of the dahlias. He seemed to be attributing to the flower as much importance as he would have attributed to a baby; it was easier to deal with a dahlia, because the dahlia did not dribble, although had it really been a baby, its mother would have been much more annoyed at its being smelt like this than was the man in shirt sleeves, who laughed and said:

"I wouldn't bother about the smell if I was you. Dahlia's don't have any smell. Size is what a dahlia's for."

"No, I was thinking it was a rose," the young man explained apologetically. The incident which had begun so rudely was ended, and except for the unseen child practising its little hymn, was ended harmoniously. The young man was taken through the house and conducted along the street as far as the next ingress to the walls. When he met Jasmine coming towards him, he felt as if he had known her for a long time, and that they were meeting like this by appointment.

"Well, that's finished," said the young man, after Jasmine had put the letters safely back in her bag. He eyed for a moment her black clothes.

"I suppose you're going to Sunday-school and all that?" he ventured.

"No, I'm just walking round the walls."

"Curious coincidence! So was I."

"Waiting for a train," she went on.

"Still more curious! So am I."

"Waiting for the 4.42."

"The final touch!" he cried. "So am I. Let's wait in unison."

They moved across to a circular bench set in an embrasure of the walls, overgrown here with ivy from which the sun drew forth a faint dusty scent. On this bench they sat down to exchange more coincidences. To begin with, they discovered that they were both going to Spaborough; soon afterward that they were both going to stay with uncles; and, as if this were not enough, that both these uncles were baronets, which even with the abnormal increase of baronets lately was, as the young man said, the most remarkable coincidence of all.

"And what's your name?" Jasmine asked.

"Harry."

She felt like somebody who had been offered as a present an object in which nothing but politeness had led her to express an interest.

"I meant your other name," she said quickly, rejecting as it were the offer of the more intimate first name.

"Vibart. My uncle is Sir John Vibart."

"Of course, how stupid of me," Jasmine murmured with a blush. "My name's Grant, of course," she hastened to add.

"Sir Hector Grant," the young man went on musingly. "Isn't he some kind of a doctor?"

"A nerve specialist," said Jasmine.

"I know," said the young man in accents that combined wisdom with sympathy.

The discovery of the baronets had removed the last trace of awkwardness which, easy though his manners were, was more perceptible in Mr. Vibart than in Jasmine, who in Sirene had never had much impressed upon her the sacred character of the introduction.

"I shall come and call on you at Spaborough," he vowed.

"Of course," she agreed; people called with much less excuse than this in Sirene.

"We might do some sailing."

She clapped her hands with such spontaneous pleasure of anticipation that Mr. Vibart remarked how easy it was to see that she had lived abroad. But almost before the echo of her pleasure had died away her eyes had filled with tears, for she was thinking how heartless it was of her to rejoice at the prospect of sailing when it was sailing that had caused her father's death. Anxious not to hurt Mr. Vibart's feelings, Jasmine began to explain breathlessly why she was looking so sad. The young man was silent for a minute when she stopped; then, weighing his words in solemn deliberation, he said:

"And, of course, that's why you're wearing black."

Jasmine nodded.

"I've brought with me all that were left of father's pictures. For presents, you know." She sighed.

"I know," said the young man wisely. He had in his own valise a cigar-holder for Sir John Vibart, the expense of procuring which he hoped would be more than covered by a parting cheque.

"And I should like to show them to you," Jasmine went on. "Perhaps we could get one out and look at it in the train."

"Hadn't we better wait until I come and call?" he suggested. "It's not fair to look at things in the train. Trains wobble so, don't they?"

9

Conversation about Sholto Grant's pictures passed easily into conversation about Jasmine's mother, because nearly all the pictures had been of her.

"She was a beautiful *contadina*, you know," Jasmine shyly told him.

Mr. Vibart, who supposed that her shyness was due to an attempt to avoid giving an impression of snobbishness in thus announcing the nobility of her ancestry, asked of what she was *contadina*. Jasmine, delighted at his mistake, laughed gaily.

"*Contadina* means country girl. Her name was Gelsomina, and she was the most beautiful girl in the island. Everybody wanted to paint her."

Mr. Vibart, struggling in the gulf between a baronet's niece and an artist's model had nothing to say, but he made up his mind to ask his uncle something about Italy. It was always difficult to find anything to talk about with the old gentleman; Italy as a topic ought to last through the better part of two bottles of Burgundy.

"And what's your name?" he asked at last.

"I was called after my mother."

"Oh, you were? Well, would you mind telling me your mother's name again, because I lost the last dozen letters?"

"Gelsomina—only I was always called Jasmine, which is the English for it."

As she spoke, all the bells in York began to ring at once, from the mastiff booming in York Minster to the rusty little cur yapping in a Methodist chapel close to where they were sitting, and with such gathering insistence in their clamour as to destroy the pleasure of these sunlit reminiscences.

"I suppose we ought to have a look at the Minster," Mr. Vibart suggested in the tone of voice in which he would have announced that he must open the door to a pertinacious caller. "Of course I'm not exactly dressed for Sunday afternoon service, but you're all right. Black's always all right for Sunday."

Jasmine's conception of going to church had nothing to do with dressing up, but it did seem to her extraordinary to go to church at this hour of the day. However, the evidence of the bells was unmistakable, and without a qualm she followed her companion's lead.

The strangeness of the hour for service was only matched by the strangeness of the congregation assembled for worship and the astonishing secularity of the interior. She could remember nothing as solemn and gloomy since she and her father had made a mistake in the time of the performance at the San Carlo Opera House in Naples and had arrived an hour early. She did not recognize the smell of immemorial respectability, and it almost choked her after the frank odours in the Duomo of Sirene—those frank odours of candles, perspiration, garlic, incense, and that indescribable smell which the skin of the newly peeled potato shares with the skin of the newly washed peasant. She did not think that the mighty organ, booming like a tempestuous midnight in Sirene, was anything but a reminder of the terrors of hell, and as a means of turning the mind toward heavenly contemplation she compared it most unfavourably with the love scenes of Verdi's operas that in Sirene provided a tremulous comment upon the mysteries being enacted at the altar. If there had been a sound of sobbing, she could have thought that she was attending a requiem; but, however melancholy the appearance of the worshipping women around, they were evidently enjoying themselves, and, what was surely the most extraordinary of all, actually taking part in the distant business of the priests, bobbing and whispering and mumbling as if they were priests themselves.

"I think I can smell dead bodies," said Jasmine to her companion.

Mr. Vibart was probably not a religious young man himself, but he had already affronted the religious sense of his neighbours by presenting himself before Almighty God in grey flannel trousers and a Norfolk jacket, and he was not anxious positively to flout it by letting Jasmine talk in church. People in the pews close at hand turned round to see what irreverent voice had interrupted their devotion, and Mr. Vibart tried to pretend that her remark had a religious bearing by offering her a share of his Prayer Book. This was too much for Jasmine. To stand up in front of the world holding half a book seemed to her as much an offence against church etiquette as when once long ago at school she had quarrelled with another little girl over the ownership of a rosary and they had tugged against each other until the rosary broke in a shower of tinkling shells upon the floor of the convent chapel.

The best solution of the situation was to go out, and out she went, followed by Mr. Vibart, who looked as uncomfortable as a man would look in leaving a stall in the middle of the row during Madame Butterfly's last song.

"I say, you know, you oughtn't to have done that," he murmured reproachfully.

"Done what?"

"Well, talked loudly like that, and then gone out in the middle of the service. Everybody stared at us like anything."

"Well, why did you joke with that Prayer Book?"

"I wasn't joking with the Prayer Book," Mr. Vibart affirmed in horror.

An emotion akin to dismay invaded Jasmine's soul. If she could so completely misunderstand this not at all alarming, this freckled and benevolent young man, how was she ever to understand her English relatives? She had been sufficiently depressed by England throughout the journey, but it was only now that she grasped what a profound difference it was going to make to be herself only half English. She was evidently going to misunderstand everything and everybody. Serious things were going to seem jokes, and, what was worse, real jokes would seem serious. She should offend with and in her turn be offended by trifles.

"I'm sorry," she said to Mr. Vibart. "You see, it was quite different from everything to which I've been accustomed all my life. Oh, do let's go and have an ice."

"Rather, if we can find a sweet-shop open."

Incomprehensible country, where ices were found in sweet-shops, and where sweet-shops were closed on Sunday! Jasmine gave it up. However, they did find a sweet-shop open, where she ate what tasted like a pat of butter frozen in an old box of soap, cost fourpence, and was called a vanilla ice-cream. She criticized it all the time she was eating it, and then found to her mortification that Mr. Vibart supposed that he should pay for it.

"In Sirene," Jasmine protested, "we all go and have ices when we have money, but we always pay for ourselves. And if I'd thought that you were going to pay, I should have pretended I thought it was very good."

The argument lasted a long time with illustrations and comparisons taken from life at Sirene, which were so vividly related that Mr. Vibart announced his intention of going there as soon as possible. Jasmine was so much gratified by her conversion of an Englishman that she surrendered about the payment for the ice, and when they got back to the station she allowed him to manage everything. It was certainly much easier. The surly cloak-room clerk handled the picture crates as tenderly as a child, and even said "upsi-daisy" when he delivered them back into their owner's possession. As for the porter with one hand he trundled his barrow along like a jolly hoop.

"I say, let's travel First," Mr. Vibart proposed, apparently the prey to a sudden and irresistible temptation towards extravagance.

"My ticket is third class," Jasmine objected.

"I know, so's mine," he said mysteriously. "But they know me on this line."

And by the way the porter and the cloak-room clerk and the guard and a small boy selling chocolates all smiled at him, Jasmine felt sure that he was telling the truth.

The journey from York to Spaborough took about two hours and a half, and the bloom of dusk lay everywhere on the green landscape before they arrived. For the first half Jasmine had been contented and gay, but now toward the end she fell into a pensive twilight mood, so that when at last Mr. Vibart broke the long silence by announcing "Next station is Spaborough" she was very near to weeping. She did not suppose that she should ever see again this companion of a few hours. She realized that she had served to while away for a time the boredom of his Sunday afternoon; but, of course, he would forget about her. Already with what a ruthlessly cheerful air he was reaching up to the rack for his luggage.

"What are those funny tools in that bag?" she asked.

"Those?" he laughed. "Those are golf clubs."

Jasmine looked no wiser.

"Haven't you ever played golf?"

"Is it a game?"

He nodded, and she sighed. How could a man who carried about with him on his travels a game be expected to remember herself? But it would never do for her to let him think that she considered his remembering her of the least importance one way or the other. Jasmine's knowledge of human nature was based upon the aphorisms in circulation among the young women of Sirene, few of which did not insist on the fact that to men the least eagerness in the opposite sex was distasteful. Jasmine had all the Latin love of a generalization, all the Latin distrust of the exception that tried its accuracy.

"I'll be very cold with him," she decided. But her coldness was tempered by sweetness, and if Mr. Vibart had ever tasted a really good ice-cream, he might have compared Jasmine with one when she said good-bye to him on the Spaborough platform.

"But isn't there anybody to meet you?" he asked, looking round.

"It doesn't matter. Please don't bother any more about me. I'm sure I've been enough of a bother already."

At that moment she caught sight of a chaise driven by a postilion in an orange jacket.

"Oh, I should like to ride in that!"

"But your people have probably sent a carriage."

"No, no!" Jasmine cried. "Let me ride in that," and before Mr. Vibart could persuade her to wait one minute while he enquired if any of the waiting motor-cars or carriages were intended for Miss Jasmine Grant, she had packed herself in and was waiting open-armed for the porter to pack her trunk in opposite.

"I shall see you again," Mr. Vibart prophesied confidently.

11

"Perhaps," she murmured. "Thank you for helping me at York. Drive to Strathspey House, South Parade," she told the postilion.

Then she blushed because she fancied that Mr. Vibart might suppose that she had called out the address so loudly for his benefit. She did not look round again, therefore, but watched the orange postilion jogging up and down in front, and the street lamps coming out one by one as the lamp-lighters went by with their long poles.

Chapter Two

THE origin of the house of Grant, like that of many another Scots family, is lost in the Scotch mists of antiquity. The particularly thick mist that obscured the origin of that branch of the family to which Jasmine belonged did not disperse until early in the nineteenth century, when the figure of James Grant, who began life nebulously as an under-gardener in the establishment of the sixth Duke of Ayr, emerged well-defined as a florist and nursery gardener in the Royal Borough of Kensington. The rhetorical questioning of the claims of aristocracy implied in the couplet:

When Adam delved, and Eve span
Who was then the gentleman?

was peculiarly appropriate to this branch, for Jamie, besides being a gardener himself, married the daughter of a Lancashire weaver called Jukes, who later on invented a loom and, what is more, profited by his talent. Although Jamie Grant's rapid rise was helped by the success of old Mr. Jukes' invention, he had enough talent of his own to take full advantage of the capital that his wife brought him on the death of her father; in fact by the year 1837 Jamie was as reputable as any florist in the United Kingdom. A legend in the family said that on the fine June morning when Archbishop Howley and Lord Chamberlain Conyngham rode from the death-bed of William IV at Windsor to announce to the little Princess in Kensington Palace her accession, the Archbishop begged a bunch of sweet peas for his royal mistress from old Jamie whose garden was close to the highway. If legend lied, then so did Jamie's son Andrew, who always declared that he was an eye-witness of the incident, and indeed ascribed to it his own successful career. Inasmuch as Andrew Grant died in the dignity of Lord Bishop Suffragan of Clapham, there is no reason to suppose that he was not speaking the truth. According to him the incident did not stop with the impulse of the loyal Archbishop to stand well with his queen on that sunny morning in June, but a few days later was turned into an event by Jamie's sending his son with another bunch of sweet peas to Lambeth Palace and asking his Grace to stand godfather to a splendid purple variety he had just raised. In these days when sweet peas that do not resemble the underclothing of cocottes without the scent are despised, the robust and strong-scented magenta *Archbishop Howley* no longer figures in catalogues; but at this period it was the finest sweet pea on the market. The Archbishop, who was a snob of the first water, liked the compliment; yes, and, anti-papist though he was, he did not object to the suggestion of episcopal violet in the dedication. He also liked young Andrew, and on finding that young Andrew wished to cultivate the True Vine instead of the Virginia creeper, he promised him his help and his patronage. James, who all his life had been applying the principle of selection to flowers, realizing that what could be done with sweet peas could be done equally well with human beings, gave Andrew his blessing, dipped into his wife's stocking, and contributed what was necessary to supplement the sizarship that shortly after this his son won at Trinity College, Cambridge.

Andrew Grant, during his career as a clergyman, was called upon to select with even more discrimination and rigour than his father before him. He had first to make up his mind that the Puseyite party was not going to oust the Evangelical party to which he had attached himself. He had later on to decide whether he should anathematize Darwin or uphold Bishop Colenso, a dilemma which he dodged by doing neither. He had also to choose a wife. He chose Martha Rouncivell, who brought him £1000 a year from slum rents in Sheffield and presented him with five children. Apart from the continual assertions of scurrilous High Church papers that he had ceased to believe in his Saviour, Andrew Grant's earthly life was mercifully free from the bitterness, the envy, and the disillusionment that wait upon success. His greatest grief was when the spiritual power that he fancied was perceptible in his youngest son Sholto, a spiritual power that might carry him to Canterbury itself, turned out to be nothing but an early manifestation of the artistic temperament. But that disappointment was mitigated by his consecration in 1890 as Lord Bishop Suffragan of Clapham, in which exalted rank he guarded London against the southerly onslaughts of Satan even as his brothers of Hampstead, Chelsea, and Bow were vigilant North, West, and East. It was a powerful alliance, for if the Bishop of Hampstead was High, the Bishop of Bow was Low, and if the Bishop of Chelsea was Broad, the Bishop of Clapham was Deep; although he preferred to characterize himself as Square.

When Archdeacon Grant was consecrated, he had to find a suitable episcopal residence, and this was not at all easy to find in South London. At last, however, he secured the long lease of a retired merchant's Gothic mansion on Lavender Hill, which after three years of fervid Lenten courses was secured to Holy Church by three appeals to the faithful rich. As soon as the Bishop was firmly installed in Bishop's House, he who had observed with displeasure the number of empty shields in the roll of Suffragan Bishops in Crockford's clergy list, applied for a grant of arms. He came from an old Scots family, and he felt strongly on the subject of coat-armour. When he first went up to Cambridge he had interested himself in heraldry to such purpose that he had been convinced of old Jamie's right to the three antique crowns of the House of Grant. And though the old boy said he should think more of three new half-crowns, he offered to use them as his trade-mark if Andrew really hankered after them. Andrew discouraged the proposed sacrilege, but all the way up from curate to vicar, from vicar to rural dean, from rural dean to archdeacon, from archdeacon to suffragan bishop, he did hanker after them, for the shadows of mighty ancestors loomed immense upon that impenetrable Scotch mist. When his eldest son was born, instead of calling him Matthew after his wife's brother, a safe candidate for future wealth, he called him Hector, because Hector was a fine old Scottish name, and most unevangelically he christened the three sons who followed Eneas, Alexander, and Sholto. When he became a bishop, he was more Caledonian than ever; perhaps the apron reminded him of the kilt. With his empty shield in Crockford's staring at him he went right out for the three antique crowns and applied to Lyon Court for a confirmation of these arms. His mortification may be imagined when he was informed that he was actually not armigerous at all, and that the coat which he proposed to wear, of course with a difference, was not his to wear. It was useless for the Bishop to claim, like Joseph, that the coat had been given to him by his father. The Reubens, Dans, and Naphtalis of the house of Grant were not going to put up with it; the three antique crowns were disallowed. For a while the Bishop pretended to exult in his empty shield. After all, he might hope to become a real bishop and contemplate one day the arms of the see against his name; in any case he felt that his mind should be occupied with a heavenly crown. But the ancestral ghosts haunted him; he could not bear the thought of Crockford's coming out year by year with that empty shield, and at last he applied for arms that should be all his own. On his suggestion Lyon granted him *Or, three chaplets of peaseblossom purpure, slipped and leaved vert;* but when for crest the Bishop demanded *A Bible displayed proper*, even that was disallowed, because another branch of the Grants had actually appropriated the Bible in the days of Queen Anne. "Then I will have the Book of Common Prayer displayed proper," said the Bishop. And the Book of Common Prayer he got, together with the Gaelic motto *Suas ni bruach*, which neither he nor his descendants ever learnt to pronounce properly, though they always understood that it meant something like *Excelsior*.

With such a motto it was not surprising that Sholto Grant's refusal to climb should upset his relations. Old Jamie must have dealt with many throwbacks when he was selecting his sweet peas; but it is improbable that any of them refused to climb at all, and though there is now a variety inappropriately called "Cupid" with scarcely more ambition than moss, these dwarfs have a commercial value. Sholto Grant had no commercial value. Sholto indeed had so little sense of profit that he actually failed to arrive in time to see his father die, and if the old gentleman's paternal instinct had not been much developed by his episcopate, and if he had not imbibed every evangelical maxim on the subject of forgiveness, he would probably have cut Sholto off with a shilling. As it was, he divided his money equally between his five children, and it can be readily imagined how indignant Hector, Eneas, and Alexander, who had all married well, had all worked hard to justify the family motto, and not one of whom could count on less than £2000 a year, felt on finding that the £20,000; which was all that the Bishop of Clapham's devotion to the Gospel had allowed him to leave to his family, was to be robbed of £4000 for Sholto, who had married an Italian peasant girl and spent his whole life painting unsaleable pictures in the island of Sirene. "Besides," as they acutely said, "Sholto does not appreciate money. He will only go and spend it." And spend it Sholto did, much to the disgust of his brothers, Sir Hector Grant, Bart., K.C.V.O., C.B.; Eneas Grant, Esq., C.M.G.; Lieutenant-Colonel Alexander Grant, D.S.O.; and even of his sister, Mrs. Arnold Lightbody, the wife of the Very Reverend the Dean of Silchester. Thus far had they climbed in the ten years that succeeded the Bishop of Clapham's death. Perhaps if they had reached such altitudes ten years before they might have been more willing to share with Sholto; but Dr. Grant of Harley Street, Mr. Grant of the Levant Consular Service, Captain Grant of the Duke of Edinburgh's Own Strathspey Highlanders (Banffshire Buffs), and Mrs. Lightbody, the wife of Canon Lightbody, were not far enough up the pea-sticks to neglect such a stimulus to growth as gold. Mrs. Hector, Mrs. Eneas, and Mrs. Alexander had their own grievance, for, as they reasonably asked, what had Sholto's wife contributed to the family ascent? They, who had followed the example set by Miss Jukes and Miss Rouncivell before them, were surely entitled to reproach the unendowed Gelsomina. It seemed so extraordinary too that a bishop should have nothing better to occupy a mind on the brink of eternity than speculating whether his youngest son would arrive in time to see him die. They had never yet observed the death of a prelate, but they could imagine well enough what it ought to be to know that a continental Bradshaw was not the book to prepare for a heavenly journey. And when a double knock sounded on the studded door of Bishop's House, the Bishop had actually sat up in bed, because he thought that it was his youngest son, arrived in time after all. But it was not Sholto, and the old man had had no business to sit up in bed and grab at the telegram like that. *"Wife dying in Paris forgive delay,"* he read out, gasping. After which with a smile he murmured, "Perhaps I shall meet poor Sholto's wife above," and without another word died. It was all very well for the chaplain to fold his arms upon his breast, but the assembled family felt that a bishop ought to have died in the hope of meeting his Maker, not an Italian daughter-in-law of peasant extraction.

During the ten years that had elapsed since then, Sholto had behaved exactly as his family had foreseen that he would behave. He had lost his wife, his money, and then most carelessly his own life, leaving an orphan to be provided for by her relatives. Luckily Sir Hector Grant, because he was the head of the family and because he had climbed a little higher than the rest, was willing to see what could be done with and what could be made of poor Sholto's daughter. Not that the others were slow in coming forward with offers of hospitality. Their letters to Jasmine were a proof of that. But they all felt that Strathspey House was the obvious place for the experiment to begin.

Strathspey House occupied what is called a commanding position on the fashionable South Cliff of Spaborough, looking seaward over the shrubberies of the Spa gardens. Sir Hector Grant had bought it about fifteen years ago, to the relief of the many ladies whom in a professional capacity he had advised to recuperate their nerves at the famous old resort. That trip to Spaborough had become such a recognized formula in his consultations that it would hardly have been decent for Dr. Grant himself to seek anywhere else recreation from his practice. In his Harley Street consulting room a coloured print of the eighteenth century entitled *A Trip to Spaborough* hung above the green marble clock that had been presented to him by a ruling sovereign for keeping his oldest daughter moderately sane long enough to marry the son of another ruling sovereign, and, what is more, cheat an heir presumptive with an heir apparent. In the caricaturist's representation a line of monstrously behooped and bewigged ladies and of gentlemen with bulbous red noses stood upon a barren cliff gazing at the sea. "Even in those days," Dr. Grant used to murmur, "you see, my dear lady ... yes ... even in those days ... but of course it's not quite like that now. No, it's—not—quite—like—that—now." The neurasthenic lady would certainly have made the prescribed trip even if it had been; but before she could express her complete subservience Dr. Grant would go on: "Air ... yes, precisely ... that's what you require ... air!... plenty of good—fresh—air! Bathing? Perhaps. That we shall have to settle later on. Yes, a little— later—on." And Dr. Grant's patients were usually so much braced up by their visit that they would begin telegraphing to him at all hours of the day and night to find out the precise significance of various symptoms unnoticed before the cure began to work its wonders.

But the claims of exigent ladies were not the only reason that determined Dr. Grant to acquire a house at the seaside. As a prophylactic against his two daughters', Lettice and Pamela, ever reaching the condition in which the majority of his female patients found themselves, their mother, who had an even keener instinct than her husband for the mode, suggested that he should build a house in the country, choosing a design that could be added to year by year as his fame and fortune increased. But when Mrs. Grant suggested building, the doctor replied, "Fools, May, build houses for wise men to live in," and forthwith bought Strathspey House to conclude the discussion. In this case the fool was a Huddersfield manufacturer whose fortunes had collapsed in some industrial earthquake and left him saddled with a double-fronted, four-storied, porticoed house, in which he had planned to meditate for many years on a successful business career put behind him. Actually he spent his declining years in a small boarding-house on the unfashionable north side of Spaborough, where he existed in a miserable obscurity, except as often as he could persuade a fellow-pensioner to walk with him all the way up to South Parade for the purpose of admiring the exterior of the house that had once been his—a habit, by the way, that vexed the new owner extremely, but for which, under the laws of England, he could discover no satisfactory remedy.

It is scarcely necessary to add that the Huddersfield manufacturer never called it Strathspey House. That was Dr. Grant's way of saying "My heart's in the Highlands a-chasing the deer," for it was down the dim glens of Strathspey that the prehistoric Grants had hunted in the mists of antiquity.

Although Mrs. Grant had never tried to persuade her husband into anything like the baronial castle that would have so well become him, she had never ceased to protest against a country seat in a popular seaside resort; but she had to wait fifteen years before she was able to say "I told you so" with perfect assurance that her husband would have to bow his head in acknowledgment of her clearer foresight. The actual date of her triumph was the first of August in the year before Jasmine's arrival, when the very next house in South Parade, separated from Strathspey House by nothing but a yard of sky and a hedge of ragged aucubas, was turned into a boarding-house and actually called Holyrood. Sir Hector Grant, K.C.V.O., C.B., would have found the proximity of a boarding-house irritating enough as he was; but a few months later he was created a baronet, and what had been merely irritating became intolerable. How could he advertise himself in Debrett as Sir Hector Grant, of Strathspey House, Spaborough, when next door was a boarding establishment called Holyrood? And if he described himself as Sir Hector Grant, of Harley Street, Borough of Marylebone, all the flavour would be taken out of the fine old Highland name and title. There was only one course of action. He must change Strathspey House to Balmoral, sell it to another boarding establishment, remove *A Trip to Spaborough* from his consulting room, buy a small glen in Banff or Elgin with a good Gaelic sound to its name, and send his patients to Strathpeffer. Yet after all, why should he bother? He had no male heir. What did it matter if he was Sir Hector Grant, of Harley Street, Borough of Marylebone? Sir Hector Grant, Bt., was good enough for anybody; he need not waste his money on glens. If old Uncle Matthew Rouncivell died soon and left him his fortune, and the old miser owed as much to his nephew's title, he should be able to buy a castle and retire from practice. Meanwhile his business was to make the most of that title while he was alive to enjoy it.

"Yes, perhaps it was a mistake to settle so definitely in Spaborough," he admitted to his wife. "But it's too late to begin building now. You and the girls won't want to keep up an establishment when I'm gone. Extraordinary thing that Ellen"— Ellen was his only sister—"should have six boys. However," he went on hurriedly, "we mustn't grumble."

The result of having no heir was that Sir Hector had to make the most of his title in his own lifetime, and he used to carry it about with him everywhere as a miner carries his gold. Journeys which a long and successful life should have made arduous at fifty-eight were now sweetened by his being able to register himself in hotel books as *Hector Grant, Bart.* Once a malevolent wit added an *S* to the *Bart*, in allusion to the hospital that produced him, and Sir Hector, gloating over the hotel book next morning, was so much shocked that he insisted upon the abbreviation *Bt.* ever afterwards. It was the second time that verbal ingenuity had made free with his titles. For his voluntary services to his country during the Boer war as consulting physician—people used to say that he had been called in to pronounce upon the sanity of the British generals on active service—he was made a Companion of the Bath, and when soon after appeared *Traumatic Neuroses. By Hector Grant, C.B.*, one reviewer suggested that the initials should be put the other way round, so old and out of date were the distinguished doctor's theories.

In appearance Sir Hector was extremely tall, extremely thin, extremely fair, with prominent bright blue eyes and a nodulous complexion. His manner, except with his wife and daughters, was masterful. Old maids spoke of his magnetism: women confided to him their love affairs: girls disliked him. It would be unjust to dispose of his success as lightly as the frivolous and malicious critic mentioned just now. He was not old-fashioned; he did keep abreast of all the Teutonic excursions into the vast hinterland of insanity; even at this period he was clicking his tongue in disapproval of the first stammerings of Freud. He was sensitive to the popular myth that alienists end by going mad themselves, and with that suggestion in view he was on his guard against the least eccentricity in himself or his family. *Mens sana in corpore sano*, he boasted that he had never worn an overcoat in his life.

He was once approached by the proprietors of a famous whisky for permission to put his portrait if not on the bottle at least on the invoice. Although he felt bound to refuse, the compliment to his typically Caledonian appearance pleased him, and now on his holiday, in a suit of homespun with an old cap stuck over with flies, Sir Hector regretted that the necessity for keeping one hand in his patients' pockets prevented his setting more than one foot upon his native heath, and even that one foot only figuratively.

Lady Grant, who had been the only daughter of a retired paper-maker and had brought her husband some two thousand pounds a year, was at fifty a tall fair woman with cheeks that formerly might not unludicrously have been compared to carnations, but which now with their network of little crimson lines were more like picotees. She was one of those women whom it is impossible to imagine with nothing on. Inasmuch as she changed her clothes three times a day, went to bed at night, got up in the morning, and in fact behaved as a woman of flesh and blood does behave, it was obvious that she and her clothes were not really one and indivisible. Yet so solid and coherent were they that if one of her dresses had hurried downstairs after her to say that she had put on the wrong one, it might not have surprised an onlooker with any effect of strangeness. At fifty her best feature was her nose, which of all features is least able to call attention to itself. Women with pretty complexions, women with shapely ankles, women with beautiful hair, women with liquid or luminous eyes, women with exquisite ears, women with lovely mouths, women with good figures, women with snowy arms, women with slim hands, women with graceful necks, all these have a property that bears a steady interest in becoming gestures. Powder-puffs, petticoats, combs, ear-rings, and a hundred other excuses are not wanting; but the only way of calling attention to a nose, at any rate in civilized society, is by blowing it, which, however delicate the laced handkerchief, is never a gesture that adds to the pleasure of the company. Lady Grant could do nothing with her magnificent nose except bring it into profile, and this gave her face a haughty and inattentive expression that made people think that she was unsympathetic. Enthusiasm cannot display itself nasally except among rabbits, and of course elephants. Lady Grant, resembling neither a rabbit nor an elephant, became more impassive than ever at those critical moments which, had she been endowed with good eyes, might have changed her whole character. As it was, her nose just overweighted her face, not with the effect of caricature that a toucan's nose produces, but with the stolidity and complacency of a grosbeak's. She was, for instance, as much gratified to be the wife of a baronet as her husband was to be a baronet itself; that intractable feature of hers turned all the simple pleasure into pompousness. It is true that by calling attention to her daughters' noses she was sometimes able to extract a compliment to her own; but at best this was a vicarious satisfaction, and when one day a stupid woman responded by suggesting that Pamela and Lettice had noses like their father, Lady Grant had to deny herself even this demand on the flattery of her friends, because Sir Hector's nose was hideous, really hideous.

Lady Grant had grumbled a good deal about her niece's arrival; actually she was looking forward to it. Several people had told her how splendid it was of her, and how like her it was to be so ready, and what a wonderful thing it would be for the niece. In fact in the ever-widening circle of her aunt's acquaintance Jasmine had already reached the dimensions of a large charitable organization. For some time Lady Grant had been protecting a poor cousin of her own, a Miss Edith Crossfield, who was so obviously an object for charity that the glory of being kind to her was rather dimmed. Miss Crossfield was so poor and so humble and so worthy that her ladyship would have had to own a heart as impassive as her nose not to have protected her. At first it had been interesting to impress poor Edith; but as time went on poor Edith proved so willing to be impressed by the least action of dear May that it became no longer very interesting to impress her. Moreover, now that she was the wife of a baronet, Lady Grant was not sure that it reflected creditably upon her to have such a poor relation. There was no romance in Edith; to speak bluntly, even harshly, she gave the show away. No, Edith must find herself lodgings somewhere in a nice unfashionable seaside town and be content with a pension. Sholto's existence in Sirene, his romantic and unfortunate marriage, his career as a painter, his death in the Bay of Salerno, such a history added to the family past, and if poor Jasmine would be more expensive than poor Edith, she would be more useful to her aunt, and more useful to darling Lettice and Pamela.

Lady Grant's daughters were tall blondes in their mid-twenties who had always hated each other, and whose hatred had never been relieved by being able to disparage each other's appearance, owing to their both looking exactly alike. They too, perhaps, were fairly pleased at the notion of Jasmine's arrival, because Cousin Edith was no use at all as a contrast to themselves; she merely lay untidily about the house like a duster left behind by a careless maid. Pamela and Lettice wanted to get married well and quickly; but since either was afraid of the other's getting married first, it began to seem as if neither of them would get married at all. Their passion was golf, and it was a pity that the pre-matrimonial methods of savages were not in vogue on the Spaborough links; Lettice and Pamela would have willingly been hit on the head by a suitor's golf club if they could have found themselves married on returning to consciousness. Such was the family to whose bosom Jasmine was being jogged along through the lamp-lit dusk of Spaborough.

It may be easily imagined that Lady Grant, after taking the trouble to send Nuckett with the car to meet her niece's arrival at Spaborough, was not pleased to find that she had driven up to Strathspey House behind an orange postilion.

"Didn't you see Nuckett?" she asked of Jasmine, whose attempt to kiss her aunt had been rather like biting hard on a soft pink sweet and finding nougat or some such adamantine substance within. Jasmine, wondering who Nuckett might be, assured her aunt that she had not seen him.

"Which means that he will wait down there for the 9.38. Hector!" she called to her husband, who was at that moment bending down to salute his niece, "Nuckett will be waiting at the station for the 9.38. What can we do about it?"

Sir Hector recoiled from the kiss, blew out his cheeks, and looked at his niece with the expression he reserved for wantonly hysterical young girls. There ensued a long discussion of the methods of communication with Nuckett, during which Jasmine's spirits, temporarily exhilarated by the ride behind the orange postilion, sank lower than at any point on the journey. Nor were they raised by the entrance of her two cousins, who were looking at her as if one of the servants had upset a bottle of ink which had to be mopped up before they could advance another step. At last the problem of Nuckett's evening was solved by entrusting the postilion with authority to recall him.

"You mustn't bother to dress for dinner to-night," conceded Lady Grant, apparently swept by a sudden gust of benevolence. "Pamela dear, take Jasmine to her room, will you?"

"Do you get much golf in Sirene?" enquired Pamela on the way upstairs.

Jasmine stared at her, or rather she opened wide her eyes in alarm, which had the effect of a stare on her cousin.

"No, I've never played golf."

It was Pamela's turn to stare now in frank horror at this revelation.

"Never played golf?" she repeated. "What did you do at home then?"

"I played picquet sometimes with father."

This was too much for Pamela, who could think of nothing more to say than that this was a chest of drawers and that that was a wardrobe, after which, with a hope for the success of her ablutions, she left Jasmine to herself.

Presently a maid tapped at the door.

"Please, miss, her ladyship would like to know where you would prefer the packing-cases put."

"Oh, couldn't you bring them up here?" Jasmine asked eagerly. "That is, of course," she added, "if it isn't too much trouble."

The maid protested that it would be no trouble at all; but her looks belied her speech.

"And if you could bring them up at once," added Jasmine quickly, "I should be very much obliged."

She had a plan in her head for softening her relatives, the successful carrying out of which involved having the crates in her room. After a few minutes they arrived.

"I'm afraid I can't open them with my umbrella," she said. She was not being facetious, for in her impetuousness she had tried, and broken the umbrella. "I wonder if you could find me a screw-driver?"

"Oh yes, miss, I daresay I could find a screw-driver."

"And a hammer," shouted Jasmine, rushing out of her room to the landing and calling down the stairs to the housemaid.

"I think I shall change my frock all the same," she decided. "Or at any rate I shall unpack; because if I don't unpack now, I shall never unpack."

In order not to lose the inspiration, Jasmine began to unpack with such rapidity that presently the room looked like the inside of a clothes-basket. Then she undressed with equal rapidity, mixing up washed clothes with unwashed clothes in her efforts to find a clean chemise. She found several chemises, but by this time it was impossible to say which or if any of them were clean, and when the housemaid came back with the screw-driver and the hammer, she spoke to her with Southern politeness:

"I say, I wonder if you could lend me a chemise. And, I say, what is your name?"

The housemaid winced at the request; but the traditions of service were too strong for her, and with no more than the last vibrations of a tremor in her voice, she replied:

"Oh yes, miss, I daresay I could find you a chemise. And, please, I'm called Hopkins, miss."

"Yes, but what's your other name?"

"Amanda, miss."

"What a pretty name!"

"Yes, miss," the housemaid agreed after a moment's hesitation. "But it's not considered a suitable name for service, and her ladyship gave orders when I came that I was to be called Hopkins."

"Well, I shall call you Amanda," said Jasmine decidedly. No doubt Hopkins thought that a young lady who was capable of borrowing a chemise from a housemaid was capable of calling her by her Christian name, and since she did not wish to encourage her ladyship's niece to thwart her ladyship's express wishes, she hurried away without replying.

While Hopkins was out of the room Jasmine attacked the crates, tearing them to pieces with her slim, brown, boyish hands as a monkey sheds a coconut. Then she took out the pictures and set them up round the room in coigns of vantage, two or three on the bed, one leaning against the looking-glass, one supported between the jug and the basin, and several more on chairs. This happened in the days before the Germans bombarded Spaborough and destroyed its tonic reputation; but between that date and this no room in Spaborough could have conveyed so completely the illusion of having been bombarded. Yet, as often happens with really untidy people, it is only when they have reduced their surroundings to the extreme of disorder that they begin to know where they are, and as soon as the room was littered with pictures, packing-case wood, and clothes, all jumbled and confused together, Jasmine was able to find not only the clean chemise she required, but all the other requisite articles of attire, so that when Hopkins came back Jasmine was able to wave at her in triumph one of her own chemises.

"Never mind, Amanda; I've found one."

"Oh yes, miss, but please, miss, with your permission I'd prefer you called me Hopkins. I wouldn't like it to be said I was going against her ladyship's wishes in private."

"Well, I like Amanda," persisted Jasmine obstinately.

"Yes, miss, and it's very kind of you to say so, I'm sure, and it would have pleased my mother very much. But her ladyship particularly passed the remark that she had a norror of fancy names, so perhaps you'd be kind enough to call me Hopkins."

"All right," agreed Jasmine, who, having only just arrived at Strathspey House, found it hard to sympathize with such servility. "But look here, the washing-stand's all covered with chips and nails. What shall I do?"

A moral struggle took place in Hopkins' breast, a struggle between the consciousness that dinner must inevitably be ready in five minutes and the consciousness that she ought to show Miss Grant where the bathroom was. In the end cleanliness defeated godliness—for punctuality was the god of Strathspey House—and she proposed a bath.

"Oh, can I have a bath?" cried Jasmine. "How splendid! But you are sure that you can spare the water? Oh, of course, I forgot. This isn't Sirene, is it?"

"No, miss," the housemaid agreed doubtfully. After seeing Jasmine's room security of location had somehow come to mean less to Hopkins; in fact she said, when she got back to the kitchen: "I give you my word, cook, I didn't know where I was."

It was a wonderful bath, and while Sir Hector downstairs kept taking his watch out of his pocket—with every passing minute it slid out more easily—Jasmine spent a quarter of an hour in delicious oblivion. At the end of it, Pamela came tapping at the door to tell her that dinner was ready, if she was. Jasmine was so full of water-warmed feelings that she leaped out of the bath, flung open the door, and all dripping wet and naked as she was assured her cousin that she herself was just ready.

"Is the island of Sirene inhabited by savages?" asked Pamela superciliously when she brought back news to the anxious dining-room.

This was considered a witty remark. Even Lettice smiled, for she already despised her cousin more than she hated her sister.

"And now," said Jasmine to herself when another quarter of an hour had gone by and she was dressed, "and now which picture shall I give them?"

She pulled down the cord of the electric light to illuminate better her choice, pulled it down so far that it would not go up again, but stayed hovering above the billowy floor like a sea-bird about to alight upon a wave. It was easy, or difficult, to choose for presentation one of Sholto Grant's pictures, because in subject and treatment they were all much alike. In every foreground there was a peasant girl among olive trees, in every middle distance olive groves, and in every background the rocks and sea of Sirene. The choice resolved itself into whether you wanted a bunch of anemones, a bunch of poppies, an armful of broom, or a basket of cherries; it was really more like shopping at a greengrocer's than choosing a picture. In the end Jasmine, who by now was herself beginning to feel hungry, chose fruit rather than flowers, and went downstairs with a four-foot square canvas.

"I ought to have warned you that in the country we always dine at half-past seven. It was my fault," said Lady Grant.

Penitence is usually as unconvincing as gratitude, and certainly nobody in the room, from Jasmine to Hargreaves the parlourmaid waiting to announce dinner, supposed for a moment that her ladyship was really assuming responsibility for the long wait.

"I thought perhaps you might like one of father's pictures," Jasmine began.

17

"Oh dear me ... oh yes," hemmed Lady Grant, who, to do her justice, did not want to hurt her niece's feelings, but who felt that the lusciousness of the scene presented might be too much for her husband's appetite. Sir Hector, craning at the picture, asked what the principal figure was holding in her basket.

"Cherries, aren't they?" suggested Lettice.

"Ah, yes, so they are," her father agreed. "Cherries.... Precisely.... Come, come, we mustn't let the soup get cold. The dessert can wait."

On the wings of a dreary little titter they moved toward the dining-room; Sir Hector, leading the way like a turkey-cock in a farmyard, murmured, whether in pity for the dead brother who could no longer feel hungry or in compassion for his art:

"Poor old Sholto. We must get it framed."

Chapter Three

JASMINE woke up next morning to a vivid acceptance of the fact that from now onward her life would not be her own. She had been too weary the night before to grasp fully what this meant. Now, while she lay watching the sun streaming in through the blind, the value of the long fine day before her was suddenly depreciated. On an impulse to defeat misgiving she jumped out of bed, sent up the blind with a jerk that admitted Monday morning to her room like a jack-in-the-box, stared out over the wide expanse of pale blue winking sea, sniffed the English seaside odour, clambered up on her dressing-table to disentangle the blind, failed to do so, descended again, and began to wonder how she should occupy herself from six o'clock to nine. And after the long morning, what a day stretched before her! A little talk with Uncle Hector about her father, a little talk with Aunt May on the same subject, a lesson in golf from her cousins, and, worst of all, the heavy foundation stones of the threatened intimacy between her and Miss Crossfield to be placed in position.

"We must get to know each other very well," Miss Crossfield had murmured when she said good night. "We must pull together."

And this had been said with such a gloating anticipation of combined effort and with such a repressed malignity beneath it all that if Miss Crossfield had added "the teeth of these rich relatives," Jasmine would not have thought the phrase extravagant.

She opened her door gently and looked out into the passage. Not even the sound of snoring was audible; nothing indeed was audible except a bluebottle's buzz on a window of ground glass that seemed alive with sunlight. She wandered on tiptoe along the pale green Axminster pile, went into the bathroom, crossed herself, and turned on the tap. The running water sounded so torrential at this hour of the morning that she at once clapped her hand over the tap to throttle the stream until she could cut it off; during the guilty quiet that succeeded, she hurried back to her bedroom, which by now was extremely hot. Before Jasmine stretched years and years of silent sunlit vacancy, in which she would be walking about on tiptoe and throttling every gush of spontaneous feeling just as she had throttled that bath tap.

"And I can't stand it," she said, banging her dressing-table with the back of her hairbrush.

She stopped in dismay at the noise, half expecting to hear cries of "Murder!" from neighbouring rooms. The pale blue sea winked below; the sun climbed higher. Jasmine sat down before the looking-glass to brush her hair. A milk-cart clinked; rugs were being shaken below. Jasmine still sat brushing her hair. The voices of gossiping servants were heard above the steady chirp of sparrows. When Jasmine's hair was more thoroughly brushed than it ever had been, she took her bath, and when her hair was dry she brushed it all over again.

At a quarter to nine Sir Hector found her waiting in the dining-room, the first down. His pleasure at such unexpected punctuality almost compensated him for the fact that she had dared to open his paper and, like all women, even his own wife, that she had turned an ordinary sixteen-page newspaper into a complicated puzzle.

"Well," he said pompously, "you wouldn't find better weather than this in Italy, would you?"

He managed to suggest that the glorious morning was Uncle Hector's own little treat, a little treat, moreover, that nobody but Uncle Hector would have thought of providing, or at any rate been able to provide.

"Yes," he went on, "and what a crime that all this should be vulgarized." He included the firmament in an ample gesture. "I expect your aunt told you that this will be our last summer in Spaborough? We didn't come here to be pestered by trippers. That boarding-house next door is a disgrace to South Parade. They were playing a gramophone last night—laughing and talking out there on the steps until after one o'clock. How people expect to get any benefit from their holidays I don't know. We'd always been free from that sort of rowdiness until they opened that pernicious boarding-house next door, and now it's worse than Bank Holiday. Some people seem blind to the beauty round them. I suppose when the moon gets to the full we shall hear them jabbering out there till dawn. What *have* you been doing to my paper? It's utterly disorganized!"

Jasmine diverted her uncle's attention from the newspaper to the basket of prickly pears that she had brought from Sirene, and invited him to try one.

Sir Hector examined his niece's unnatural fruit as the night before he had examined his brother's unnatural fruit.

"Well, I don't know," he hemmed. "We're rather old-fashioned people here, you know."

"I think the prickles have all been taken out," said Jasmine encouragingly, "but you'd better be careful in case they haven't."

Sir Hector had been on the verge of prodding one of the pears, but at his niece's warning he drew back in alarm; and just then the clock on the mantelpiece struck nine. Before the last stroke died away the whole family was sitting down to breakfast. Jasmine's punctuality was evidently a great satisfaction to her relatives, and if she did look rather like a chocolate drop that had fallen into the tray reserved for fondants, she felt much more at home now than she had at dinner last night. Nothing occurred to mar the amity of the breakfast-table until Lady Grant's fat fox-terrier began to tear round the room as if possessed by a devil, clawing from time to time at his nose with both front paws and turning somersaults. Lady Grant, who ascribed all the ills of dogs to picking up unlicensed scraps, rang the bell and asked severely if Hargreaves, whose duty it was to supervise the dog's early morning promenade, had allowed him to eat anything in the road; but it was Jasmine who diagnosed his complaint correctly.

"I think he has been sniffing the prickly pears," she said.

"But what dangerous things to leave about!" exclaimed her aunt. "Hargreaves, take the basket out into the kitchen and tell cook to empty them carefully—carefully, mind, or she may hurt herself—into the pineapple dish. She had better wear gloves. And if she can't manage them," Lady Grant called after the parlourmaid, who was gingerly carrying out the basket at arm's length, "if she can't manage them, they must be burnt. On no account must they be thrown into the dustbin. I'm sorry that we don't appreciate your Italian fruit," she added, turning to her niece, "I'm afraid you'll find us very stay-at-home people, and you know English servants hate anything in the least unusual."

"How they must hate me!" Jasmine thought.

"And what is the programme for to-day?" asked Sir Hector suddenly, flinging down the paper with such a crackle that Jasmine would not have been more startled if like a clown he had jumped clean through it into the conversation.

"Well, we *were* going to play golf," said Lettice disagreeably.

"Oh then, please do," said Jasmine hurriedly, for she felt that a future had been mutilated into imperfection by the responsibility of entertaining herself.

"Jasmine and I have a little business to talk over after breakfast," Sir Hector announced. "So you girls had better be independent this morning, and give Jasmine her first lesson this afternoon."

The girls looked at their father coldly.

"We've got a foursome on with Dick Onslowe and Claude Whittaker this morning, and if George Huntingford turns up this afternoon," said Lettice, "I've got a match with him. But if Pamela isn't engaged, I daresay she will look after Jasmine, that is if she can find her way to the club-house."

"But Roy Medlicott said he might get to the links this afternoon," protested Pamela. "And if he does, I shan't be able to look after Jasmine."

"Well, we might get Tommy Waterall to give her a lesson," proposed Lettice. Something in her cousin's intonation made Jasmine realize that Tommy Waterall was the charitable institution of that golf club, and she vowed to herself that she at any rate would not be beholden to him, even if she were successful in finding her way to the club-house, which was unlikely.

Jasmine's little talk with her uncle was the smallest ever known. Sir Hector, as a consulting nerve specialist, was accustomed to ask more questions than he answered, and since the only positive information he had to impart to his niece was the fact that she had not a penny in the world, the theme did not lend itself to eloquence.

"Yes, that's how your affairs stand," said Sir Hector. "But you mustn't worry yourself." He was just going to dilate on the deleterious effects of worry, as though Jasmine were a rich patient, when he remembered that whether she worried or not it was of no importance to him. His observations on worry, therefore, those very observations which had won for him a fortune and a title, were not placed at his niece's disposal. The little talk was over, and Sir Hector strode from the study to proclaim the news.

"We've had our little talk," he bellowed. Lettice and Pamela, delightfully equipped for golf in shrimp-pink jerseys, passed coldly by. It was one of those moments which do give a nose an opportunity of showing off, and Sir Hector, afraid of being snubbed, drew back into his study. When he heard the front door slam, he emerged again, and shouted louder than ever: "We have had our little talk!"

Lady Grant appeared from another door further along the hall, her hand pressed painfully to her forehead.

"Couldn't you wait a little while, dear, until I have finished doing the books?"

"Sorry," said Sir Hector, retreating again. He was wishing that he had at Strathspey House his Harley Street waiting-room into which he could have pushed Jasmine to occupy herself there with illustrated papers a month old and not disturb him by her presence. "Perhaps you might care to go and wait for your aunt in the drawing-room," he suggested finally. "I know she's very anxious to say a few words to you about your father—your poor father." The epithet was intended to be sympathetic, not sarcastic, but Jasmine bolted from the room with her handkerchief to her eyes.

"A leetle overwrought," murmured Sir Hector, as if he were talking to a patient. But soon he lighted a cigar and forgot all about his niece.

There are few places in this world that cast a more profound gloom upon the human spirit than a sunny English drawing-room at 9.45 a.m. Its welcome is as frigid as a woman who fends off a kiss because she has just made up her lips.

"If I feel like this now," said Jasmine to herself, "*Dio mio*, what shall I feel like in a month's time?"

She put away the handkerchief almost at once, for even grief was frozen in this house, and memories that yesterday would have brought tears to her eyes were to-day so hardly imaginable that they had no power to affect her. "I'm really just as much dead as father," she sighed to the Japanese blinds that rustled faintly in a faint breeze from the sea. On an impulse she rushed upstairs to her bedroom, took off her black clothes, and came down again to the dining-room in a yellow silk jersey and a white skirt.

"My dear Jasmine!... Already?..." ejaculated her aunt, when the household accounts were finished and she found her niece waiting for her in the drawing-room. "I don't know that your uncle will quite approve, so very soon after his brother's death."

"I don't believe in mourning."

"My dear child, are you quite old enough to give such a decided opinion on a custom which is universally followed—even by savages?"

"Father would perfectly understand my feelings."

"I daresay your father would understand, but I don't think your uncle will understand."

And one felt that Sholto's comprehension in Paradise was a poor thing compared with his brother's lack of it on earth.

"Anyway, I'm not going to wear black any longer," said Jasmine curtly.

"As you will," her aunt replied with grave resignation. "Oh, and before I forget, I have told Hopkins to show you exactly how the blind is pulled up in your room. I'm afraid you didn't keep hold of the lower tassel this morning. They're still trying to get it down, and I am very much afraid we shall have to send for a carpenter to mend it. If you pull the string on the right without holding the lower tassel——"

"I know," Jasmine interrupted. "I'm rather like that blind myself."

Lady Grant hoped inwardly that her niece was not going to be difficult, and changed the subject. "You have no doubt gathered by now exactly how you stand," she went on. "I know you've been having a little talk with your uncle, and I know that there is nothing more galling than a sense of dependency. So I was going to suggest that when we went back to Harley Street in September you should take Edith Crossfield's place and help me with my numerous—well, really I suppose I *must* call them that—my numerous charities. At present Cousin Edith only answers all my letters for me; but I daresay you will find many ways of making yourself much more useful than that, because you are younger and more energetic than poor Edith. Though, of course, while we are at Spaborough I want you to consider yourself as much on a holiday as we all are. Do make up your mind to get plenty of good fresh air and exercise. The girls are quite horrified to hear that you have never played golf, especially as they're so good at it themselves. Lettice is only four at the Scottish Ladies'. Or is it five? Dear me, I've forgotten! How angry the dear child would be!"

"I'm D—E—A—D, dead," Jasmine was saying to herself all the time her aunt was speaking.

And perhaps it was because she looked so much like a corpse that her aunt recommended a course of iron to bring back her roses. Lady Grant was so much accustomed wherever she looked, even if it were in her own glass, to see roses that Jasmine's pallor was unpleasant to her. Besides, it might mean that she really was delicate, which would be a nuisance.

"It's almost a pity," she said, "that your uncle did not postpone his little talk, so that you could have gone with the girls to the links. They have such wonderful complexions, I always think."

"Please don't worry about me," said Jasmine quickly. "I can amuse myself perfectly well by myself."

"My dear," said Lady Grant, asserting the purity of her motives with such a gentle air of martyrdom as Saint Agnes may have used toward Symphronius, "you misunderstand me. You are not at all in the way; but as I have some private letters to write, I was going to suggest that you and Cousin Edith should take a little walk and see something of Spaborough."

"Little walks, little talks, little talks, little walks," spun the jingle in Jasmine's mind.

At this moment the companion proposed for Jasmine floated into the room. Miss Crossfield was so thin, her movements and gestures were so indeterminate, and her arms wandered so much upon the air, that indoors she suggested a daddy-longlegs on a window-pane, and out of doors a daddy-longlegs floating across an upland pasture in autumn. It was perhaps this extreme attenuation that gave her subservience a kind of spirituality; with so little flesh to clog her good will, she was almost literally a familiar spirit. She materialized like one of those obedient genies in the Arabian Nights whenever Lady Grant rang the bell, and she endowed that ring with as much magic as if it had been the golden ring of Abanazar.

"Edith," said Lady Grant magnanimously, "I am writing my own letters this morning to give you the opportunity of taking Jasmine for a little walk. You had better take Spot with you—on the lead, of course."

That at any rate would tie Cousin Edith to earth, Jasmine thought, for Spot was so fat and so porcine that he was unlikely to run away and carry Cousin Edith with him in a Gadarene rush down the face of the cliff. Yes, with Spot to detain her, not much could happen to Cousin Edith.

But Jasmine was wrong. Spot had a fetish: the sensation of twigs or leaves faintly tickling his back gave him such exquisite pleasure that to secure it he would use the cunning of a morphinomaniac in pursuit of his drug. He would put back his ears and creep very slowly under the lower branches of a shrub, so that Cousin Edith, who in her affection for the family felt bound to indulge the dog to the whole length of his lead and even further, was lured after him deep into the chosen bush, so that finally, immaterial as she was, she was herself entangled in the upper branches.

"I think I'm getting rather scratched," she would cry helplessly to Jasmine, who would have to come to the rescue with a sharp tug at Spot's lead. This used to give such a shock to the bloated fox-terrier that, torn from his sensation of being scratched by canine houris, he would choke, while Cousin Edith, dancing feebly on the still autumn air, would beg Jasmine never again to be so rough with him.

The music of the Spa band grew louder while they were descending the winding paths of the cliff, until at last it burst upon Jasmine with the full force of an operatic finale and gave a throb of life to her hitherto lifeless morning. The music stopped before they reached the last curve of the descent, where they paused a moment to watch the movement of the dædal throng, above which parasols floated like great butterflies. From the sands beyond, above the chattering, came up the sound of children's laughter, and beyond that the pale blue winking sea was fused with the sky in the silver haze of August so that the furthest ships were sailing in the clouds.

And then, just when it really was beginning to seem worth while to be alive again, Cousin Edith's hand alighted uncertainly like a daddy-longlegs on Jasmine's arm and jigged up and down as a prelude to whispering in what, were that insect vocal, would certainly have been the voice of a daddy-longlegs:

"Do you think we can communicate with the dead?"

"No, I don't," said Jasmine sharply. "And if we could, I shouldn't want to."

Cousin Edith opened wide her globular eyes, which, like those of an insect, were set apparently on her face rather than in it. But before she could combat the blasphemy she had been lured by Spot deep into a privet bush, so deep that the old rhyme came into Jasmine's head about the man of Thessaly who scratched out his eyes in bushes and at his own will scratched them in again in other bushes. He must have had eyes like Cousin Edith's—external and globular.

"Poor old Spot," she murmured, disengaging her lips from a cobweb as genteelly as possible. "He so enjoys his little walk. Up here now, dear," she added, seeing that Jasmine was preparing to go down to the promenade.

"But shan't we go and listen to the music?"

"We have Spot with us."

"Well?"

Cousin Edith came very close to her and whispered:

"Dogs are not allowed on the promenade."

"Then let's tie him up and leave him here," suggested Jasmine.

Cousin Edith laughed. At least Jasmine supposed it was a laugh, even if it did sound more like the squeaking of a slate pencil. Indeed she was pretty sure that it was a laugh, because when it was finished Cousin Edith's fingers danced along her arm and she said:

"How droll you are! We'll go out by the north gate. Unless," she added, "you would like to sit in this summer-house for a little while and listen to the band from here."

There was a summer house close at hand which, with the appearance of a decayed beehive, smelt of dry-rot and was littered with paper bags.

"I often sit here," Cousin Edith explained. Jasmine was tempted to reply that she looked as if she did; but a sense of inability to struggle any longer against the withering influence of the Grants came over her, and she followed Cousin Edith into the summer-house. There on a semicircular rustic seat they sat in silence, staring out at the dim green world, while Spot seduced a few strands of the tangled creeper round the entrance to play upon his back paradisal symphonies. Then Cousin Edith began to talk again; and while she talked a myriad little noises of insect life in the summer-house, which had been temporarily disturbed, began again—little whispers, little scratches, little dry sounds that were indefinable.

"You have no idea how kind Cousin May is. But, of course, she isn't Cousin May to you, she's Aunt May, isn't she?" Again the desiccated titter of Cousin Edith's mirth sounded. The myriad noises stopped in alarm for a moment, but quickly went on again. "Already she has planned for you a delightful surprise."

Jasmine's impulsive heart leaped toward the good intention of her aunt, and with an eager question in her eyes she jumped round so energetically that she shook the fabric, bringing down a skeleton leaf of ivy, which fluttered over Spot's back and gave him the finest thrill of the morning.

"What can it be?" she cried, clapping her hands. This was too much for the summer-house. Skeleton leaves, twigs, dead flies, mummied earwigs began to drop down in all directions.

"It's quite dusty in here," said Cousin Edith in a perplexed tone. "I think perhaps we had better be moving along."

"But the surprise?" Jasmine persisted.

Cousin Edith trembled with self-importance, and her long forefinger waved like an antenna when she bade Jasmine follow her in the direction of the promised revelation. They strolled along the winding paths of the shrubberies above the promenade until they reached the main entrance of the Spa.

"Will you hold Spot for a tiny minute? I have a little business here," Cousin Edith pleaded. Having adjured Spot to be a good dog, and promised him that she would not be long, Cousin Edith engaged the ticket clerk in a conversation, and so much did she appear to be pecking at her purse and so nearly did she seem to be ruffling her feathers when she bobbed her hat up and down that if she had presently flown into the office through the pigeon-hole and perched beside her mate on the desk inside it would have appeared natural. Jasmine might have wondered what Cousin Edith was doing if she had not been too much occupied with Spot, who in default of a convenient bush was trying to extract his dorsal sensations from a little girl's frock. When he was jerked away by a heavier hand than Cousin Edith's he began to growl, whereupon Jasmine smacked him with her glove, which so surprised the fat dog that he collapsed in the path and breathed stertorously to attract the sympathy of the passers-by. Cousin Edith came back from her colloquy with the clerk, and in a rapture of esoteric benevolence she pressed into Jasmine's palm a round green cardboard disk.

"Your season ticket," she murmured. "Cousin May—I mean Aunt May—asked me to buy you one while we were out."

Jasmine felt that she ought to jump in the air and embrace the gate-keeper in the excess of her joy. As for Cousin Edith, she watched her as one watches a child that has been given a sweet too large for its mouth. She seemed afraid that Jasmine would choke if she swallowed such a benefaction whole.

"And now," she said, as if after such a display of generosity it were incredible that there might be more to come, "and now Aunt May—there, I said it right that time!—Aunt May suggested that we might have a cup of chocolate together at the Oriental Café afterwards."

"Hullo!" cried a cheerful voice, which brought Jasmine back to earth from the dazzling prospects being offered by Cousin Edith. "Why, we've met even sooner than I hoped we should."

Jasmine's sandy-haired railway companion, looking delightfully at ease, every freckle in his face twinkling with geniality and pleasure, shook hands. For the first time she regretted that it was Cousin Edith's duty to hold Spot. If Cousin Edith had not been detained by the fat fox-terrier, she might have floated away like a child's balloon, such evident dismay did Mr. Vibart's irruption create in one who was under the obsession that all the young men in the world fit to be known were already friends of Lettice and Pamela. Jasmine introduced Mr. Vibart without any explanation, and poor Cousin Edith, who was too genteel, and had been too long dependent to know how to escape from an acquaintanceship she did not wish to be forced on her, allowed Mr. Vibart to shake her hand. When, however, he calmly suggested that they should all turn back and listen to the band, she pulled herself together and declared that it was quite impossible.

"The dog...." she began.

"Oh, we'll leave the dog with the gate-keeper," said Mr. Vibart.

"I'm afraid, Jasmine, your friend doesn't understand that dear old Spot is quite one of the family." And turning with a bitter-sweet smile to the intrusive young man: "Spot is a great responsibility," she added.

"I should think so," Mr. Vibart agreed, regarding with unconcealed disgust the fox-terrier, who, having been rolling on his back in the dust, looked now more like a sheep than a pig. Jasmine understood at once what Mr. Vibart wanted, and as she wanted the same thing so much herself she nearly answered his unspoken invitation by saying, "Very well, Mr. Vibart and I will go and listen to the band for half an hour, and when you've finished your chocolate at the café, we'll meet you here." She felt, however, that such independence of action was too precipitate for Spaborough.

"I'm afraid that we were just going to the Oriental Café," Cousin Edith had begun, when Mr. Vibart interrupted her.

"Capital! Just what I should like to do myself!"

Before Cousin Edith could do anything about it they were all on their way to the town; but by the time the café was reached she had perfected her strategy.

"Thank you very much for escorting us," she murmured. "Miss Grant and I are much obliged to you. You, of course, will prefer the smoking-room. We always go into the ladies' room."

The Oriental Café included among its appropriate features a zenana, outside the door of which, marked *LADIES ONLY*, Mr. Vibart was left disconsolate, although before it closed Jasmine had managed to whisper, "Strathspey House, South Parade."

Within the zenana, to which Spot was admitted as little boys under six are admitted to ladies' bathing-machines, Cousin Edith warned a young girl against the wiles of men.

"I shan't say anything to Aunt May about this unpleasant little business," she promised Jasmine, who was convinced that she would take the first opportunity to tell her aunt everything. "No, I shan't tell Aunt May," Cousin Edith went on, "because I think it would pain her. She's so particular about Lettice and Pamela, and we always have such nice men at Strathspey House." But lest Jasmine should suppose that the presence of nice men there implied a chance for her in the near future, she made haste to add:

"Though, of course, we must always be careful, even with the nicest men. I must say that it seems to me a dreadful idea that a young girl like you should be able to meet a man in the train, travel with him unprotected, and actually be accosted by him the next day. Ugh! I'm so glad we had Spot with us! Brave old Spot!" And in her gratitude to Spot for the preservation of their modesty she gave him half of one of the free biscuits that the Oriental Café allowed to the purchaser of a cup of chocolate.

"Do you know," went on Cousin Edith, flushed by the thought of their narrow escape and by the deliciously hot chocolate, "do you know that once, nearly five years ago, a man winked at me in a bus? I was quite alone inside, and the conductor was taking the fares on the top."

"What did you do?" Jasmine asked with a smile.

"Why, of course I rang the bell, got out almost before the bus had fully stopped, and walked the rest of the way. But it made such an impression on me that when I reached my friend's house she had to give me several drops of valerian, my heart was in such a state, what with walking so fast and being so frightened. Perhaps I oughtn't to have told you such a horrid story. But I'm older than you, and I want you to feel that I'm your friend. Oh yes, the things men do! Well, I was brought up very strictly, but I have a very strong imagination, and sometimes when I'm alone I just sit and gasp at the wickedness of men. And now," Cousin Edith concluded with an uneasy glance round the zenana, "I think we ought to hurry back as fast as we can. Come, Spot! Good old Spot! I'll show you the Aquarium, dear, as we go home. You can see the roof quite well when we turn round the corner from Marine Crescent."

Perhaps Cousin Edith thought that Jasmine's indiscretion would be more valuable as a weapon for herself if it was unrevealed, for she did not say a word to Lady Grant about the meeting at the gates of the Spa; indeed all the way home she talked about nothing except the wonder of possessing a season ticket of one's own, ascribing to the round green cardboard disk a potency such as few talismans have possessed.

"You will be able to go and see the fireworks on gala nights," she explained, "and you'll be able to go and hear concerts—though, of course, if you want to sit down you have to pay extra—and you'll be able to go and drink the waters—though, of course, you have to pay a penny for the glass—and you'll be able to take a short cut from South Parade to the beach—though, of course, you won't care for the beach, because it's apt to be a little vulgar—and then the promenade is far the best place to hear the pierrots from—though I'm afraid that even they have been getting vulgar lately. I'm so glad that Cousin May thought of making you this present. It makes me so happy for you, dear."

While Cousin Edith was extolling its powers, the green cardboard disk, which was originally about the size of a florin, seemed to be growing larger and larger in Jasmine's glove, until by the time South Parade was reached it seemed the size of a saucer. In fact it was only after Jasmine had warmly thanked her aunt for the kind thought that it shrank back into being a small green cardboard disk again. At least she was no longer aware of its burning her palm; but when she came to take off her gloves she found that this was because the ticket was no longer there. The loss of the Koh-i-nur diamond could not have been treated more seriously. The house was turned upside down, and small parties were sent out into South Parade to examine carefully every paving stone and to peer down the gratings of the drains. Sir Hector, who had been in charge of the operations conducted inside the house, suddenly became overheated and announced that it was useless to search any longer, but that when he paid his own afternoon visit to the Spa he would go into the question with the authorities, and if necessary actually buy another ticket.

"And perhaps your uncle will take you with him," said Lady Grant.

Cousin Edith clasped her hands in envious amazement. "Jasmine!" she exclaimed. "Do you hear that? Perhaps Sir Hector will take you with him!"

Lettice and Pamela did not come back to lunch, and at four o'clock Sir Hector sent Hargreaves up to Jasmine's room to inform her that he was ready. Two minutes later he sent Hargreaves up to say that he was waiting. Four minutes later he sent Hargreaves up to say that he would walk slowly on. Six minutes later, Jasmine, not quite sure which way her hat was facing or whether her dress was properly fastened, found Sir Hector, watch in hand, at the nearest entrance of the gardens.

"If there is ever any doubt about the time," he told her, "we always follow the clock in my room. Let me see. You have lost your season ticket, so that at this entrance you will have to pay. Wait a minute, however; I will see if the gate-keeper will let you through for once."

The gate-keeper was perfectly willing to trust Sir Hector's account of the accident to the season ticket, and Sir Hector, carrying himself more upright even than usual, observed to Jasmine as they walked along towards the main entrance, "You see they know me here."

"Now where are you going to keep this ticket so that you don't lose it like the other one?" asked Sir Hector when he had presented Jasmine with the second small green disk, for which the management had regretfully but firmly exacted another payment.

Jasmine proposed to put it in her purse.

"Yes," said Sir Hector judicially, "that might be a good place. But be very careful that you don't drop it when you want to take out any money."

"There's only tenpence halfpenny to take out," said Jasmine. "But I can put the ticket in the inside compartment, which is meant for gold."

"Good Heavens! I hope you don't carry much gold about with you," exclaimed her uncle.

"No, not very much," she replied. "A broken locket, that's all."

On the way to the promenade Sir Hector was saluted respectfully by various people; and several ladies sitting on sunny benches quivered as he went by, with that indescribable tribute of the senses which they accord to a popular Lenten preacher who passes them on the way to the pulpit.

"Some of my patients," Sir Hector explained.

Jasmine wondered if it would be more tactful to say that they looked very well or that they looked very ill; not being able to decide, she smiled. At that moment Sir Hector stopped beside a bath-chair.

"Duchess," he proclaimed in a voice sufficiently loud to be heard by all the passers-by, most of whom turned round and stared, first at the Duchess, then at Sir Hector, then at Jasmine, and finally at the chairman, "you are looking definitely better."

"Ah, Sir Hector, I wish I felt better."

"You will.... You will...." Sir Hector prophesied, and, raising his hat, he passed on.

"That," he said to Jasmine, "is Georgina, Duchess of Shropshire. Yes ... yes ... it's odd.... They're all my patients.... The Duchess of Shropshire, ... Georgina, Duchess of Shropshire, ... Eleanor, Duchess of Shropshire."

Jasmine, who came from Sirene, where any summer Italian duchesses bathing are to be found as thick as limpets on the rocks, was less impressed than she ought to have been.

"What's the matter with her?" she enquired.

Sir Hector never encouraged his patients to ask what was the matter with themselves, and he certainly did not approve of his niece's enquiry.

"You would hardly understand," he said severely, and then relapsed into silence, to concentrate upon threading his way through the crowd of the Promenade.

Sir Hector, who wished to be the cynosure of the promenaders floating with the opposite current, kept on the extreme edge of the downward stream, so that Jasmine, with two feet less height than her uncle and no title, found it difficult to make headway, so difficult indeed that in trying to keep up with him she got too much to the left and was swept back by the contrary stream, in which, though she managed to keep her season ticket, she lost herself. Several times during this promenade eternal as the winds of hell, she caught sight of her uncle's neck lifted above the swirl like a cormorant's, and once she managed to get to the outside of the stream and actually to pluck at his sleeve as he went by in the opposite direction; but her voice was drowned by the music, and he did not notice her. She was beginning to feel tired of walking round and round like this, and at last, finding herself working across to the right of the current, she struggled ashore, or in other words went into the concert room.

The concert room of the Spa looked like a huge conservatory full of dead vegetation. The hundreds of chairs stacked one upon another in rows seemed a brake of withered canes; the music-stands on the platform resembled the dried-up stalks of small shrubs; while the few palms and foliage plants that preserved their greenery only served to enhance the deadness all round, and were themselves streaked with decay. Outside, the gay throng passing and repassing like fish added a final touch to the desolation of the interior. Two small boys, with backward uneasy glances, were creeping furtively through the maze of chairs. Jasmine thought that they like herself had been overcome by the mystery haunting this light and arid interior, until a dull boom from the direction of the platform, followed by the screech of hurriedly moved chairs and the clatter of frightened feet made her realize that their cautious advance had been the preliminary to a daring attempt to bang, if only once, the big drum muffled in baize. No sooner had the boys successfully escaped than Jasmine was seized with a strong desire to bang the drum for herself, to bang it, however, much more loudly than those boys had banged it, to raise the drumstick high above her and bring it down upon the drum as a smith brings his hammer down upon the anvil. The longer she sat here, the harder she found it to keep away from the platform. Finally the temptation became too strong to be resisted; she snatched the baize cover from the instrument, seized the drumstick, and brought it down with a crash.

"I wish I could do that at Strathspey House," she sighed; and then, hearing a voice at the back of the hall, she turned round to see an indignant man in a green baize apron looking at her over folded arms.

"Here! you mustn't do that," he was protesting.

"I'm sorry," said Jasmine. "I simply couldn't help it."

"It isn't as if I didn't have to spend half my time as it is chasing boys out of here, but I never reckoned to have to go chasing after young ladies."

"No; I'm sorry," said Jasmine. She hesitated for a moment what to do; then she thought of her talisman and fumbled in her purse. The attendant wiped his hands on the apron in preparation for the half-crown that he estimated was the least remuneration he could receive for the loudest bang on that drum he had ever heard, and when Jasmine produced nothing but a season ticket he was inclined to be nasty.

"You needn't think you can come in here and rattle all the windows and fetch me away from my work just because you're a season ticket holder, which only makes it worse in my opinion, and I'll have to take your name and number, miss, and complain to the management. That's all there is to it. I've been asking to have this place closed when not in use, and now perhaps they'll do it. Only this morning I barked my shins something cruel trying to catch hold of a boy who was playing the banjo on the double bass. I've got your number, miss, 17874, and you'll hear from the management about it; and that's all there is to it."

He wiped his other hand on the apron and waited a moment; when Jasmine did not seem to understand what he wanted, he invited her to leave the hall forthwith, and retired to formulate his complaint. As for Jasmine, she rejoined the throng; but by now, in whatever direction she looked, she could not even see Sir Hector's long red neck, much less meet him face to face. She began to be bewitched by the continuous circling round the bandstand. It was really delicious on this golden afternoon to be borne round upon these mingled perfumes of scent and asphalt. The asphalt, softened by the heat, was pleasant to walk on, like grass, and it was only after circling for about half an hour that she realized how tiring it was to the feet. At this moment the music stopped; the opening bars of *God Save the King* were played; a patriotic gentleman next to her planted his foot on her own in his desire to remind people that he was an old soldier. Two minutes later the Promenade was empty, and Jasmine, with any number of chairs to choose from now, sat down.

She had not been there more than five minutes when round the corner came Mr. Vibart, walking in the way people walk when they have an object.

"I hoped I should find you on the Spa," he said. "I've just called at your home. Don't be frightened," he went on at Jasmine's expression of alarm, "I didn't ask for you. I rang the bell and asked if they had a vacant apartment, and how much the board was a day. Luck was on my side. The maid was just coming to from her swoon when an old boy looking like a turkey that's nearly had its neck wrung came shouting through the garden that he had lost Jasmine on the Promenade. I didn't wait to hear any more, but hurried down as fast as I could. And here I am, full of schemes. But I decided not to put any of them into practice until I'd seen you again."

"Oh, but it's all turned out much worse than what I expected," said Jasmine hurriedly. "You mustn't come and call or do anything like that. Why, I'm almost frightened to ring the bell myself, and if I heard any of my friends ring a bell I don't know what I should do. I'm not a bit of a success. I heard my aunt say *sotto voce* that she distrusted dark people. I lost a season ticket this morning which cost I don't know how many shillings. I've lost my uncle now. If you come and call, *sarò perduta io*. And now I must say good-bye and go back."

"Well, don't break into Japanese like that. Let's sit down and talk over the situation."

"No, no, no! I must say good-bye and hurry back."

"I don't want to compromise you and all that," the young man protested, "but it seems a pity not to enjoy this weather."

"No, please go away," Jasmine begged. "It's all perfectly different to anything I ever imagined. Quite different. I'm sorry I gave you my address this morning."

Jasmine was getting more and more nervous. She had an idea that Cousin Edith would be sent to look for her; if Cousin Edith found her talking to Mr. Vibart by the deserted bandstand she would suppose that the assignation had been made that morning. All sorts of ideas swirled into Jasmine's mind, and she began to hurry towards the winding path up the cliff.

"At any rate you might let me walk back with you as far as the entrance," he suggested.

"No, please, really. You make me nervous. You don't in the least understand my position."

Mr. Vibart looked so sad that Jasmine hesitated.

"Don't you play a game called golf?" she asked.

"Yes, I do play a game called golf," he laughed.

25

"Well, I believe they're going to teach me, so perhaps we might meet on the golf grounds," said Jasmine. "My cousins went there this morning and didn't come back for lunch, and I think they go every day."

"I see the notion. I must get to know them, what?"

"Yes, I don't think it will be very difficult," Jasmine answered. She was speaking simply, not maliciously. "They seem to know lots of people who play this game. But if you do meet them, for goodness' sake don't say you know me. Turn round! Turn round!" she cried in agony. "Turn round straight away in the other direction without looking back! Do what I tell you! Do what I tell you!"

Round the next bend of the laurel-edged walk Jasmine met Cousin Edith, who, unencumbered by Spot, was floating towards her as a daddy-longlegs floats towards a lamp.

Jasmine found it difficult to make her uncle understand how she had been lost.

"I cannot think where you got to," he said. "I looked about everywhere. Most extraordinary!"

"I'm sure she didn't mean to get lost, Sir Hector," Cousin Edith put in with just enough accent on the intention to create a suspicion of Jasmine's sincerity.

"No, of course she didn't mean to get lost," Sir Hector gobbled. "Nobody means to get lost. But you'll have to learn to keep your head, young lady. However, all's well that ends well, so we'll say no more about it. Where are the girls?"

Just then the girls came in, and Jasmine hoped that she was going to be invited to partake of the mysterious game that occupied so much of their time. All indeed promised well, for several allusions were made in the course of dinner to the necessity of introducing her to the joys of golf. Next morning, however, Lettice and Pamela went off as usual, and as an intoxicating treat for Jasmine it was proposed that Cousin Edith should show her the Castle.

"It might be a little far for Spot," Cousin Edith humbly objected.

"Yes, I think you are right," Lady Grant agreed. "So Spot shall take a little walk with his mother."

It was supposed to be necessary for Cousin Edith to translate into baby language for Spot his mother's wishes, after which she turned to Lady Grant and proclaimed intensely:

"He knows."

Spot was standing on three legs and scratching himself with the fourth, which was presumably his method of acknowledging the success of Cousin Edith's interpretation.

The walk up to the Castle was long and hot; the Castle was a little more uninteresting than most ruins are. Cousin Edith poetized upon the romance of the past; Jasmine counted two hundred and nine paper bags.

When they got back to Strathspey House it was obvious that something unpleasant had occurred during their absence. Cousin Edith tried all through lunch to give her impression of the delight Jasmine had tasted in going to the Castle; but her account of the morning's entertainment was received so coldly by her patrons that in the end she was silent, shrinking into such insignificance and humility that the faint clicking of her false teeth was her only contribution to actuality. After lunch a few whispers were exchanged between her and Lady Grant, at the conclusion of which she danced on tiptoe out of the dining-room, and Lady Grant turned to her niece.

"Your uncle wishes to speak to you," she announced gravely.

Sir Hector, who during these preliminaries had been hiding behind the newspaper, jumped up and took a letter from his pocket.

"Can you explain this?" he demanded.

His wife had moved over to the window and was looking out at the sky in the way that ladies look at the East window when something in the preacher's sermon is particularly applicable to a neighbour. Jasmine read the letter, which was from the director of the Spa:

Spa Gardens Company, Limited,
Spaborough,
August 15th.

Dear Sir Hector Grant,

I am writing to you personally and confidentially to ask you whether season ticket 17874 is really held by one of your family party. The caretaker of the Concert Room has complained to me that a young lady holding season ticket 17874, which was traced to the name of Miss Jasmine Grant, Strathspey House, removed the green baize cover from the big drum yesterday afternoon the 14th inst. and struck it several times. We have not been able to trace any reason for her behaviour, and I should be much obliged if you would give the matter your kind attention. The Company has of course no wish to take any action in the matter, and is content to leave all the necessary steps in your hands. I may add that the drum has been examined carefully, and I am glad to be able to assure you that it is quite uninjured. At the same time we rely on our season ticket holders to set an example to the casual visitors, and I am sure you will appreciate the delicacy of my position.

Believe me, my dear Sir Hector Grant,
Yours very faithfully,
John Pershore,
Managing Director.

"Yes, I did bang the drum," Jasmine confessed.

Now if Sir Hector Grant had been asked by one of his patients to cure an uncontrollable impulse to beat big drums he would have known how to prescribe for her, and within a week or two of her visit ladies would have been going round each asking the other if she had heard of Sir Hector Grant's latest and most wonderful cure. His niece, however, did not present herself to him as a clinical subject; he had no desire to analyse her psyche for her own benefit or for the elucidation of the Flatus Complex.

"No wonder you were lost," he said bitterly. "I don't suppose you expected me to look for you among the drums? I don't wish to make a great fuss about nothing, but I should like to point out that you cannot accuse me of being backward in coming forward to ... er ... show our ... er ... affection, and we look, not unreasonably, I hope, for a little ... er ... sympathy on your side. I shall write to Mr. Pershore and explain that you were brought up in Italy and did not appreciate the importance of what you were doing. That will, I hope, close the matter. I cannot think why you don't go and play golf with the girls," he added fretfully.

"I should love to go and play golf," Jasmine declared.

Lady Grant now came forward from the window: perhaps, during this painful scene she had made up her mind that her niece must be added to the list of her charities.

"You must try to realize, my dear child," she said, shaking her head, "that our only idea is for you to be happy. Have you already forgotten that you lost your first season ticket? Have you forgotten even that it was your Uncle Hector himself who immediately offered to buy you another one? He has not said very much about the drum; but his restraint does not mean that he has not felt it all dreadfully. And he has had other things to upset him this morning. Only yesterday one of his oldest patients jumped out of a fourth storey window and was dashed to pieces. So we must all be a little considerate. Don't you think that you're too old to play with drums? What would you think if I went about beating drums? However, enough has been said."

Sir Hector blew his nose very loudly, and Jasmine on her way up to her room thought that if she could trumpet like that with her nose, she should be content to let drums alone.

Chapter Four

IT seemed to be the general opinion of Strathspey House that Jasmine was reckless, and in order to counteract a propensity that might one day cause serious trouble to her protectors it was decided to sow the seeds of prudence by making her a quarterly allowance of £10, on which she was to dress and provide herself with pocket money. The announcement of the largesse was made in such a way that if the first ten golden sovereigns had lain within her reach Jasmine would have been tempted to pick them up and fling them back at the donors. In order, however, that the possession of wealth might bring with it a sense of wealth's responsibilities it had been decided to open an account for her at the Post Office Savings Bank, and without even so much as an account book to throw, Jasmine found that all her verbal protestations were interpreted as a becoming sign of gratitude.

To say that Jasmine longed for the freedom of Sirene is to express nothing of the fierce ache she suffered every moment of the day for that happy island. Adam and Eve when their sons first began to quarrel could not have looked back with a sharper bitterness of desire to their childless Eden. The possibility of ever being able to go back there did not present itself even in the most distant future, and the thought that with each year the sound of Sirenian mandolins, the scent of Sirenian roses, and the brilliance of Sirenian moonlight would grow fainter dabbled Jasmine's pillow with tears when she fell asleep in the sentimental night-time, and when she woke made of the sun a heavy brass dish that extinguished instead of illuminating the new day.

Jasmine's last hope was that her cousins would offer to take her to the links; but a fortnight passed, on every evening of which it was decided that she should accompany Lettice and Pamela the following morning, and on every morning of which it was decided at the last moment that she had better wait until to-morrow. Her time was spent partly in dreary walks with Cousin Edith, partly in what Lady Grant euphemistically called checking her accounts, a process that consisted in Jasmine's having to be at her elbow for whatever assistance she required in managing the household and several of her exacting charities. In a rash moment Jasmine alluded to Aunt Ellen's suggestion about learning to typewrite. Aunt May declared that this was a capital notion, and presently Cousin Edith, on one of what she called her little expeditions, discovered in an obscure part of the town a second-hand typewriter that was really very cheap. A long discussion ensued whether or not Lady Grant was justified in spending the £3 10s. asked by the shopman. Cousin Edith for three successive days wrestled with him penny by penny until for £3 7s. 6d. she secured that typewriter, of which she was as proud as she would have been proud of her eldest child, that is, of course, with marriage previously understood. Once she even described it as graceful; and she used to play upon it ghostly sonatas, occasionally by mistake pressing too hard upon one of the stops and uttering a rudimentary scream of affright when she beheld an ambiguous letter take shape upon the paper. Jasmine, who was seriously expected to become proficient upon this machine, was not so fond of it. She put forward a theory that, when it had ceased to be a typewriter, it had been used by children as a toy, which shocked Cousin Edith.

"Or perhaps it was saved from a wreck," Jasmine went on.

"Oh, hush!" Cousin Edith breathed. "How can you say such things?"

Gradually Jasmine mastered some of the whims of the instrument; she learnt, for instance, that if one wanted a capital A, the birth of a capital A had to be helped by pressing down S at the same time; she also learnt to control the self-assertiveness of the Z, which used to butt in at the least excuse as if for years it had resented the infrequency of its employment and, thriving on idleness, was able now when the more common stops rattled like old bones to dominate them all.

Jasmine's mastery of the instrument was fatal to her. Nobody else could use it; and Lady Grant was so pleased with the effect of typewritten correspondence upon the dignity of her charities that Cousin Edith, deposed from whatever secretarial state was left to her, found herself betrayed by her own purchase. Sir Hector, with what was impressed upon Jasmine as unusual magnanimity even for Sir Hector, had invited his niece to accompany him once more upon his afternoon walks; but the arrival of the typewriter kept her so busy that Lady Grant began to say 'To-morrow' to these walks as her daughters said 'To-morrow' to the links. Finally Jasmine, in a rage, decapitated the Z stop, thereby producing such a perfect specimen of correspondence that her aunt, much moved, announced that she really should go to the links on the very next day, and that she herself would go with her. What happened to the typewriter between five o'clock that evening and the following morning was never known; but that epistle was its swan-song. Perhaps the execution of the Z stop, on whom the others had come to rely so completely, put too great a strain on their old bones, or perhaps Cousin Edith in the silence of the night severed the machine's spinal cord. Anyway, next morning, when Lady Grant, having proposed for the fifteenth time that visit to the links, asked Jasmine if she would be so kind as to type out a schedule of the rules of her club for Tired Sandwichmen, Jasmine announced that the machine was no longer working. Her aunt seemed unable to believe her, and insisted that the schedule should be done. Jasmine showed her the first four lines, which looked like a Magyar proclamation, and Lady Grant exclaimed, "What a waste of £3 7s. 6d.!" Cousin Edith, whose *amour propre* was wounded by this imputation, observed with the bitter mildness of pale India ale:

"Not altogether wasted, May. Jasmine has learnt typewriting. I wish that when I was young I had had such an opportunity."

"Well, perhaps we can go to the links after all," Lady Grant sighed. "The girls always take the tram, but we'll drive in the car. I don't think that you had better come, Edith. The last time, don't you remember, you received that nasty blow with the ball. Hector," she called, "you wouldn't mind if Cousin Edith gave you your lunch?"

Sir Hector bowed gallantly, and vowed that he should be delighted to be given his lunch by Cousin Edith. He was in a good temper that morning, for he had just been reading the obituary of a rival baronet of medicine. Cousin Edith did her best to make Jasmine sensible of the gratitude she owed to her aunt for this wonderful treat, and herself came as far as the front gate, holding Spot by the collar and waving until the car was out of sight.

Jasmine did not much enjoy her drive, because every time they turned a corner or a child crossed the road a quarter of a mile ahead, or a dog barked, or a sparrow flew up in front, her aunt gasped and clutched her wrist. And even when the road was straight and clear as far as they could see the drive was tiresome, because her aunt could talk about nothing except Nuckett's carefulness.

"Nuckett is such a careful driver. But of course he knows that your uncle would not keep him for a moment otherwise. We hesitated for a long time before we bought the car, and in fact it wasn't until we had given Nuckett a month's trial.... Oh, now there's a flock of sheep! Thank goodness it's Nuckett, who's always particularly careful with sheep ... ah!..."

And so on, in a mixture of complacency and terror, until they reached the links and Jasmine was really there.

Travellers have often related the alarm they felt at first when some savage chief, wishing to pay his distinguished visitors a compliment, arranged for a war-dance by the young men of his tribe. It was that kind of alarm which Jasmine felt when she found herself for the first time on golf links. She knew that it was a game. She kept assuring herself that it was only a game. But the Italian strain in her was continually asserting itself and making her wonder whether people who behaved thus in jest might not at any moment be seized with an extension of their madness and take to behaving thus in earnest.

Lady Grant, however, made her way calmly toward the club-house and put her name down for lunch with one guest, explaining to Jasmine that no doubt the girls would have arranged a luncheon party on their own account. Then she went into the ladies' room, picked up a ladies' paper, advised Jasmine to do the same, and ensconced herself comfortably in a wicker chair on the verandah, where she seemed inclined to stay for the rest of the morning. Half an hour later she looked up from the fifth paper and asked Jasmine how she liked golf.

"I don't think I understand it very well yet."

"It's an interesting game," said her aunt. "Your uncle wanted me to take it up last year, and I did have two lessons; but I think it's really more a game for young people, and your uncle decided that it was bad for my rheumatism. Still, I was beginning to realize its fascination—the holes, you know, and all that—and I believe that when you actually do hit the ball each time it's much less tiring. I tried to persuade your uncle to take it up himself, but he felt it was too late to begin, although of course he's a member of the club and plays bridge here every Thursday afternoon."

Another half-hour went by.

"Really," Lady Grant declared, "I think the advertisements nowadays are wonderful. Dear me, how you'll enjoy your first visit to London. You mustn't spend your allowance too quickly, my dear. You mustn't believe everything you see in the advertisements."

While Lady Grant was speaking, the rich voice of Lettice close at hand was unmistakably heard.

"He stimied me on the ninth."

Jasmine looked up apprehensively on an impulse to warn Lettice of her mother's presence before she gave herself away any more; but at that moment Lettice saw them and exclaimed rather crossly:

"Hullo, mother! Are *you* here?"

"Yes, dear, I have paid our long-promised visit. Did you have a good game?"

Lettice made a gesture of indifference, and there was a short pause. "I suppose you'll be going home for lunch?" she enquired.

"No, I've ordered lunch for Jasmine and myself here. But don't let that disturb you, dear. We shall amuse each other if you and Pamela are already engaged. We shall understand, shan't we, Jasmine?"

"As a matter of fact," said Lettice, "we are lunching with Harry Vibart and Claude Whittaker. We've a foursome on afterwards."

"Delightful," said her mother genially. "Don't you bother about us. I don't think I've looked at this week's *Country Life* yet; have you finished with it?" she asked Jasmine, who, having for some time been listlessly turning over the pages had suddenly found *Country Life* to be of such absorbing interest that she had buried her face in its faint oily smell. Lady Grant never really enjoyed looking at a paper unless she had taken it away from somebody else, and when her niece surrendered it she smiled at her.

"My dear Jasmine, how pale you are!" she exclaimed, and bade her ring the bell for a glass of water.

Jasmine, with a reproach for her treacherous Southern heart, tried to appear composed.

"No, really please, Aunt May," she murmured.

"But I insist, Jasmine. If you won't look after yourself, I must look after you. Ring the bell at once, there's a good girl, and you shall have a glass of water."

Jasmine, to conceal her emotion, accepted the excuse that her aunt offered, and did as she had been told.

"A glass of water for my niece, please, Frank," said Lady Grant to the waiter, and she managed to convey in the tone of her command that a glass of water for her niece would be different somehow from ordinary water. Perhaps it was, for when Frank brought it, all the people round looked up to watch Jasmine drinking it; and everyone who has drunk water in similar circumstances will know that it does then have a peculiar taste of its own, rather like that positive nothingness which is the flavour of permanganate of potash and peroxide of hydrogen.

Soon after this Pamela came out on the verandah, and she, like her sister, had to be reassured of the sanctity of her lunch.

"But at least," Jasmine thought, "he'll be able to see me, and perhaps when he sees me he'll ask to be introduced to Aunt May."

At this moment Frank appeared again and asked Lady Grant in an awe-struck whisper if she had not ordered cold chicken.

"Yes, Frank. Cold chicken for two."

"The head steward asks me to say, my lady, that unfortunately there is no more cold chicken left."

"Dear me," Lady Grant exclaimed, "what a disappointment! Well, perhaps Jasmine and I had better go home to lunch after all."

Neither Lettice nor Pamela made any attempt to detain her; and Jasmine decided to forget all about Mr. Vibart, and all about everything indeed that could ever for one moment lighten her future.

But Frank protested:

"I beg pardon, my lady, only the head steward requested me to inform your ladyship that there is cold duck."

"Then in that case I think we may as well stay," said her ladyship.

"The ducks are very tough," Lettice snapped.

"I beg pardon, Miss Grant," Frank respectfully argued, "the head steward is now procuring our ducks for the club from another farm. Will you take apple sauce, my lady?"

Lady Grant nodded decidedly.

"Very good, my lady."

And Frank glided away, leaving in Jasmine's mind the thought of a powerful and sympathetic personality.

Ten minutes later they went into the dining-room of the club, where a quantity of women with bright woollen jerseys and bright harsh voices shouted across the room the tale of their prowess, or gobbled down their food in a hurry to get off before the links became crowded. The men too seemed much excited by what they had achieved so far that morning. For the first time since she had been in England Jasmine divined that underneath the stolid Anglo-Saxon exterior palpitated ambition and romance and the dark emotions of Southern passion. These rosy barbarians who vied with one another in making their legs ridiculous with fantastic knickerbockers, whose cheeks were rasped by east winds, who illustrated with knife and fork and salt-cellar the vicissitudes of their pastime, became intelligible to her as the leaders of civilization. In Sirene she had always been proud of being English; but hitherto in Spaborough she had congratulated herself on being far more Italian. Now with the consciousness that one of these paladins had turned aside from his purposeful sport to observe herself, she was eager to join in all this; and if to smite a ball farther than other women was to be accounted desirable in the eyes of men, or if to stand on a hillock looking like a scarecrow in a gale was an invitation to love, then so be it; she should not disdain such wiles.

Lady Grant had chosen a small table in the window, one of those small tables with such a large vase of flowers in the middle that the feeder is left with the impression that he is eating off the rim of a flower-pot. Moreover, with the excuse that she did not like so much light, she had placed herself in a recess of the window, with the result that Jasmine had her back to the room and the light full in her eyes.

"I'm afraid you've got the light in your eyes," said her aunt, and she made signs with her nose that her niece should move over to the left, where at the next table a fat man with a back like the nether part of a rhinoceros was taking up so much space that it was obviously impossible for Jasmine to squeeze her chair between his back and the side of their table. She hesitated for a moment, hoping that her aunt would indicate the other side of the table where she herself had been sitting; but she did not offer to move her bag, which took up what space was left by the vase of flowers, and Jasmine was too anxious to have a view of the room to take the risk by moving it herself of being advised to stay where she was.

Frank, the waiter, who had come to her rescue once already, was the instrument chosen by destiny to preserve her a second time from disappointment. For just as he was handing the duck to Lady Grant, the fat man at the next table, outraged by some piece of news in the paper he was reading, threw himself back in his chair so violently that he swept the dish out of Frank's hand. The noise made everybody look in their direction, and Lady Grant and Jasmine, who had jumped up in affright, were conspicuous to the world. It was thus that Mr. Vibart, lunching at the far end of the room, perceived Jasmine, learned who Lady Grant was, and without a moment's hesitation came across and insisted that they should all lunch at his table. Lettice and Pamela did not dare to look as disagreeable as they felt, for each knew from her sister's countenance how ugly ill-temper made her. The host was so boisterously cheerful that the luncheon party appeared to be going splendidly, and when about two o'clock Lettice glanced at her watch and asked if they ought not to be getting along with the foursome before the links filled up, Jasmine thought that she could have no idea how old such fussiness made her seem.

"I say, Claude, do you know," Mr. Vibart said gravely to his companion, a young man to find any other adjective for whom would be a waste of time, "I say, Claude, I believe I did strain my leg in the ravine before the eighth. Most extraordinary! It's gone quite stiff." He called to another friend who was passing out of the dining-room unaccompanied. "Ryder! Are you engaged this afternoon? I wish you'd take my place in a foursome, like a good chap. I've strained my leg."

"Oh, let's postpone it," Lettice begged, with a desperate attempt to hide with an expression of concern the chagrin she felt.

"Oh no, don't do that," said Vibart. "Ryder might think you were trying to snub him. He's an awful sensitive fellow."

Claude Whittaker, whom Vibart had been kicking under the table with his strained leg, urged the prosecution of the foursome, and the two sisters, with a reputation of jolly good-fellowship to maintain, had to yield. When they were gone, Vibart turned to Lady Grant and asked if he could come and sit with her on the verandah. He said that he thought he could manage to limp as far as that.

"But how are you going to get home?" she asked.

"Oh, I shall get a lift in a car from somebody."

Lady Grant hesitated. She was wondering if she should offer to drive him in hers, or rather she was wondering if she could not manage to get him and Lettice into the car.

"Didn't I see you at York railway station about a fortnight ago?" Mr. Vibart was saying to Jasmine. "On a Sunday afternoon it was."

"My niece did pass through York," Lady Grant admitted unwillingly.

"I thought I recognized her. Are you staying long at Spaborough?"

"My niece is staying with us indefinitely," said Lady Grant. "But how long we stay in Spaborough will depend rather upon the weather. Besides, my husband's patients are waiting for him."

"They will become impatients if he doesn't go back soon," the young man laughed.

Lady Grant had never heard anybody make a joke about Sir Hector's profession, and if Mr. Vibart had not been the heir of an older baronetcy than her husband's she might have resented it.

"How long will it be before my daughters get back?" she asked after a while, when she found that the conversation between Jasmine and Mr. Vibart was steadily leaving her behind.

"I should guess in about an hour and a half."

"Well, in that case I think my niece and I ought to be getting home now," said Lady Grant. "Perhaps if I sent back the car," she added, "you would let my daughters drive you home?"

"Thank you very much," said Mr. Vibart. "I really think I ought not to wait so long as that. My leg seems to be getting stiffer every second. But that's all right. I shall get a lift. May I come and call on you one afternoon, as soon as my leg's a little better?"

"But of course we shall be delighted," said Lady Grant graciously. "Perhaps you will arrange a day with my daughter Lettice so that we are sure to be in? Good-bye, Mr. Vibart. I do hope your leg will soon be all right."

"Oh yes, I think it will," said Mr. Vibart. Nor was his optimism unjustified, for the very next afternoon it was well enough for him to call at Strathspey House, where, having forgotten to make any arrangement with Lettice, he found that Sir Hector had just gone out, that Lady Grant was lying down, and that Jasmine was by herself in the drawing-room. He knew that Lettice and Pamela were safely engaged on the links, and before Cousin Edith divined that something was going on in the house, he had had five minutes alone with Jasmine.

Mr. Vibart spent most of that five minutes in telling Jasmine how much he disliked her cousins; he was just going to demonstrate how much he must like her in order to put up with the company of such cousins for a whole fortnight of foursomes when Cousin Edith came in. Naturally in what she called her intimate heart-to-heart talks with the dear girls, and what they called keeping Cousin Edith from feeling too keenly her position, she had been told a good deal about young Mr. Vibart, nephew and heir of Sir John Vibart; and in her anxiety to stand well with Lettice and Pamela she had committed a kind of vicarious bigamy, so earnestly had she encouraged both of the girls to believe that she was the chosen of Mr. Vibart. The moment she heard—and she heard these things by being as tactful with the servants as she was with the family—that Mr. Vibart was in the house and was shut up in the drawing-room with Miss Jasmine, she was alert to defend the honour of her patrons. She knew, of course, that such an insignificant girl as Jasmine had no chance of rivalling either dearest Lettice or darling Pamela; but at the same time Cousin Edith's profound distrust of all men disinclined her to run any risks. Besides, she saw no reason why Jasmine should be puffed up with an undue sense of her own importance by being allowed to suppose that she was capable of entertaining anybody like Mr. Vibart.

It may well be imagined, therefore, with what dismay Cousin Edith discovered that Mr. Vibart was identical with what had already been magnified by time's distorting hand into an agent of White Slavery, which was the only kind of appeal she could allow Jasmine to be capable of making.

She was now in a dilemma: if she revealed the secret of that meeting in the Spa, she would have implied that the impression made by Jasmine was capable of enduring, though it had been stamped and surcharged over and over again by the images of Lettice and Pamela; on the other hand, if she kept quiet, and if by any inconceivable chance—and men were men—this young man should really prefer Jasmine to her cousins, she would run the risk of being suspected as an accomplice. On the whole, Cousin Edith decided that it was far safer to betray both parties. She resolved, while assuring Jasmine of her intention to keep the secret of her previous acquaintance with Mr. Vibart, to do her best to prevent its ripening into anything more permanent, and at the first opportunity, by somehow involving Jasmine with her aunt, to procure her banishment from the family, and thus remove what seemed likely to be a rival to Lettice, Pamela, and herself. Thanks to Cousin Edith's discretion nobody suspected that the two young people were interested in one another. Indeed it would have needed a considerable display of affection to have convinced Lettice and Pamela Grant that anybody so foreign-looking as Jasmine was capable of attracting anybody so English-looking as Harry Vibart. So Lettice and Pamela supposed that his now daily visits were paid for them, and though they would have been better pleased to observe his admiration wax daily on the links, they were much too fond of him to let him play golf a moment before his leg was completely healed; moreover, since they did not want him to feel that he was depriving them of a pleasure, they protested that as a matter of fact they were growing tired of golf, and that one round in the morning was enough for anybody. There was a charming display of sisterly affection when Lettice entreated Pamela and Pamela implored Lettice not to give up golf on her account.

"Poor Claude Whittaker will feel quite deserted," Lettice declared spitefully.

"Yes," Pamela replied. "Only this morning he asked me why you always went home for lunch nowadays."

"I don't know why he should ask that," Lettice exclaimed.

"Don't you, dear?" her sister sweetly marvelled.

31

"For he can't be missing me," said Lettice, "because he's so devoted to you."

"Oh no, my dear, he's much more devoted to you," replied Pamela.

"They're such affectionate girls," Lady Grant whispered to Mr. Vibart. "They really do admire each other, and that's so rare in sisters nowadays." Lady Grant always implied by her disapproval of the present that she and all to do with her were survivals of the Golden Age. "And really," she went on in a low voice, "everybody likes them. I know that as a mother I ought not to talk so fondly, but I do believe that they are the most popular girls anywhere."

Mr. Vibart nodded in absent-minded sagacity.

"I never met your uncle, Mr. Vibart," Sir Hector said importantly.

"No, sir, he keeps very much to himself."

"Quite so. Quite so." Sir Hector wanted Vibart to realize that baronets had certain instincts and habits which he, as one of the species, emphasized in his own manner of life. "No, when I get away for a few weeks' rest," he went on, "I like to rest; and as I know that your uncle comes to Spaborough for the same reasons as myself, I haven't disturbed him with a card. A fine name, a fine name! Fourteenth in precedence, I believe? A Jacobean creation? Yes, to be sure." Sir Hector wished that he were a Jacobean creation himself, and he often thought when he saw himself in the glass that he looked like a Jacobean creation. So he did, just as Jacobean furniture in Tottenham Court Road looks very like the real thing.

"My title dies with me," he sighed, "and to me there's always something very sad in the thought of a title's becoming extinct. You, I believe, are the last representative?"

Vibart nodded.

"You ought to marry," said Sir Hector, and though the advice was given by the baronet, it sounded as though it were given by the doctor.

"I certainly must," Vibart agreed lightly. "By the way, you haven't forgotten that to-night's a gala night at the Spa?"

"Indeed no," said Lady Grant. "Aren't we expecting you to dinner, so that you can escort us afterwards to see the fireworks?"

Later, when the composition of the evening's party was being discussed, Jasmine perceived a suggestion hovering on her aunt's lips that she should stay at home and keep her uncle company. But Sir Hector on this occasion was somewhat obtuse for a man who had won rank, money, and reputation by his ability to indulge feminine whims, and he decided that contrary to his usual custom he would himself attend the gala.

"I like Vibart," he affirmed when the guest had gone home to dress. "A very decent fellow indeed. It must be a great consolation to Sir John to feel that the title will be in good hands. A very fine young fellow indeed! I shall quite enjoy going to the fireworks with him."

There was only the problem of Spot's loneliness to be considered, which it was decided that Cousin Edith should be called upon to solve.

"Poor old Spot," said Cousin Edith deprecatingly. "Spot shall stay with me. Yes, he shall, the good old dog! Poor Spot! Good old Spot! I shall be able to see the rockets beautifully from my window. And Spotticums will be able to see the rockets too. Yes, he will, the clever old Spot!"

It was a fine night; the gardens of the Spa were crowded with people, the sky with stars. Sir Hector, who was tall enough to be independent of his place in the largest crowd, kept ejaculating, "What a splendid view we have got! We really are remarkably lucky to have found such an excellent place! By Jove, that was a magnificent shower of gold! Upon my soul, I'd forgotten how good the Spa fireworks were."

Every time Sir Hector applauded a new pyrotechnic effect, the people in his immediate neighbourhood all stretched their necks and stood on tiptoe to see if they too could not catch a glimpse of what had aroused his enthusiasm. The result of this continual straining and struggling by the crowd was to separate one from another the various members of the Strathspey House party.

"Don't bother about the fireworks," said Vibart to Jasmine when one of Sir Hector's loud expressions of approval had been followed by a kind of panic of curiosity in his neighbourhood and Jasmine, in order not to be swept down over the slope of the cliff, had been compelled to catch hold of Mr. Vibart's arm. "Let's get out of this squash and take a breather."

It was only when they had pushed their way through to the outskirts of the crowd that they discovered the full enchantment of the night. A hump-backed moon, the colour of an old guinea, was lying large upon the horizon; fairy lamps bordered the paths that wound about the bosky cliffs; and from time to time bursting rockets were reflected in streaks of colour upon the tranquil and hueless sea. They strolled along until they found a deserted corner of the promenade, where, leaning over the parapet, they watched swarming on the sands below the people who were come to watch the fireworks as freely as they might watch the stars every night of their lives. Beyond the crowd stretched a wide expanse of wet sand, already glimmering faintly in response to the rising moon. From the beach below a shadow under the parapet breathed up to them in a hoarse voice:

"Lovely night for a sail, sir."

"Why, there's not a breath of wind," Vibart contradicted.

"Lovely breeze about half a mile out, sir. Better have a couple of hours' nice sail, sir."

"It would be rather jolly," Vibart suggested with a glance at Jasmine. She, her eyes brimming with memories of the South, could not gainsay him.

"The whiting's biting something lovely to-night, sir," tempted the hoarse voice again. "There's a party just come in, sir, took 'em by the dozen in half an hour."

A tempting exit to the sands was visible close to where they were standing, the tall iron turnstile of which was like a gate to the moon. Vibart hurried through.

"And now you must come," he pointed out, "because I can't get back."

"That's right, lady," breathed the voice. "He can't get back."

A maroon crashed overhead, and before the echoes had died away Jasmine was on the free side of the turnstile. The voice, which belonged to a burly longshoreman, led the way seaward, and when they were clear of the crowd on the beach shouted:

"*Mermaid*, ahoy! Jonas Pretty is my own name," he added.

Some of the crew flopped toward them like walruses and helped them along planks over the ribbed and rippling sands to the *Mermaid's* dinghy; and presently they were aboard with the crew grunting over the oars to catch the legendary breeze half a mile off shore.

In the last act of *The Merchant of Venice* Shakespeare has said all that there is to say about moonlight and its effect upon young people, and if Harry Vibart was less expressive than young Lorenzo, Jasmine Grant was at least as susceptible as pretty Jessica. She had a moment's sadness in the recollection of her father's death after such a night in the Bay of Salerno; but it was no more than a transient gloom, like a thin cloud that scarcely dims the face of the moon in its swift voyage past. Indeed, the sorrowful memory actually added something to her joy of the present; for fleeting though the emotion was, it endured long enough to stir the depths of her heart and to make her more grateful to her companion for the beauty of this night.

The skipper of the *Mermaid* had spoken the truth; the light breeze he had promised did arrive, and presently the grunt of oars gave place to the lisp and murmur of water and to airy melodies aloft.

"Magnificent, eh what?" Vibart asked.

"Glorious," Jasmine agreed.

Pointing to a small craft half a mile away to starboard, he quoted two lines of verse:

A silver sail on a silver sea
Under a silver moon.

"That really exactly expresses it, don't you think?"

"Perfectly," she agreed.

"Funny that those lines should come so pat. I don't usually spout poetry, you know. It really is awfully good, isn't it?—

A silver sail on a silver sea
Under a silver moon!"

He marked the beat more emphatically at the second time of quoting. "It's really awfully musical. You know, I admire a chap who can write poetry like that. Some people rather despise poets, but if you come to think what a lot of pleasure they give....

A silver sail on a silver sea
Under a silver moon!"

"Who wrote it?" asked Jasmine idly.

"Oh, great Scott, don't ask me. It's extraordinary enough that I should remember the lines. I must have learnt them at my dame's school. Years ago. Quite fifteen years ago. Terrific, isn't it? I'm twenty-four, you know. That's the worst of being an heir. I wanted to go out and try my hand at coffee in British East, but my old great-uncle kicked up a fuss. He's a funny old boy. Likes to have me around, and then grumbles all the time because I'm not doing anything. Says my conversation would cure a defaulting solicitor of insomnia. I bucked him up rather, though, by talking about Italy. Do you know, I think he'd rather like you.

A silver sail on a silver sea
Under a silver moon.

"Dash it, I can't get those lines out of my head. It's worse than a tune. Yes, I think he'd rather like you, Miss Grant. Miss Grant! That sounds absurd on a night like this. Now, I think Jasmine's a charming name. Jasmine! It seems to fit in so well with ... *a silver sail* ... look, here, do you mind stopping me if I begin again? Jasmine! Would you jump overboard if I called you Jasmine?"

"I'd rather you called me Jasmine."

"And of course you'll return the compliment? My name's Harry. It's a perfectly normal name, so you needn't blush."

Mr. Jonas Pretty interrupted any embarrassment with the news that the whiting were biting. Presently the boat was in a confusion of fish. As fast as they dropped the lines they had to tug them in again with half a dozen iridescent victims squirming and leaping and flapping on the hooks, and in half an hour the bottom of the boat was aglow with silver fire.

"Well, I think we've caught enough," said Harry Vibart. "And I mustn't keep you out late, Jasmine. Better sail back now, Skipper."

"Aye, aye, sir."

Mr. Pretty shouted a number of unintelligible and raucous commands, and the breeze immediately died away.

"Lost that nice little wind we had," he grumbled. "That means a bit of a pull back. You wouldn't like to stay out all night, sir, with the whiting biting so lovely? There's a lot of gentlemen likes to do that and come back with the sunrise."

"No, no, this lady has to get home."

Mr. Pretty shook his head reproachfully at such a lack of adventurous spirit.

"It'll be a long pull back, sir."

Indeed the lights of Spaborough did look very far away.

"Can't be helped. We must get back. How long will it take?"

"About a couple of hours, sir."

"What?"

"We'd better steer for the harbour."

Jasmine did not blame Harry—in the excitement of pulling up her line she had fallen easily into calling him by his Christian name—for the flight of the wind.

"I say, it's awfully sporting of you to be so decent about it," he said, turning her behaviour into an excuse to take her hand.

"It's not your fault."

During the long pull back to the harbour Harry Vibart quoted no more poetry; indeed he hardly seemed to notice the moonlight, so deeply was he engaged in telling Jasmine all about his early life and his present life, and what he should do when he inherited his uncle's title and estate.

"Of course I shall have to get married."

"Of course," she agreed.

They looked at each other for a brief instant; but almost simultaneously they looked away again and began to count the whiting. Soon afterward they reached the harbour.

The clocks of Spaborough were striking the apprehensive hour of one when Jasmine and Harry Vibart, each carrying a large bunch of fish, disembarked at the pier of the old harbour.

"I'm afraid that they really will be very cross," said Jasmine. "But never mind, I've had a glorious evening, and I've enjoyed myself, more than I ever have since I left Sirene."

"They might be cross if we hadn't got these whiting," Harry pointed out. "But you can't go against evidence like this. I don't see a carriage anywhere, do you?"

"Perhaps it's too late."

From the old fishing town to South Parade was at least an hour's walk uphill all the way. The whiting began to weigh rather heavily. It was obvious that Jasmine would not be able to carry her bunch, and Harry relieved her of it. After climbing for about five minutes he began to feel that the bunches were more than even he could manage, and pulling off four fish as he would have pulled off four bananas, he offered them to a policeman who was standing at the corner.

"Just caught," he explained cheerfully.

"Thank you, sir," said the constable. "I'll wrap them up and leave them on this window-sill."

"Don't lose them," said Vibart. "They're fresh."

"That's all right, sir. I'll wrap them up in the evening paper. I'm not off duty till six."

"They'll still be quite fresh then," said Vibart encouragingly.

He looked round to see if there was anybody else to whom he could make a present of fresh fish; as there was nobody else in sight, he advised the constable to have two more, and so make up the half-dozen. Another five minutes of slow ascent passed, during which the whiting seemed to have grown into cod. A wretched old woman asleep in an archway, her head bowed in her lap, offered a good opportunity for charity, and Harry was just going to lay a couple of whiting in her lap when Jasmine suggested that if the old woman put her head down any lower she would touch them with her face, which might startle her too much and spoil the pleasure of the surprise.

"Well, I'll lay them on the pavement beside her," said Harry. He also put a couple on her other side, so that she would be sure to see them and not miss her breakfast.

"It's jolly to think how happy she'll be when she wakes up."

"But if she hasn't got anywhere to sleep," Jasmine objected, "I don't suppose she's got anywhere to cook whiting."

"Oh yes," he assured her, "she'll get them cooked all right. Oh, rather! She'll find some workmen who are mending the road."

"But how will that help her to cook whiting?"

"Oh, they always have a fire. I don't know why, but they always do. Still not a carriage to be seen!"

The clocks struck a quarter-past one. The whiting had grown from cod to sharks. They toiled on without meeting a soul till the clocks struck the half-hour, and the whiting from sharks were become whales.

"It would be a pity to go back without these confounded fish," said Vibart, "because it really was a remarkable catch. Besides, fresh whiting's tremendously good for breakfast. It does seem a most extraordinary thing that there's not a carriage anywhere. I think I'll try another way of carrying them—one on each end of my stick, and then I'll put my stick over my shoulder like a milkmaid."

He was demonstrating how much easier it was to carry whiting in this way, and saying what an extraordinary thing it was that he had not thought of doing so before, when both bunches slipped forward, the front one falling into the road and the second one only being prevented from joining its companion by Vibart's shoulder.

"That's a pity," he said. "But I don't think we ought to pick them up, do you? They're rather dusty, and I really think we've got enough. There must be at least sixty left. Only it seems rather wasteful to leave a lot of whiting in a road."

"Come along," Jasmine urged. "For goodness' sake let's leave them and get back. Now, if you give me one end of the stick and take the other yourself we can easily carry the rest between us."

Just as the clock struck two they reached Strathspey House. It seemed as dead in the moonlight as a spent firework; and Jasmine's heart sank.

"It does look as if they were very angry indeed," she said.

"They'll soon cheer up when they see the whiting," Vibart prophesied. "I'll ring."

He rang repeatedly, but there was no answer.

"Perhaps I'd better knock."

He knocked repeatedly; several windows in Balmoral were opened, and dim heads stared down inquisitively; but Strathspey House remained mute.

"Why doesn't that beastly dog bark?" complained Vibart. "It barks all day long. Perhaps I'd better shout."

"Oh no, don't shout."

"Will you ring the bell while I knock again?"

The orchestral effect achieved what the solo had failed to achieve. Sir Hector put out his long neck and asked severely if that were his niece.

"We got slightly becalmed, sir," said Vibart. "But we had a splendid catch. You'll be delighted when you see all the whiting we've brought back for you. Between sixty and seventy. They're so fresh that you'll be able to have them for breakfast both to-morrow and the day after."

But Sir Hector did not reply, and for nearly ten minutes Strathspey House gave no further sign of recognition. Then the front door was opened by Hargreaves, so completely dressed that it was hard to believe that she had really been roused from bed by Sir Hector's method of internal communication.

From a landing above Lady Grant's voice was heard. "You'd better go up to bed at once, Jasmine, and we will talk about your escapade in the morning."

"I'm afraid there's not much I can do," said Harry, somewhat abashed by the discouraging reception. "But I'll get round as soon as I can in the morning and explain that it was all my fault. You mustn't be angry with Miss Grant, Lady Grant," he called up. "I'm the only person to blame. Can you see our haul of whiting? You ought to have a look at them before they're cooked."

The slamming of a distant door was Lady Grant's reply to this.

"Bit annoyed, I'm afraid," he said, shaking his head, and then, turning to the parlourmaid, he asked her where she would like to put the fish.

The question was answered by the fish, because the main string broke, and they went slithering all over the hall.

"I don't know, sir, I'm sure where they'd better be put," said Hargreaves, looking rather frightened.

"Can't you get a dish or something from the kitchen?"

"No, sir, I'm afraid I can't. Cook always has her ladyship's orders to take the key of the basement door up to bed with her, and she's rather funny about being woke up."

"But look here," Vibart protested, "we can't leave all these splendid fish to get trodden on. They're whiting! You know, those fish they usually serve like kittens running after their tails. They won't have any tails left if they're going to be walked over by everybody."

He looked round the hall, and his eye fell upon the card-tray.

"Here's the very thing," he cried, and emptying the cards into the umbrella stand, he began to heap as many whiting as he could on the tray. "Well, that's saved enough for breakfast. We'll put the rest in a corner. Lend me your apron."

The prim Hargreaves was as much taken aback by this suggestion as her colleague Hopkins had been taken aback by Jasmine's attempt to borrow a chemise on the evening of her arrival. But mechanically she divested herself, and the whiting were hung up in a bundle on the hat-rack.

"I'll be round very early," Harry promised Jasmine. "Sorry I've let you in for trouble. I enjoyed myself—well, tremendously."

"So did I," she said. "Tremendously."

Hargreaves without her apron seemed scarcely willing to open the door for him; but she managed to do it somehow, and Jasmine went slowly upstairs to the sound of bolts being driven home, of chains clanking, and latches clicking. It was like being taken back to prison.

Immediately after breakfast the next morning Lady Grant showed her sense of the gravity of the occasion by postponing her household duties until she had had what she called an explanation with her niece about her behaviour last night. As soon as they were closeted in the drawing-room, Jasmine, supposing that she really was anxious for an explanation, began to give a perfectly straightforward account of the misadventure. Lady Grant, however, cut her short before she had time even to explain the accident by which she and Vibart were separated from the rest of the party.

"I am sorry, my dear Jasmine, to find that your only object is to make excuses for your behaviour. There is nothing I dislike so much as excuses."

"But I haven't begun to excuse myself yet," Jasmine retorted.

Her aunt smiled patiently. "Perhaps you will allow me to say without interruptions what I was going to say. I am willing to make every allowance for you, remembering that you have been brought up in a wild island in the south of Italy, and remembering that your poor father had odd notions about the education of young girls. But you are old enough to realize that Spaborough is not Sirene, and that to come back at two o'clock in the morning after spending the whole night sailing about with a young man on the open sea is not a very kind way of showing your affection for your relations, who have been only too anxious to do everything on their side to help you. You cannot complain of the warmth of your welcome in England, and you must admit that your Uncle Hector and I showed ourselves ready to do all we could to rescue you from the condition in which you found yourself after your father's death. I do not wish to say too much about Mr. Vibart's conduct. I can only express my surprise that Sir John Vibart's nephew should so absolutely deceive us in this way. And I blame Cousin Edith greatly. Please do not think that I have not already spoken to her very severely for the part she played in what I can only call a vulgar intrigue. She should, of course, have let me know at once that you and this young man had made each other's acquaintance at a railway station. The idea of it! I should have thought that your natural nice-minded feelings, if not your conscience, would have told you that casual conversation with young men at railway stations is not the way in which young girls in your position behave."

"I don't see any difference between speaking to a young man at a railway station and speaking to a young man at a golf club," Jasmine argued.

"Please do not add to your faults by being rude," Lady Grant begged. "Your rudeness only shows that you are, as I suspected, insensible to kindness. I have had so much ingratitude in the course of my various charities from all sorts and conditions of people whom I have tried to help that I no longer expect gratitude. But if I do not expect gratitude I certainly do not expect rudeness. I do not wish to recapitulate what your uncle has done for you; but I hope that when you come to yourself and think over what he has done for you you will realize how much there has been. Who was it sent you your fare from Sirene to Spaborough? Your uncle. Who was it, when you lost your season ticket before you had even used it once, bought you another one? Your uncle. Who was it that was so glad to give you an opportunity of learning the typewriter? Your uncle. Who was it that did his utmost to get us the best view of the fireworks yesterday evening? Your uncle. Finally, who was it, when the servants had gone to bed and the house was locked up, rang the bell in Hargreaves' room? Your uncle. I shall not go on, Jasmine, because I see by your face that you are hardening your heart. Well, luckily you have other uncles and aunts who have come forward to help you. I have just telegraphed to your Aunt Cuckoo at Hampstead to find out if she will be ready to receive you to-morrow. And although I think that you deserve that she should be told of your behaviour here, I am not going to tell her anything about it. I am not going to say a single word to prejudice your Aunt Cuckoo against you. But I most earnestly beg you, my dear Jasmine, to behave a little differently in Hampstead. Your Uncle Hector and I, who have daughters of our own, will always understand girls better than your Uncle Eneas or your Aunt Cuckoo can. Frankly, I do not think you will enjoy yourself as much in Hampstead as you have enjoyed yourself here, or as you might have enjoyed yourself here, if you had not displayed such a wilful spirit. What puzzles me is your unwillingness to make friends with Lettice and Pamela. It cannot be *their* fault, because they are friends with everybody. Even Mr. Vibart, who must be almost without any decent feelings of any kind whatsoever, liked Lettice and Pamela. Well, I am glad we have had this little explanation. When next you come to stay with us—for although at present your uncle is so much annoyed at being woken up last night that he has said quite positively that he will never have you to stay with us again, I am sure, knowing his goodness as I do, that he will ask you—when next you come to stay with us, I say, perhaps in London, I hope you won't go sailing about with young men half through the night. Of course you would not be able to do any actual sailing in London, but I mean the equivalent of sailing, like riding about on the outside of omnibuses at all hours. I fear that in your present hardened mood nothing can touch you, but I think that at least you might express your sorrow at making poor Spot so ill."

"Is Spot ill?" asked Jasmine.

"He is not ill any longer," said her aunt. "But you know how careful I am about his diet. Apparently he found one of those fish which you left lying about in the hall and was sick seven times this morning."

The explanation was over. The next morning Jasmine left Strathspey House, and late that afternoon was met at King's Cross by her Aunt Cuckoo. Cousin Edith shook her head a great deal at Jasmine's disgrace, but she was so glad to see the last of her that she could not resist waving her handkerchief to the departing car. As for Mr. Vibart, he called five times during the day, and every time Hargreaves, thinking of her apron, was glad to be authorized to inform him with cold politeness that nobody was at home.

Chapter Five

JASMINE's first experience of being succoured by rich relatives might have discouraged her from expecting a happy result from the second. Yet, although the Eneas Grants would be as much her patrons as the Hector Grants, there was something in the sound of 'Aunt Cuckoo' that suggested to her mind the anticipation of a positively more congenial atmosphere. It showed considerable elasticity to feel even subconsciously cheerful on this journey, with the weather south of York becoming overcast and a hundred miles of London breaking into a drench of rain, which turned to dripping fog on the outskirts of the city and made King's Cross an inferno of sodden gloom. In the first confusion of alighting from the train, Jasmine felt like a twig precipitated toward the drain of a gutter. In this din, in this damp and dusky chill made more obscure by fog and engine smoke and human breath, it hardly seemed worth while to have an opinion of one's own upon destination. Swept along toward the exits, Jasmine would soon have found herself astray in the phantasmagoria of the great squalid streets outside had she not been rescued by a porter whose kindly interest and paternal manner persuaded her to consider with due attention the advantages and disadvantages of the various routes from King's Cross to Hampstead.

A complicated but economical itinerary had no sooner been settled than a woman glided up to Jasmine with what in the press of the traffic seemed an almost ghostly ease of movement and asked in an appropriately toneless voice if she were her niece.

Jasmine, without thinking that amid the incalculable permutations and combinations of city life it was at least as probable that she was not this woman's niece as that she was, replied without hesitation that she was.

"Then how do you do?" said Aunt Cuckoo, offering first her right hand, then her left hand, and finally a cheek, the touch of which was like menthol on Jasmine's warm lips.

"I'm very well, thank you," she assured her aunt, transforming the conventional greeting into an important question by the gravity with which she answered it.

"Yes, it's a pity you got a porter," Aunt Cuckoo continued. "A great pity. Because I've got a porter as well. And it doesn't seem worth while, does it, to have two porters?" Jasmine agreed helplessly. "Unless your luggage is very heavy indeed," Aunt Cuckoo added, "and if it *is* very heavy indeed, we can't take it back with us in the brougham, and then I don't know what to do. Yes, it's a pity really you got a porter so quickly. Aunt May wrote us that you were rather impulsive."

She sighed; the rival porters waiting for a decision sighed too. Finally Jasmine took a shilling from her bag, presented it to her porter, and said "Thank you very much."

"Thank *you* very much, miss," said the porter, respectfully touching his cap and retiring from the contest. Aunt Cuckoo without commenting upon Jasmine's action, asked wearily if her luggage was in the back or the front of the train. By good luck Jasmine did know this, because Sir Hector's last bellowed words at Spaborough had been: "Don't forget that your luggage will be in the back part of the train! You are in a through carriage!"

By this time Jasmine's luggage had been reduced to one trunk. The crates with her father's pictures had on her uncle's advice been left at Strathspey House to be brought to London with the rest of the furniture when the family moved. The carpet bag had been presented to Hopkins as a parting gift, because Hopkins had once said how much it would appeal to a little niece of hers in Battersea. The basket of prickly pears had long ago been burnt, because Aunt May had supposed it capable of introducing subtropical insects into Strathspey House. There was therefore nothing left but her trunk, which Aunt Cuckoo decided was neither too large nor too heavy for the brougham. In fact, as a piece of luggage she made light of it altogether, and only gave her porter twopence, at which he said: "I shan't argue about it, mum. It's not worth arguing about."

"Are you dissatisfied?" asked Aunt Cuckoo.

The porter called upon Heaven with upturned eyes to witness his treatment and invited Aunt Cuckoo to keep her twopence.

"You want it more than I do, mum," he said.

The drive from King's Cross to Hampstead took a long time. No doubt the horse and the coachman were both tired, for Aunt Cuckoo explained that she had been shopping in London all day and that really she ought to have gone home much earlier. The small brougham looked like one of those commercial broughams in which old-fashioned travellers drive round to exhibit their wares to old-fashioned firms. Nor did the coachman look like a proper coachman, because he had a moustache, which somehow made the cockade in his hat look like a moustache too. When he stood up to push the trunk into place, Jasmine noticed that he was wearing baggy trousers under his coat, and for a moment she wondered if it could possibly be Uncle Eneas himself who was driving them. Afterward she discovered that he was really the gardener who consented to drive the brougham occasionally, because the horse was useful to his horticulture.

The climb up to the summit of the Heath seemed endless; Jasmine was glad when they got on to level ground again and the cardboard boxes fell back into place. Every time the rays of a passing lamp splashed the brougham Jasmine felt that she ought to say something, but before she had time to think of anything to say it was dark again; and the next splash of light always came as a surprise, so that in the end she gave up trying to think of anything to say and counted the lamp-posts instead. Driving in a brougham with Aunt Cuckoo reminded her of playing hide-and-seek in a wardrobe, when, although one was delighted to have found a good place in which to hide, one hoped that the searchers would not be long in finding it out.

Half-way down the tree-shaded slope of North End Road on the far side of the Heath the brougham turned aside down a short drive and pulled up before an irregular and what appeared in the darkness a rather attractive house. When the door was opened by a sallow butler, Jasmine perceived that the reason for her aunt's prolonged silence during the drive back was a large black respirator, of which she unmuzzled herself before she asked the butler something in a language which Jasmine did not understand, but which she afterwards found was Greek. Then, turning to her niece, she divulged as if it was a family secret that Uncle Eneas had gone to dine at his club that night.

Jasmine was not sorry to be spared the anxiety of another introduction so soon, and she eagerly accepted her aunt's proposal to dine earlier than usual so that she could get a good night's rest after the tiring journey.

"I've ordered *pilau* for you," Aunt Cuckoo announced. Jasmine wondered what this was and hoped it would not be too rich a dish. The oriental hangings in the dining-room portended an exotic type of food, and she had been rather shaken by the train.

"But it's just like our own *risotto*," she exclaimed when the heap of well-greased rice sown with morsels of meat was put before her.

"Very likely," said Aunt Cuckoo, and the tone in which she accepted Jasmine's comparison was so remote and vague that if Jasmine had likened the *pilau* to anything in the scale of edibility between Chinese birds' nests and ordinary bread and butter, she would probably have assented with the same toneless equanimity.

Jasmine liked her bedroom at The Cedars much better than her bedroom at Strathspey House. Uncle Eneas' consular career had naturally set its mark on his possessions. Strathspey House had been furnished first with all the things that were not wanted in Harley Street and then with the new and inexpensive suites that were considered appropriate to a holiday house. Moreover, Strathspey House itself was a creation not much older than Sir Hector's baronetcy. The Cedars was a century and a half years old, a rambling irregular countrified house with a large garden leading directly to the Heath; it possessed externally a colour and character of its own which in combination with the oriental taste of Eneas Grant produced an effect that Jasmine much esteemed after the newness of Strathspey House. In this bedroom there were Turkish and Persian rugs, thread-bare, but rich in hues; photographs with cypresses and minarets along the sky-line; paintings on rice-paper of bashi-bazouks and many other elaborate old Eastern costumes; and hanging by the fireplace a horse's tail set in an ivory handle to whisk away the flies. The Cedars was not Italy, but at least it seemed to recognize that somewhere there was sunlight. Jasmine fell asleep almost happily, and coming down to breakfast next morning after a struggle with punctuality she found to her relief that breakfast at The Cedars consisted of the civilized coffee taken in bed and that she alone was expected to devour eggs and bacon at the unnatural hour of nine a.m. After this first breakfast she, like her uncle and aunt, kept to her room.

Eneas Grant was obviously the brother of Sir Hector; and when Jasmine found that there was a tendency among her relatives to insist upon the importance and value of this family likeness, so much so indeed that it was crystallized into a phrase: 'A Grant! Oh yes, he's obviously a Grant,' she realized that her father had probably alienated himself from the esteem of his family as much by his outward dissimilarity as by the divergence of his tastes. Eneas was tall and thin; but neither his tallness nor his thinness ever reached the impressive ungainliness of angularity that was Sir Hector's outstanding characteristic. Eneas, like his brother, was intensely proud of his good health, and in the contemptuous way he alluded to anybody who lacked good-health he suggested that the ill-health was due to a moral lapse. He was a non-smoker and a teetotaller, and to both abstentions he attributed the moral value that so many ascetics attribute to any abstention from life's minor comforts. He was good enough, however, to allow as much to human weakness as not to condemn any man for moderate indulgence in either nicotine or alcohol, although to any man who fell a prey to the major human failings, like women or cards, he was merciless.

"I see no reason why a man should run after women," Uncle Eneas used to declare; and there hung about Mrs. Grant after twenty years of married life such an aura of antique virginity that one felt quite sure he was speaking the truth. Like many men who boast of their immunity from all the fleshly attacks of the tempter, Eneas Grant was greedy; indeed he was more than greedy, he was a glutton. A dish of curried prawns roused the glow of concupiscence in his milky blue eyes. Jasmine found it embarrassing at first to watch her uncle's tongue rubescent with all that vaunted good-health titillate itself in anticipation along the sparse hairs of his grey moustache, just as Spot titillated his back upon the leaves of shrubberies. Uncle Hector had been greedy with the frank greed of a man who at the beginning of a meal sharpens his knife upon the steel with a preliminary bravura and gusto. This greed of Uncle Eneas was colubrine. It really did seem as if he actually were fascinating the new dish; as if the curried prawns would presently rise of their own accord and abjectly, one after another, jump into his mouth. Jasmine would look up apprehensively to see if Niko the butler were not observing contemptuously this display of greed. But Niko seemed to encourage his master; one felt that, if the curried prawns should presume to show the slightest hesitation at coming forward to be devoured, Niko would complete with his fingers what his master's snakish eyes had failed to effect.

Like most teetotallers and non-smokers Eneas was a ruthless talker. He had innumerable stories of his career which, to do him justice, were at a first hearing entertaining enough; but after one had wandered with him on his famous expedition to negotiate with the Mirdite clan in Albania, had watched the eagles soaring above the gorges of the Black Drin or the passes of the Brseshda, had noticed curiously the mediæval costumes of the inhabitants, had been regaled with gigantic feasts by hospitable chieftains, and had heard mass said by moustachioed priests whose rifles were leaning against the altar, one tired of Albania; at the third time of hearing one became as it were mentally saddle-sore and yearned to be back home. It was entertaining, for the first time, to hear him tell how once, in the old days, while walking like God in his garden at Salonika, inhaling the perfumed breeze of the Balkan dusk, there had suddenly fallen at his feet, flung over the garden wall, a matchbox which when opened was discovered to contain a human ear. That story, heard for the first time, provided a genuine shudder. But when one had heard it six or seven or eight or nine times one was stifled by the preliminary perfumes, dazzled by the preliminary sunset, and prayed for some change in the weather and some new bit of anatomy in the matchbox, a human eye or a human finger—anything rather than a human ear.

"A perfectly ordinary matchbox," Mr. Grant used to say. "I just stooped down to open it and found inside a human ear. You of course see the point of that?"

The first time Jasmine had not seen the point, and had been interested to be told that the ear belonged to some British subject under the protection of her uncle who had refused to pay his ransom to the brigands that held him captive on Mount Olympus. But once the point had been seized, and repetition gave the poor gentleman as many ears as the breasts of the Ephesian Diana, the story became grindingly, exasperatingly tiresome.

Even more tiresome were those stories that turned upon the listener's acquaintance with official etiquette. Uncle Eneas cherished the memories of former grandeur, and he was never tired of counting over for Jasmine the number of guns to which a consul was entitled when he paid a visit of ceremony to any warship that visited the port to which he was accredited. The echoes of their booming still rumbled among the files and dockets of his brain. He had preserved even more vividly the memory of one or two occasions on which these grandeurs had been denied him by mistake, for like most consuls of the Levant service, whether they be or be not teetotallers and non-smokers, Eneas Grant was an aggrieved and disappointed man who had retired with that disease of the mental outlook which is known as consulitis. Yet Eneas Grant had less to complain of than most of his colleagues. The bitterness of finding himself in a post where he must come into direct competition with embassies or legations had not often fallen to his lot. He had indeed spent two galling years as Chief Dragoman at Constantinople, where he was responsible for all the practical work of the Embassy and considered that he was treated with less respect than an honorary attaché. But he had had Salonika; he had taken an important part in the Aden demarkation; he had reported a massacre of Christians in Southern Asia Minor and had been commended by the Foreign Office for his diligence; his name had been blessed by the fig merchants of Smyrna. He had eaten rich food in quantity for a number of years, and he possessed a rich wife, who had never given him a moment of uneasiness, neither when the bulbuls were singing to the roses of Constantinople nor amid the murmurous gardens of Damascus.

Aunt Cuckoo was a daughter of the wealthy old Levantine family of Hewitson, who brought her husband such a handsome dowry that he was able ever afterward to claim by some obscure process of logic that he had really served his country for nothing.

"The point is," he used to argue, "the point is that I can give up my consular career when I choose." And the student-interpreters, vice-consuls, and consuls of the Levant service, some of whom had rashly married lovely but penniless Greeks, wondered why the deuce he didn't hurry up and do so and thus give them a lift all round.

Aunt Cuckoo, being without children, had devoted herself to cats—Angora cats, a breed to which she became attached during the time that her husband was consul in that city. Angora cats lack even as much humanity as Persian cats; compared with Siamese or Javanese cats they are not human at all- Indeed, as a substitute for the emotions and cravings of womanhood they are not much more effective than bundles of cotton-wool would be. In the eyes of the world Aunt Cuckoo's childlessness was atoned for by the purity and perfection of her Angora breed; but she herself had to satisfy her own maternal instincts more profoundly by coddling, almost by cuddling for twenty years a bad arm. And really what better substitute for a baby could a childless woman find than a bad arm? Sometimes, of course, it really does hurt; but then sometimes a baby cuts its teeth, has convulsions or croup, is prone to flatulence and breaks out into spots. An arm exhibits the phenomena of growth and decay, and if a baby becomes an inky little boy, and an inky little boy becomes an exigent young man, an arm gets older and becomes as exigent as its owner will allow it to be. A bad arm can be shown to people even by an elderly lady without blushing, whereas children after a certain age cannot be exhibited in their nudity. Aunt Cuckoo's bad arm was the chief consolation of her loneliness, and it was only natural that the morning after Jasmine's arrival she should take her niece aside and enquire in a whisper if she should like to see her bad arm. Jasmine welcomed the introduction with an unspoken hope that there was nothing nasty to see. Nor was there. It was apparently the perfectly normal arm that any woman over fifty might possess. Age had blunted the contours; twenty years of testing the efficiency of various lotions and liniments had gradually stained its pristine alabaster; but there was nothing whatever to see, no tumour malignant or benign, no ulcer indolent or irritable.

"I am going to try a new system of massage," Aunt Cuckoo confided. "And I can't help thinking how nice it would be if you could have a few lessons."

And as Uncle Eneas for his part was convinced that a more valuable lesson would be the art of jiu-jitsu, in whatever direction she looked Jasmine could see nothing before her but muscular development.

"The point about jiu-jitsu," Uncle Eneas explained, "is the independence it gives you. My own feeling is that women should be as far as possible independent."

Aunt Cuckoo looked up at this. It had never struck her before that such was her husband's opinion.

"Now don't *you* suggest learning jiu-jitsu," he said quickly.

"I don't think my arm would let me," his wife replied.

"And you ought to get plenty of walking," Uncle Eneas added, turning to Jasmine. "At your age I always walked for an hour and a half before breakfast. I remember once at Broussa...." and he was off on one of his entirely topographical stories, dragging his listeners through landscapes that for them were as shifting, as uncertain, as nebulous and confused as the landscapes of other people's dreams.

Perhaps Aunt Cuckoo yielded less to her husband than superficially she appeared. Certainly nothing more was said about jiu-jitsu, whereas the massage scheme made considerable progress. Two days later a gaunt blonde, with that look professional nurses sometimes have of being nuns who have succumbed to the temptations of the flesh, invested The Cedars. She advanced upon poor Aunt Cuckoo with such a grim air that Jasmine began to think that it was rather a pity that she had not learnt jiu-jitsu in order to defend herself against this barbarian.

"This is Miss Hellner," said Aunt Cuckoo, timorously offering the introduction in the manner of a propitiatory sacrifice. "Miss Hellner," she went on imploringly, "who has made such a wonderful improvement in my bad arm. I want my niece to get a few hints from you, Miss Hellner. She is anxious to take up massage professionally."

Miss Hellner's cold blue eye, as cold and blue as one of her Scandinavian fjords, was fixed upon the victim; no amount of talk about Jasmine's future was going to deter her from her duty.

"Will you please unbutton the sleeve?" she requested in a guttural voice, which Aunt Cuckoo prepared to obey.

"The arm has been rather better the last few days," the patient suggested. "So perhaps it won't be necessary to repeat last week's treatment."

"Three times that treatment is repeated," said Miss Hellner inexorably. "That is the rule."

"Oh dear," Aunt Cuckoo murmured with a dolorous little giggle. "I'm afraid I'm going to have rather a painful time. But don't go away, Jasmine. It's going to hurt me very much, but it will be very interesting for you to watch. Miss Hellner is so expert."

But flattery was impotent against Miss Hellner, who by now had seized the arm and was kneading it, pinching it, digging her knuckles into it—and bony knuckles they were too—trying to tear it in half apparently with her thumbs, burrowing and boring, while all the time Aunt Cuckoo ejaculated "Ouch!" or "Ah!" and to one viciously penetrating use of the forefinger as a gimlet "Yi! Yi!"

At last Miss Hellner stopped, and Aunt Cuckoo lay back on the sofa with a sigh, occasionally giving a glance of ineffable tenderness to where her bad arm, as red as a new-born baby, lay upon her breast.

"If your arm is not well after one more treatment...."

"One more treatment," echoed Aunt Cuckoo dutifully, "Yes?"

"You will have to take the oil cure."

"The oil cure?" asked the patient, pleasantly excited at the prospect of a new treatment. "What does that consist of?"

"First you take an ice bath."

"Yes," said Aunt Cuckoo, "our bathroom is *very* nice."

"Ice bath," repeated the nurse severely.

"Oh, I see," said Aunt Cuckoo with less enthusiasm. "You mean a cold bath."

"Ice bath," Miss Hellner almost shouted. "With lumps of ice to float. Then I rub you with oil of olives."

Aunt Cuckoo nodded gratefully; after the ice such a proceeding sounded luxurious.

"Then with nothing on you will do the gymnastic. Up and down the room. Backwards and forwards. So."

"Dear me, with nothing on? Absolutely nothing? Couldn't I keep a small towel?"

"Nothing on," repeated the masseuse obstinately. "Then you sit for ten minutes in the window with the fan."

"But surely not with nothing on except a fan?"

"With nothing on," the masseuse insisted. "Then——" She paused impressively, while Aunt Cuckoo looked excessively agitated, and Jasmine wondered what ultimate ordeal she was going to prescribe. Surely she could not intend to make the patient sit in the garden or drive in the brougham with nothing on?

"Then you will drink a large glass of lemonade and absorb the oil," Miss Hellner announced.

"Good gracious! Not a very large glass of oil?"

"It is the lemons who drink the oil. It was not you yourself," Miss Hellner explained scornfully.

"Jasmine," said Aunt Cuckoo with one finger lifted in solemn admonition, "don't let me forget to order the lemons in good time."

The lemonade was such a simple and peaceable climax that Aunt Cuckoo was evidently anxious to try it; she did not ask her niece to remind her about the ice, and in order to prevent Miss Hellner's reminding her she suggested that Jasmine should have a short lesson in the art of massage.

"Oh, but I think watching you has been enough lesson for to-day" objected Jasmine, who feared the example that is better than the precept. "I don't think I could take in any more at first."

"She must come to the school of Swedish culture," Miss Hellner decided.

Thus it was that Jasmine found herself engaged on Mondays, Wednesdays, and Fridays to travel from Hampstead to Baker Street, with every prospect, unless fate should intervene to save her, of becoming by profession a masseuse, the last profession she would ever have chosen for herself.

On the days when she did not go to Baker Street she had to comb the cats. To comb seven Angora cats was almost as tiring as massage.

"I suppose this is the way your arm got bad?" she once suggested to her aunt.

"Oh, no, dear," said Aunt Cuckoo. "When I was young I used to write a great deal. I wrote six novels about life in the Levant, and then I had writer's cramp."

That evening when she went up to her bedroom Jasmine found her aunt's novels waiting to be read—eighteen volumes published in the style of the early 'nineties and the late 'eighties, with titles like *The Sultan's Shadow* and *The Rose of Sharon*. She read bits of each one in turn, and then abruptly felt that she had had enough, just as one feels that one has had enough Turkish-delight. Unfortunately Aunt Cuckoo said there was nothing she liked better than really intelligent criticism. So between reading the novels, learning massage, and combing the cats there was not much leisure for Jasmine, and what leisure she had was more than filled by rapid walks with Uncle Eneas over the Heath. Sirene is not a place that predisposes people to walk fast, and Uncle Eneas was continually being amazed that a niece thirty-five years younger than himself should be unable to quicken her pace to suit his own. Sometimes he said this in such a severe tone that Jasmine was half afraid that he would buy a lead and compel her to keep up with him. Luckily she was not expected to talk, and she soon discovered that she was only expected to say once in every ten minutes 'What an extraordinary life you have had, Uncle Eneas,' to maintain him in a perfectly good temper.

Aunt May had written Jasmine a long letter from Spaborough expressing her delight at the news that she was treating Uncle Eneas and Aunt Cuckoo with more consideration than she had shown towards Uncle Hector and herself, announcing the imminent return of the family to Harley Street and magnanimously offering to give Jasmine lunch on her 'massage days,' inasmuch as Harley Street was, as no doubt she knew, quite close to Baker Street. Cousin Edith also wrote warmly and effusively; but the paleness of the ink, the thinness of the pen, and the flimsiness of the paper made the letter seem like an old letter found in a secret drawer and addressed to somebody who had been dead a century. She did not hear from Harry Vibart, and she wondered if he had written to her at Strathspey House and if her relatives there had kept back the letter. She supposed that she should never see him again, and she began to fear that she, like so many other girls, should drift into a profession to which she was not particularly attracted, or into a marriage for which she was not particularly anxious, or perhaps, worst of all, that she should merely shrink and shrink and shrink into a desiccated old maid like Cousin Edith. It was not an exhilarating prospect; Mustapha, the patriarch of the Angora cats, had his fur combed out less gently than usual that morning.

Life was seeming unutterably dreary when Aunt Cuckoo came into the room, her eyes flashing with anticipation, her being rejuvenated by excitement, to say that one of the maids had a stiff neck, and to ask if Jasmine would immediately go to her room and operate on it.

Jasmine followed her aunt upstairs, and expressed her sense of life's disillusionment by the vigour with which she manipulated, man-handled indeed, the neck and shoulders of the young woman, who after numerous vain protests burst into hysterical tears and gave a month's notice.

"Funny, isn't it," said Aunt Cuckoo when they left the room, "what little gratitude you find among the lower classes nowadays?"

"I think I did rather hurt her," said Jasmine, who was by now feeling rather penitent.

"*I* think you did it very well," said Aunt Cuckoo, "and *I* am very pleased with you. And of course her shoulders are so much harder than my poor arm."

Aunt Cuckoo, for all her folly, had for Jasmine a certain pathos, and during the late autumn and winter while she stayed at The Cedars she to some extent grew accustomed to the atmosphere of cold storage which prevailed there; she began to contemplate the slow freezing of herself during the years to come into an Aunt Cuckoo; she preferred the notion of a frozen self, which after all would always be liable to melt, to the notion of a withered self like Cousin Edith's, which would indubitably never bourgeon again. She did sometimes lunch with the Hector Grants at Harley Street, and she found them more insufferable every time she went there. Aunt Cuckoo could not help feeling gratified by this, because for many years now she had been jealous of Lady Grant.

"Of course I should not like to appear as if I was criticizing her," she would say to Jasmine. "But I understand what you mean about Lettice and Pamela, and I can't help feeling that they have been spoilt. It's the same with cats," she murmured, in a vague effort to elucidate the moral atmosphere.

When Aunt Cuckoo talked like this, Jasmine began to wonder if she could confide in her about Harry Vibart; but when she had to frame the words, her account of the affair began to seem so pretentious and exaggerated that she could not bring herself to the point, would blush in embarrassment, and hide her confusion by an energetic combing of Mustapha.

In the middle of the winter Aunt Cuckoo began to throw out hints of what Jasmine might expect from herself and Uncle Eneas in the future. She never went so far as a definite statement that they intended to make her their heiress; the prospect of future wealth was merely hinted at like the landscape under a false dawn. Yet even this glimmer over something beyond was enough to alarm Jasmine with the idea that her uncle and aunt would suppose that she was aiming at an inheritance. She tried by diligent combing of cats, by concentration upon the massage of Aunt Cuckoo's arm, and by the rapidity of her walking pace, to show that she appreciated what was being done for her in the present; but the moment Aunt Cuckoo began to talk of the future she was discouragingly rude. Nevertheless these hints, notwithstanding Jasmine's reception of them, would probably have taken a more definite shape if on the anniversary of the conversion of Saint Paul Aunt Cuckoo had not taken shelter from a sudden storm of rain in a small Catholic mission church at Golders Green. Here she felt vague aspirations at the sight of half a dozen poor people praying in the rich twilight of imitation glass windows; but she was more particularly and more deeply impressed by the behaviour of a woman in rusty mourning in bringing a pallid little boy to the feet of a saintly image that was attracting Aunt Cuckoo's attention and everybody's attention by lifting his habit and pointing to a sore on his leg. After praying to an accompaniment of maternal prods the child was bidden to deposit at the base of the image a bandage of lint, after which he stuck six candles on the pricket, lighted them, and followed his mother out of the church with many a backward glance to observe the effect of his illumination. Aunt Cuckoo was puzzled by all this, and overtaking the woman in the porch asked what it meant. She was told that the saint's name was Roch and that he had miraculously cured her little boy of an ulcerous leg. Aunt Cuckoo's arm immediately began to pain her acutely. On feeling this pain she went back into the church and prayed shyly, for she was not a Catholic and she had only heard the saint's name for the first time. The pain vanished as abruptly as it came, and Aunt Cuckoo, thrilled by the miracle, hurried home to tell Jasmine all about it. As soon as her mind had turned its attention to miracles Aunt Cuckoo began to fancy that she was being specially favoured by Heavenly manifestations.

"Of course one has said 'How miraculous!' before," she assured her niece. "But one employs terms so loosely. I learned that when I used to write." Aunt Cuckoo's voice, from many years of tonelessness, was, now that she was able to feel a genuine excitement, full of astonishing little squeaks and tremolos which had she been a clock would have led the listener to oil the works at once. "And the healing of my bad arm wasn't the only miracle," she hurried on. "Oh no, dear. I assure you it stopped raining the moment I came out of church, and you know how difficult it is to find a taxi when one requires one. Well, would you believe it, lo and behold, one pulled up just outside the church, and the moment I was inside it started to pour again. I'm so glad that you're a Catholic, dear. There, you see I'm already learning not to say Roman Catholic...."

It was at this point that Jasmine became discouraging. Her religion had always been such a matter-of-fact business in Sirene and the existence of Protestants so natural in a world divided into rich touring English folk and poor dear predatory Italians that her aunt's intentions shocked her.

"You're not thinking of becoming a Christian—I mean a Catholic," she gasped.

"Who knows?" said Aunt Cuckoo in the vague and awful tones of a Sibyl. "And I should have thought, Jasmine, that you would have been the first to rejoice."

Jasmine felt that her aunt was presenting her out of a profusion of miracles with one all for herself; but realizing what everybody would say she was so ungracious that Aunt Cuckoo went and offered it to the parish priest instead.

Father Maloney was at first inclined to resent Aunt Cuckoo's suggestion that St. Roch should have healed a Protestant; but when her ardour and humility had been sufficiently tried, he agreed to receive her into the Church, and though he did not encourage her to believe in any more miracles, he was privately inclined to hold the pious opinion that a well-to-do convert's arrival in the unfinished condition of the new sacristy was as nearly miraculous as anything in his career.

A month later, notwithstanding Uncle Eneas' severe indictment of the crimes of the papacy, Aunt Cuckoo became a Catholic. Miss Hellner was dismissed; Jasmine was bidden to consider massage an invention of the devil; the Angora cats were sold; Aunt Cuckoo was confirmed. Her husband who in the course of their married life had successfully cured her of singing after dinner, of writing novels, of spiritualism, of Christian science, of a dread of premature burial, of a belief in the immortality conferred by sour milk, and of eating nuts the last thing at night and the first thing in the morning, was defeated by this craze; her ability to resist her husband's disapproval convinced Aunt Cuckoo more firmly than ever that she was the recipient of a special dose of grace. Yet although Catholicism supplied most of Aunt Cuckoo's emotional needs, it could not entirely stifle her unsatisfied maternal instinct, so that sometimes, when St. Roch was busy with other patients, she looked back regretfully to the days when her arm really hurt, and her faith was exposed to the insinuations of the Evil One. She turned her attention to juvenile saints and became much wrapped up in St. Aloysius Gonzaga until she found that he objected to his mother's seeing him undress when he was eight years old and that he had fainted because a footman saw him with one sock off at the age of four. St. Aloysius evidently did not require her maternal love, and she lavished it on St. Stanislas Kostka instead; but even with him she felt awkward, until at last St. Teresa, most practical of women, came to her rescue in the middle of the Sursum Corda. Three months after her conversion Aunt Cuckoo arrived home from mass on Lady Day with an expression in her pale blue eyes that would have required the cobalt of Fra Angelico to represent.

"Eneas," she announced, "I have decided to adopt a baby."

To the consular mind of Mr. Grant such a procedure evoked endless complications in the future. His mind leaped forward twenty years to the time when this baby would require a passport, and he wondered if there were a special form for adopted babies. He seemed to fancy vaguely that there was, and he asked what the nationality of the baby would be.

"A Catholic baby," Aunt Cuckoo proclaimed.

Her husband explained to her that she must not confuse religion with nationality, and then suddenly with a grimace of real ferocity he said:

"I hope you don't intend to adopt an Irish baby?"

"A Catholic baby," Aunt Cuckoo repeated obstinately.

"This kipper is rather strong," said Eneas.

But it was not strong enough to divert Aunt Cuckoo from her own trail.

"I spoke to Father Maloney about it this morning after mass," she persisted.

"Damn Father Maloney!" said Eneas.

Jasmine was wondering to herself what part she would be called upon to play with regard to the baby. But whatever she had to do would be less tiring than combing Angora cats or trying to keep up with Uncle Eneas on the slopes of Hampstead Heath. Uncle Eneas protested all day for a week against the baby; Aunt Cuckoo appealed to St. Teresa, secured her support by a novena, and defeated him once more. Father Maloney discovered a Catholic bank-clerk, the victim of chronic alcoholism, who with the help of a tuberculous wife had brought into the world twelve children, the youngest of which, now ten months old, he secured for Aunt Cuckoo. At the formal conveyance of the baby Uncle Eneas asked whether it were a boy or a girl, and when Aunt Cuckoo replied that she did not know, he, apostrophizing heaven, wondered if ever since the world began a vaguer woman had walked the earth.

"It's a boy," said Father Maloney soothingly.

"What's his name?" asked Aunt Cuckoo.

"Michael Francis Joseph Mary Aloysius," said Father Maloney.

"Good God!" exclaimed Uncle Eneas.

"We'll call him Frank," Aunt Cuckoo decided, and her husband was almost appeased. He had not realized that anything so ordinary could be extracted from that highly coloured mosaic of names.

At first Aunt Cuckoo was glad of Jasmine's help, and of the advice of the very latest product in professional nurses. But when she found that the nurse had theories in the bringing up of babies that by no means accorded with her own sentimental views, and that Jasmine was inclined to support the nurse, she began to be a little resentful of her niece.

"You don't understand, my dear," she said. "You see you aren't a mother."

"Well, but nor are you," Jasmine pointed out. This retort so much annoyed Aunt Cuckoo that she began to hint, much more obviously than she had hinted at future prosperity, at the inconvenience of Jasmine's presence in The Cedars.

Possibly Aunt Cuckoo's desire to be relieved of any responsibility for her niece's future might not have matured so rapidly had not Uncle Eneas been converted if not to the baby's religion at any rate of its company by the obvious pleasure his entrance into the room caused the creature. No man is secure against flattery; the cult of the dog as a domestic animal proves that. No doubt if on its adopted father's entrance into a room the baby had shrieked, turned black in the face or vomited, he would have been tempted to take refuge in the society of his niece from such implied contempt. But the baby always demonstrated rapture at the approach of Uncle Eneas. Its toes curled over sensuously; its fingers clutched at strings of celestial music; it dribbled and made that odd noise which is called crowing. It said La-la-la-la-la very rapidly and tried to leap in the air. Probably it was fascinated by a prominent and brilliantly coloured red wen on Uncle Eneas' cheek, because if ever he bent over to pay his respects the baby would always make distinct efforts to grasp this wen with one hand, while with the other it would try to grasp his tie-pin, a moderately large single ruby not unlike the wen. Luckily for itself the baby could not express what exactly kindled its young enthusiasm, and Uncle Eneas naturally began to believe that the infant was exceptionally intelligent. His wife encouraged this opinion; all the servants encouraged this opinion; even the professional nurse encouraged this opinion. It was obvious that the baby would be henceforth ineradicable. Moreover by acquiring a baby already ten months old, what Uncle Eneas called the early stewed raspberry stage of babyhood had been passed elsewhere, and the exciting first attempts at conversation and locomotion were already in sight. As yet neither Uncle Eneas nor Aunt Cuckoo had gone beyond hints about the problem of Jasmine's future, but she began to feel sensitive about staying longer at The Cedars and to ask herself what she was going to do presently. At this point the baby, with what had it not been a baby might have been called cynical coquetry, roused the demons of jealousy by suddenly making shameless advances to Jasmine. Nothing would please the infant now but that Jasmine should play with it continually: Uncle Eneas and Aunt Cuckoo were greeted with yells of disapproval. With Spring rapidly coming to the prime it was felt that such an unnatural preference indicated the need for a change of air. Jasmine sensed an exchange of diplomatic notes among her relatives. She shrank within herself at the thought that none too much willingness was anywhere being displayed to receive her.

"I thought it would be rather nice for you to go down to Curtain Wells and stay with your Uncle Alexander for a while in this beautiful spring weather," said Aunt Cuckoo. "But it appears that the only spare room is in the hands of the decorators."

And on another day she said: "I am rather surprised that your Aunt May doesn't invite you to stay with her in Harley Street for the season. They have become so ultra-fashionable nowadays that one might have supposed that they would have invited you to Harley Street to share in the general atmosphere of gaiety. I do hope that dear little Frank is not going to grow up quite so self-absorbed as Lettice and Pamela."

"If you want me to go away," said Jasmine desperately, "why don't you say so? I never wanted to come to England. I'll go back to Sirene with what massage I know and earn my living there."

"But who has given you the least idea that you are unwelcome?" said Aunt Cuckoo. "It was of you I was thinking. I am afraid that dear baby's arrival has made us less able to amuse you than we were. And I don't like to suggest that you should take entire charge of him."

At this moment Uncle Eneas came blustering into the room.

"I've had a letter from Uncle Matthew," he proclaimed. "He's got an idea into his head that he wants to go down to the seaside. Some fool of a doctor's been stuffing him up with that notion. He says he thinks we ought to go to the seaside, and says it would be a good idea to share expenses, we paying two-thirds and he paying one-third. The mean old screw! How like him that is! And if we take baby he'll only want to pay a quarter."

"Oh, but I think Uncle Matthew would be too frightening for dear baby," said Aunt Cuckoo. "Why shouldn't Jasmine go and stay with him?" she suggested.

"That wouldn't suit his plan," said Uncle Eneas. "If Jasmine went he would have to pay for her as well as for himself."

"But don't you think that if Jasmine went to stay with him at Muswell Hill, she would do as well as a change of air?"

"By Jove, that's quite a notion," said Uncle Eneas, looking at his niece as people look at the sky to see if it is going to rain. Jasmine was trying to remember what she knew about Uncle Matthew. He existed in her mind as an incredibly old gentleman of boundless wealth who years ago had bought a picture of her father.

"I think you would like Uncle Matthew so much," Aunt Cuckoo was saying persuasively. "Of course he's very old and he's a little eccentric. I think old people often are eccentric, don't you? But he's very well off, and it really does seem a wonderful solution of the difficulty."

"You mean the difficulty of having me on your hands?" Jasmine bluntly demanded.

"Please don't say that," Aunt Cuckoo begged. "Surely you heard what your uncle said? Our difficulty is that we don't want to disturb Uncle Matthew with precious Baboose. I don't think he would quite understand how the little pet came to us."

So long as she was to be tossed about like a ball, Jasmine thought she might just as well be tossed into an old gentleman's lap as anywhere else, and soon after this, gathering from a fragment she overheard of a low colloquy between her uncle and aunt that her introduction to Uncle Matthew would intensely annoy the Hector Grants, she made up her mind not to oppose, but even to press forward the proposed visit.

"Where is Muswell Hill?" she asked.

"Oh, it's on a hill," said Aunt Cuckoo vaguely. "I don't know what bus you take. It's a large house, and as he has only one servant everything gets a little dusty. Whenever I go there I always take a duster with me, because Uncle Matthew so appreciates a little attention. At least I'm sure he does really appreciate it, though of course he's reached that age when people don't seem to appreciate anything. What do you think, dear?" she turned to ask her husband. "We might invite him to dinner."

It was extraordinary how much the baby's arrival had strengthened Aunt Cuckoo's position in the household. In the old days she would never have dreamed of asking anyone to dinner; but her vicarious maternity gave her as much importance as if she had really borne a child at the age of fifty-two. Eneas had correspondingly shrunk with regard to his wife, though with everybody else he was as pompous as ever.

"Now I'm going to give you a few hints," said Aunt Cuckoo to Jasmine. "Dear old Uncle Matthew is very fond of pictures."

"Yes, I remember he bought one of father's years and years ago."

"Oh, hush, hush!" Aunt Cuckoo breathed. "He's not at all fond of buying anything now. You must *give* him one of your father's pictures. In fact, if I might suggest it, you had better give him all that you have left. We shall send the brougham over to fetch him, and I don't see any reason why you should not drive back with him to Muswell Hill after dinner. We could put the pictures on the luggage rack, and your trunk could be sent over by Carter Paterson the next day. You could put what you wanted for the night in quite a small bag, which I will lend you."

Religion was making Aunt Cuckoo as practical as St. Teresa herself. Perhaps it was lucky for Uncle Eneas that she had adopted a baby; he would have found a new order of nuns much more expensive.

The invitation was sent to Uncle Matthew, and the next day the answer came back written on the back of the same sheet of paper. In a postscript he had added: "*I wish you wouldn't seal your envelopes to me, as I cannot turn them so easily. People nowadays seem to have no idea of economy. Every envelope should be used twice over.*"

"It's really not avarice," Aunt Cuckoo explained. "It's only eccentricity."

She was longing more than ever to get Jasmine out of the house. That afternoon darling baby had pulled Uncle Eneas' moustache with a suggestion of viciousness, and though Uncle Eneas had said in a fatuous voice, "Poor little man, he doesn't know that it hurts," Aunt Cuckoo was inclined to think that Baby did know it hurt, and that he had been prompted to the outrage by Jasmine's influence.

Uncle Matthew was apparently a difficult person to entertain at dinner because he liked to be well fed and at the same time he did not like to see anything wasted. If the least bit too much was given him, he would overeat himself rather than let anything be wasted, which often made him ill afterwards. Aunt Cuckoo's dinners in the past had usually been failures, because in those days her temperament was far too vague to calculate nicely the necessary quantity of food. The development of her practical qualities promised greater success now. Besides, now that Jasmine was here, she could not make a mistake, because if there was too much Jasmine could be given a larger helping than she wanted, and if there was too little Jasmine could be given less. It was debated whether it would be wise to warn Uncle Matthew in advance of Jasmine's existence, of which he was probably unaware, inasmuch as the Hector Grants had every interest in not telling him; and it was finally decided to say nothing about her until she was introduced to him. Aunt Cuckoo was anxious to explain that Jasmine had come all the way from Sirene to lay at his feet her father's dying wish in the shape of four pictures; but Uncle Eneas' more cautious consular nature did not approve of this plan. There was also some discussion whether anything should be said about Baby. Aunt Cuckoo in the pride of maternity had no doubts; but Uncle Eneas with the approach of Uncle Matthew's visit was feeling more and more like a nephew and less and less like a father.

"I don't think the old boy will understand our deliberately procuring a child in that way. I know he has always regarded children as unpleasant accidents."

"But suppose darling Baboose cries?"

"Well, he mustn't," the adopted father decided. "Or if he does, we must say that it's a baby in the street outside. It's impossible really to arrange a suitable reception in advance. That last tooth has been giving him a good deal of trouble, you know, and he may ... well, he may in fact take it out of the old gentleman. No, I feel sure that a meeting between them would be most inappropriate."

Aunt Cuckoo gave way. She was too anxious to palm off Jasmine on Uncle Matthew not for once to sacrifice Baby's dignity as the heir of The Cedars.

Chapter Six

UNCLE Matthew Rouncivell was not of course so old as his relatives boasted that he was, but he was old enough to be considered incapable of lasting much longer and old enough to justify any member of the family in adding a few years to the correct total, which was seventy-six. He had been fifteen years younger than the wife of the Bishop of Clapham, and though he had scoffed at his sister for marrying a parson, he had to admit in the end that Andrew had made the most of a poor profession. Uncle Matthew's mean and acquisitive boyhood had been the consolation of his father's declining years, and he started life with a comfortable fortune notwithstanding what had been robbed from him as a dowry to marry off his sister. Their father, Samuel Rouncivell, had invested largely in property that seemed likely to put difficulties in the way of far-off municipal improvements, or as he preferred to put it, lay along the lines of future urban development. He and his son after him had a remarkable flair for buying up decrepit slums that would afterward turn out to be the only possible site for a new town hall or public library. And then the keen eye old Samuel had for the arteries of traffic! Why, it was as keen as an anatomist's for the arteries of the human body. In whatever direction tramlines or railroads desired to flow, there stood Samuel ready to apply his tourniquet, which was sometimes nothing more than one tumbledown cottage plastered with signs of ancient lights. This sense of direction was transmitted to Matthew, who when one of the big London termini had to be enlarged trebled his fortune at a stroke. Now, at seventy-six, he could not be worth less than fifteen thousand a year, and as he did not spend five hundred, every year he lived was making him wealthier. Long ago he had married a beautiful young woman who a few months later was killed in a riding accident. Since then he had spent a solitary and misanthropic life, grinding his tenants, amassing a quantity of unusual walking-sticks and bad modern pictures, and collecting what he called antiques. His only amusement was the malicious delight he took in leading the various groups of his relations to suppose one after another that he was contemplating them as his beneficiaries. Thin-lipped and beaky, he had a fat flabby back and pale flabby cheeks, and the skin of his neck was mottled and scaly as a snake's slough. He usually wore a frock-coat that resembled the green slime on London railings in wet weather; but when he dined out he took with him a black velvet smoking cap worked in arabesques of yellow silk and a pair of slippers made of leopard's fur to which moth had given a mangy appearance. He liked to dine early, and it was six o'clock of a fine evening in early May when he arrived at The Cedars, his frock-coat reinforced by a grey muffler long enough and thick enough to have kept a Zulu moderately warm at the North Pole. He did not seem in a good temper, and when Niko helped him to disengage himself from the muffler, he asked with a growl if the fool thought he was spinning a top. However, when he entered the dining-room and saw poor Sholto Grant's pictures all aglow in the rich horizontal sunlight, he cheered up for a moment, until a suspicion that his nephew Eneas was proposing to sell him the pictures intervened and spoilt his pleasure. He at once began to criticize and cheapen the pictures so ruthlessly that Jasmine could hardly keep back her tears. In Crispano's Café at Sirene she had once heard a futurist painter criticizing her father's pictures, and she had been so angry that she had upset the coffee over him on her way out. To hear Uncle Matthew one might suppose that such bad pictures had never been painted since the world began; yet she could say nothing.

"I'm sorry you don't like them," said Aunt Cuckoo, "because Jasmine has brought them back for you all the way from Sirene."

"Eh? What's that?" demanded Uncle Matthew, twisting round on one of his sticks and thumping the floor with the other. "Who's Jasmine?"

"Jasmine is poor Sholto's daughter."

"What? Another?" the old gentleman growled.

"No, he only had one."

"I can't think why people want to have children at all," Uncle Matthew sniffed. Eneas congratulated his wife with a complacent glance on their reserve about Baby. "So you brought back these pictures for me, did you?" the old gentleman continued. "Humph! I did buy one of your father's pictures a long time ago, and I don't say it was bad, but he asked too much for it. And now if I accept these I shall have to buy frames for them," he concluded indignantly.

But the insistency of Sholto's pictures, the indubitable, the positive proclamation of their being what they were, the full value they gave of blue water, bright flowers, and rosy cheeks, softened the old gentleman's heart. They really did express for him his own taste in art, and inasmuch as they were a present he could not quite conceal his gratification.

"I hope you haven't gone and ordered a very extravagant dinner for me," he said gruffly to hide as far as possible the least amenity in his manner.

Aunt Cuckoo reassured him, and, the gong ringing at that moment, they moved toward the dining-room. Uncle Matthew disdained an arm, preferring to rely upon his two sticks.

"Wonderful how he bears himself for an old gentleman, isn't it?" whispered Uncle Eneas to Jasmine. "We're a long-lived family. There's no doubt about that." He was too anxious for the success of the evening to brag more particularly about his own athletic qualities.

The dinner consisted of various Eastern dishes, on all of which the old gentleman looked with an approving eye, because each dish gave the impression of being a hash of something unfinished the day before. The richness of their flavouring appealed to his palate, and the zest with which his nephew filled up his own plate had its effect upon his own appetite. Jasmine got into disgrace early in the meal by leaving half a plate of *pilau* untouched, but she was able to recover some of her lost ground by refusing wine.

"Good girl!" Uncle Matthew exclaimed, and turning to his nephew he asked why there was wine on the table when he knew that there was nothing of which he disapproved so much as wine. Eneas glared angrily at his wife. It was only since Father Maloney had been dining with them occasionally that wine had been seen at The Cedars. The offending decanter was removed, and everybody finished what water was left in his tumbler with an expression of critical enjoyment.

"Have you written about those rooms yet?" Uncle Matthew asked presently.

Eneas shook his head weightily. "The trouble is I shall have to stay in London until the end of July. I've been asked by the Foreign Office to do some work for them—expert work in Turkish which nobody else can do at present." Then he wavered. "But perhaps Cuckoo...."

His wife cut him short. "I shan't be able to get away until July," she said; but she went on roguishly: "So we thought that perhaps if you were very good, Uncle Matthew, we'd lend you Jasmine for a little while."

Eneas could not withhold a glance of admiration; he even resolved not to allude to the mistake over the wine when Uncle Matthew was gone. He admitted to himself that he should never have thought of suggesting that Jasmine was a loan, or of putting Uncle Matthew in the position of a little boy being given a treat.

"Lend me Jasmine?" the old gentleman repeated. "And what am I to do with Jasmine, pray?"

"She's invaluable," said Aunt Cuckoo, leaning across the dining table and squeezing her niece's hand. "And I wouldn't lend her to anybody else but you. Everybody's clamouring for her."

Uncle Matthew looked at his great-niece with the expression that for many years he had been wont to accord to proffered bargains.

"You told us you wanted a change," Aunt Cuckoo persisted. "And as soon as you told us we made up our minds that whatever it cost us *you* should have Jasmine."

Throughout the evening Aunt Cuckoo made it appear that Jasmine really was indispensable, and by dint of never committing herself to anything without asking Jasmine if she agreed with her and of never formulating any plan without asking Jasmine first if she approved of it and of never wanting anything without asking Jasmine if she would fetch it for her, she really did manage to impress Uncle Matthew that by taking away Jasmine from The Cedars he would be robbing a nephew and niece. This was too keen a pleasure for the old gentleman to deny himself, and when he left that evening he went away with a solemn promise that Jasmine should be delivered to him at eleven o'clock the following morning.

"We don't usually let the carriage go out two days running," said Aunt Cuckoo in a final burst of abnegation, "but for dear Jasmine's sake we will."

"A very successful evening, my dear," Uncle Eneas observed when the visitor was gone.

"And that precious lamb upstairs never made a sound."

"The young rascal! He knew. *He* knew," the adoptive father idiotically chuckled.

Jasmine wondered what he was supposed to know—perhaps, she thought with a shade of malice, that he might one day inherit Uncle Matthew's fortune if Uncle Matthew died in ignorance of his existence. She could not bring herself to imagine that any money would be left to Lettice and Pamela. Ah, but there were others whom she had not yet seen, those six boy cousins at Silchester, and Uncle Alexander with his lunatic prince. Why had she ever consented to leave Sirene? Whichever way she looked in England there was nothing to be seen except an endless vista of servitude. Girls in books always struck out for themselves, but perhaps they were the only girls who were written about. There must be hundreds of others like herself who remained slaves. Not at all, they finally got married; they worked hard and....

"It's really a ghastly prospect," she exclaimed aloud.

"*Uscirò pazza!* I'm like some cheap novel in a circulating library gradually getting more and more dog's-eared, more and more dirty and greasy, and all the time being passed on and on—oh! I can't stand it much longer...."

Jasmine did not set out to Muswell Hill with much hope in her heart. She felt as if she was being posted to Matthew Rouncivell, Esq., and the kisses of her uncle and aunt remained on her cheeks like postage stamps.

Rouncivell Lodge was a double-fronted, two-storied house which was built of brown brick in the first quarter of the nineteenth century, probably by some prosperous city merchant, as a country residence. It had remained what was practically a country residence until a few years ago, when old Matthew Rouncivell sacrificed the couple of acres of garden behind the house and built on the site large blocks of bright red flats, leaving no land to his own house except the shrubbery in front, which was divided into three segments by a semicircular drive; in the largest of these stood a Doric summer-house converted by Mr. Rouncivell into a smoking-room. The proximity of the flats and the amount of sky they cut off added to the gloom of the shrubbery, which was a mass of rank ivy and euonymus bushes, of American rhododendrons, lilacs that never flowered, privets, and Portuguese laurels. Moreover, although the flats were what the agent called high-class residential flats, the landlord, possibly with the vague notion of guarding what was left of the privacy he had himself destroyed, had had them planned to present to anybody entering the gates of Rouncivell Lodge their domestic windows, which, with dish-cloths drying on every sill, gave them the squalid appearance of tenement buildings.

The old gentleman himself, when, wearing his velvet smoking-jacket, his tasselled smoking-cap, and a pair of goloshes over his fur slippers, he visited the smoking-room to smoke his weekly cigar, found the flavour of the cigar was enhanced by calculating how much a year each window in sight brought him in. This meditation was so comforting that he used really to enjoy his smoke, although the cigars, which were of poor quality when he bought them, had not been improved by their storage in the damp Doric summer-house. However, he smoked them literally to the bitter end; this bitter end he used to stick upon a penknife, and even when each puff nearly blistered his tongue he still enjoyed it, because he had made a calculation that merely by the amount more of a cigar he smoked than anyone else he had gained on the whole year two complete cigars. He was always making calculations. He would even calculate how much each spine of the shark's backbone that was the only decoration of the walls of his smoking-room cost him. And as for the cost of Jasmine's food, he could have told you to a spoonful of soup.

The centre of Rouncivell Lodge was occupied by a very wide staircase lighted from above by a large skylight and bounded by walls the entire area of which was covered with a collection of astonishingly banal pictures. The visitor realized with a shock of knowledge that the pictures from the exhibition of the Royal Academy went every year to accommodation provided by staircases like this. The most rapid, the most inattentive glance at these pictures was enough to produce a sense of almost intolerable fatigue, because each picture was so obviously what it set out to be that the eye was not allowed a blink between a Sussex down, a Devonshire harbour, a Dorset pasture, and a London slum, and the amount of narrative compressed into the space was as if a dozen bad novelists had simultaneously read a dozen of their worst chapters. The massed effect was as confused and brilliant as a wall covered with varnished scraps. The brightness of the staircase and the gaudiness of the pictures were accentuated by the comparative gloom of the rooms on either side, particularly those at the back of the house, which from having been designed to look over a spacious garden were some of them now only six feet from the walls of the new flats. The still close atmosphere created by windows that were never opened from one year's end to the other was tainted by the odour of varnish and stale sunlight; the rooms on the ground floor smelt perpetually of half-past-two on Sunday afternoon, partly of clean linen, partly of gravy.

There were six bedrooms, all of them with large four-poster beds, and all of them haunted by that strange frigidity, that frigidity almost of death which is produced by the least superfluity of china. They were furnished in an eclectic style, but the china was kept strictly to its own kind; thus one bedroom would be red, blue, and gold with Crown Derby; another, and this the most attractive, rose and lavender with Lowestoft; and there was one nightmare of a room filled with black and rose Sèvres.

"I don't like the idea of your sleeping in any of these rooms," Mr. Rouncivell grumbled to Jasmine. She thought at first that he meant to suggest their discomfort, but he went on: "You'll have to be very careful not to break anything. Just because there are three toilet sets, it doesn't mean that you can break what you like. This china has taken me a long time to collect, and it has cost me a great deal of money, what's more. Look at that slop-pail. You dare use that slop-pail!"

"Couldn't I have a less valuable set in my room?" Jasmine suggested.

"Less valuable?" the old man echoed fiercely. "What do you mean by less valuable? Do you want me to provide you with china you can throw about the room?"

"Which bedroom do you use?" she asked to change the subject.

"Bedroom? Did you say bedroom? I don't sleep in a bedroom. I sleep in the bathroom."

He took her to the furthest door along the passage and showed her what she thought was the most depressing room she had ever seen in her life. It was such a small bathroom that having chosen it for a bedroom Uncle Matthew had actually to sleep in the bath itself, or rather on a box mattress which he had fixed on top of it. The window of the room, already sufficiently gloomy from looking out on the flats, was made still more gloomy by its panes being plastered with ferns and the faded plumage of tropical birds. A board was nailed to the sill on which was a brush with scarcely more bristles than Uncle Matthew had hairs, a comb with four teeth, and a safety razor. Safety razors had brought a peculiar pleasure into the old man's life, because since their introduction he had been able to calculate every morning how many less blades he used than anybody else would have used.

After seeing this room Jasmine began to be rather apprehensive where she should sleep; but with many admonitions she was finally awarded the Lowestoft room, which, if she had to live surrounded by china, was the ware she would have chosen. There was only one servant in the house, an elderly woman with a yellow face called Selina, to whom Uncle Matthew presented Jasmine with a solemnity that was accentuated by a din of multitudinous clocks striking noon all over the house with an accompaniment of cuckoos, chimes, and musical voluntaries.

"Twelve o'clock," Uncle Matthew announced.

"At least," said Jasmine. And then she blushed, because she had not meant to be anything more than anxious to please the old man by an assumption of cheerful interest. "I meant ... I was surprised to find it was so early."

"You'll be more surprised than that before you leave this house," said Selina bitterly. "You'll be more surprised than that. You'll have the surprise of your life. You'll be so surprised that you won't know whether you're on your head or your heels."

After this prophecy, the application of which Jasmine could not guess, Selina did not speak to the guest except in monosyllables, and she passed a dreary enough week in being shown Uncle Matthew's antiques and in trying to hold the balance between greediness and wastefulness at their sombre meals. At the end of the week he chose from his collection of walking-sticks a Jersey cabbage-stalk, which he offered to lend her for promenades about the shrubbery.

"You've taken his fancy," said Selina, grabbing her arm when Jasmine, cabbage-stalk in hand, was pretending to enjoy walking up and down the drive.

"I wish I could take yours," she replied.

"You have," said the housekeeper. "And you're going to have tea with me this blessed afternoon. It isn't the surprise I intended for you."

"But it's a very nice surprise," said Jasmine.

"It's a surprise to me. Which is God's way," she added more enigmatically than ever.

Selina belonged to one of those small religious sects which have done so much to solve, to their own satisfaction at any rate, the obscure problems of eschatology. Ceaseless meditation upon the fact that ninety-nine per cent of the human race were damned made Selina gloomy, for she was not naturally a misanthropist and took no pleasure in the thought. Sometimes, moreover, she had doubts even about her own salvation, and on such days the household suffered. Jasmine's arrival at Rouncivell Lodge induced her to proclaim her conviction that with no exception at all the whole of the human race was to be damned eternally. Gradually, however, she realized that in any case she could not hope to inherit the whole of Uncle Matthew's fortune, and she decided that the few years between Uncle Matthew's death and her own projection into eternal torment would be more pleasantly and more profitably passed with Jasmine than alone on what might be an inadequate pension. No sooner had she reached this conclusion than she heard a voice in the night telling her that she was saved; the following morning she cooked some cakes and invited Jasmine to tea with her in the kitchen, the character of which accounted, Jasmine felt, for the housekeeper's yellow complexion; the room was as warm and nearly as dark as the inside of an oven. A large American clock, which only had to be wound up annually, was ticking over the high black mantelpiece; crickets were clicking somewhere behind the range; a green Norwich canary was pecking at his seeds; the hostess was rustling the tea in a canister.

Selina came to the point at once, and postponing the discussion of Jasmine's chances in the eternal future asked her frankly how she proposed to provide for the temporal future.

"That's a question we're both entitled to ask, as you might say. Don't eat those cakes too fast, or you'll have indigestion. What I mean to say is Mr. Rouncivell's rich and you're not. You'll excuse the familiarity? As soon as I saw your box, I said to myself: 'She's not rich.' Well, that's nothing, is it? I'm not rich myself. But that doesn't say we shouldn't live in hope. And that doesn't mean that I'm not provided for in a manner of speaking. Well, I like your looks, and I don't mind telling you that a lady friend of mine in Catford has taken two rooms for my retirement when Mr. Rouncivell's earthly troubles are over; for I wouldn't have you think he's not going to have worse troubles in the next world. That's neither here nor there. He can't expect to keep me for ever, that's a sure thing. If I'm one of the elect, he must just lump it. Only as soon as I heard you was coming I said to myself: 'Now, don't take an instant dislike to her before you've seen her. Make friends and talk things over quietly in your own kitchen.' You're eating those cakes too fast. Oh yes, I know they're very light and eat theirselves in a manner of speaking, but you're eating them too fast. Wait a bit and you shall have a cup of tea before you eat another one. You help me and I'll help you. That's all there is to it. Yes, now you're choking, you see. Supposing Mr. Rouncivell was to leave you everything, you *would* take care, wouldn't you, that those two rooms of mine in Catford which my lady friend is occupying at present was nicely furnished with what you might call any little tit-bits I chose for myself? Now, there's the clock in the hall, for instance. I've been listening to that clock these twenty years, and I've a fancy I should like to go on listening to it until I die. The beds you can have. Well, I mean to say, I never really cared for sleeping in a four-post bed. Too human altogether, I'm bound to say. The posts, I mean."

49

Jasmine had made several attempts to interrupt this stream of conversation, and once she would have succeeded if Selina had not filled her mouth at the moment of speech with a small tart. At last, however, she managed to protest that she expected nothing from Uncle Matthew.

"And that's where you're quite right," said Selina. "Don't expect nothing, and you won't be disappointed. If I expected, I shouldn't be taking you into my confidence, as it were, like I am doing. But if you'll only do what I say and follow my advice, you can have it all. There's that Lettice and that Pamela coming down with their darling Uncle Matthew here and their darling Uncle Matthew there. But he sees through it. Oh yes, he sees through all of them, the same as anybody else might see through glass. He wants to leave his money to somebody who'll look after it and not go and spend it. All you've got to do is to scrimp and scrape and let him see as you're like himself. I suppose you think he paid for those cakes you're eating? Not at all. They're paid for out of my savings to show you I'm your friend. You help me and I'll help you; and you can't say that's going against the Gospel, can you? Do unto others as you would they should do unto you. So what you've got to do is keep on admiring the way I save money, and I won't let any chance go by of whispering in his ear that his money is safer with you than with any of them. All I ask for myself is a few tit-bits when the poor old gentleman's in the ground. He's got *no* religion; he hates dogs, he hates poor people, he hates hospitals, he hates public parks, he hates everything. So there you are. I've been very plain spoken with you, and you can't say the contrary; very plain spoken, I've been. I'm one of the elect, and I can afford to be plain spoken. It doesn't matter what I say or what I do, our loving heavenly Father's waiting for me at this very moment, because He told me so last night. So far as I can see at present, you're not one of the elect. I'm sorry for it, because I've taken a rare fancy to you. But if we don't meet, in the heavenly courts, we can be friends so long as we're on earth. Oh yes, it's all in the Gospel."

The housekeeper's frankness was not displeasing to Jasmine, although she was much amused at the idea of inheriting money from anybody. However, for the first month of her stay with Uncle Matthew she was, without realizing it, quite a success, because having no money to spend, she gave him the impression that she was of a saving disposition. It never entered his head that anybody could be actually without one halfpenny, and he applauded her disinclination to visit shops and theatres, her habit of walking to where she wanted to go rather than of riding on omnibuses, her transformation of a spring hat into a summer hat, as admirable economies.

"You're doing a treat," whispered Selina cunningly. "Last night I peeped through his keyhole, and he was reading his will."

It was a strange existence for a girl of nineteen, this life with Uncle Matthew, and there were moments when she really did have daydreams about inheriting a vast fortune and going back to Sirene. It was not so much the idea of the money as of the return to her beloved island which twined itself round her thoughts. There would be such delightful things to do. She would buy that villa her father had always talked about buying one day; she would buy up all the pictures of her father that she could find and have a permanent exhibition of them in a large studio; she would invite Lettice and Pamela to stay with her and make their visit much more pleasant than they had made hers; she would invite Aunt Cuckoo and Uncle Eneas to bring the baby to Sirene, and she would make *their* visit very pleasant; and, above all, she would always take care that no people ever had to leave Sirene just because they could not afford to go on living there. Oh yes, and then there was Cousin Edith. She would certainly make an allowance to her so that she need never again be snubbed by Aunt May. Poor Cousin Edith, how polite she would be if she did inherit all Uncle Matthew's money. She would be so sorry about the way she had behaved about Harry Vibart. Harry Vibart? What could she do for him? She would never be able to marry him if she were an heiress, because she would always be afraid that he only wanted to marry her for her money. What a pity he did not propose to her before she inherited. She would not accept him, of course, but if he did not marry anybody else, and if he asked her again when she was rich, why perhaps ... but what nonsense all this dreaming was! She ought to be ashamed of herself.

And then she would jump up from the chair in which she was sitting, jump up so abruptly that all the knick-knacks would rattle and clink, and taking her Jersey cabbage-stalk, she would wander up and down the drive and become interested by such dull little incidents. Far the most exciting thing that happened all that month was a white butterfly that went dancing past and seemed to be flying south; and once an errand boy tried to stand on his head in his empty basket just outside the gates of Rouncivell Lodge. But that was only moderately exciting. Sometimes Uncle Matthew would come and stump up and down beside her and tell her how much a square foot the wood of whatever walking-stick he was using that morning fetched. And then he would think that it was too cold to be out of doors, and she would have to go in with him and mount a crazy step-ladder to lift down some ornament that he wanted to move. Or else she would have to wind up all the twelve tunes in his musical box, an elaborate instrument with little drums, the parchment of which was illuminated with posies, as much unlike real drums as the tinkling music from old operas was unlike a real band. When all the tunes had been played, Uncle Matthew always told her to be careful how she closed the lid, because the case was worth a lot of money and the tunes had been favourites of his wife.

That young wife of Uncle Matthew who died so long ago! It was difficult to think of her as his wife. Her portrait, in a full-skirted riding habit and wearing a hat such as only undertakers and mutes wear nowadays, hung over the mantelpiece in the dining-room, and Uncle Matthew used to talk about her as Clara, which made it seem all the more absurd to think that were she alive now Lady Grant would be calling her Aunt Clara. Jasmine had never disliked Uncle Matthew, and his devotion to the memory of his dead wife kindled the beginnings in her of a genuine affection. She divined now why he slept in that bleak uncomfortable bathroom, divined that it was due to a sentimental horror of occupying any room that contained relics of her too intimate to be spoken of. Jasmine used to ponder the old trunks, locked and strapped and full no doubt of mouldering clothes, that stood in every bedroom except her own. And even in her own bedroom the chests of drawers had both of them two locked drawers, containing who should say now what souvenirs of girlhood? Jasmine asked the housekeeper about Clara; but Selina knew no more than herself.

"I've never caught so much as a tiny glimpse of anything," she said. "And of course she was dead almost before I was born, though not before I was thought of, because my Pa was set on having a little girl of his own a considerable number of years before he actually did. Yes, Mr. Rouncivell cherishes her memory very dearly, and if ever he unlocks any of her boxes or drawers, he always takes care to bolt himself in first. In the room that is, of course. She was well-born too. Oh yes, an undoubted lady—the only daughter of an esquire."

One day Uncle Matthew took from the middle of his walking-sticks a slim malacca cane, the silver handle of which was cut to represent a mailed hand grasping a pistol.

"Loaded with lead," he observed, "just like a real pistol. That was Clara's favourite stick, and it's stood in this stand ever since she had it first. If you like...."

But he thought better of his offer and recommended Jasmine to look well after her Jersey cabbage-stalk. Jasmine liked to think that the unpleasant side of Uncle Matthew had not been developed until Clara's death. She tried to get accustomed to his meanness, making all sorts of excuses for it, and sometimes she actually encouraged him in it, as one humours an invalid's petulance and selfishness. She never felt nearly so much of a poor relation with him as with the others, and it was a satisfaction to feel that he regarded all of them as every bit as much poor relations as herself. Well, time was passing: already people were writing less frequently from Sirene. The city sunlight glittered upon the dusty leaves of the shrubs; Selina was a perpetual diversion; Jasmine was as happy as a Java sparrow in a cage, and almost as happy as the sparrows on the roof of Rouncivell Lodge. As for Uncle Matthew, he became less grumpy every day.

"Which means you suit him," said Selina. "You suit him the same as I suit him. Yes, in a manner of speaking, I fit that man like a glove."

Uncle Matthew had other reasons for supposing that in Jasmine he had discovered a treasure, for no sooner had the information that she was staying with him gone the round of her relatives than she received pressing invitations to come and stay with them as soon as dear Uncle Matthew could spare her. Perhaps Aunt Cuckoo, who had always been considered the most foolish of the family, had proved herself the wisest. The more the others wrote to ask Jasmine to stay with them, the more Uncle Matthew expressed himself content with her company, and the more Selina, with knowing looks and headshakes, implied her success.

"You'll be his heir, you'll be his heir, you'll be his heir!" she breathed exultingly. "And I've written to Mrs. Vokins she can rent the kitchen an extra two days a week as from per now. What did he do yesterday? Sent me out for a bottle of indelible ink. Indelible ink is only used for two things—wills and washing. Oh, there's not a doubt about it."

The yellow-faced housekeeper was so confident of success that when Lady Grant visited Rouncivell Lodge a few days later she alarmed her by open references to Jasmine's good fortune. Lady Grant hurried home and told Lettice and Pamela that, whatever their engagements during the crowded end of June, they must be prepared to sacrifice themselves. Nothing could be allowed to interfere with the affection they owed Uncle Matthew. The poor old gentleman was in his dotage; he was on the edge of the grave; he was being got at by that odious housekeeper and Jasmine.

"After all our kindness," Lady Grant lamented. "It does seem a little hard that she should turn the poor old dear against us. It's a crime."

"It's worse than a crime," declared Cousin Edith fervidly, "it's a———" But she could not think of anything worse than a crime except the sin against the Holy Ghost, and fond though she was of Cousin May, she did not think that Jasmine's behaviour was that—no, not quite that ... but worse than a crime.... "it's an unnatural sin," she triumphantly concluded after a little longer reflection.

"Don't be ridiculous!" This was from Sir Hector.

"Lettice and Pamela must go and stay with him," their mother decided. "Now please, dear children, don't look so disagreeable."

Lady Grant sat down at once and wrote to propose the visit. Next morning Uncle Matthew tossed the letter across the breakfast table to Jasmine.

317 Harley Street, W.
June 20.

My dearest Uncle Matthew,

Poor Lettice and Pamela are both getting so tired of gaiety that ever since they went and had tea with you last they've been at me to ask you to invite them to stay with you at Rouncivell Lodge. If three are too many for you (or even two) Jasmine could come here and stay with either Lettice and Pamela, whichever you didn't have with you. If Lettice came now, Pamela could come in July, and I thought that you would like to come and spend the summer holidays with us wherever you liked. We thought of going to Littlehampton, but anywhere will suit us. Do send a p.c. to say you expect either or both. I'll send you all our news by the girls. Hector has been awarded an honorary degree by the University of Cambridge. He has just been trying on his robes. How expensive such things are! And of course his brother's affairs cost him more than he could well afford. But he never grumbles, though sometimes after a hard day he talks of giving up his cigars.

Ever your affectionate niece,
May Grant.

"Oh, I hope you won't send me away," Jasmine begged. She was not perhaps actually enjoying herself at Rouncivell Lodge, but she greatly preferred walking about the shrubbery with her Jersey cabbage-stalk to walking round the Chamber of Horrors with Cousin Edith, which had been the last dissipation provided for her at Harley Street.

Therefore, when Uncle Matthew told her to write and say he could not have either Lettice or Pamela, she was overjoyed to do so. It did not strike her that it was a good opportunity to score off the Hector Grants, and she wrote so simply that her letter gave the impression of a security that irritated her relations much more than an attempt on her side to be clever.

"She's perfectly sure of herself," Lady Grant gasped. "She's wormed herself in."

"I always thought she was deeper than she pretended," Cousin Edith said with a shake of her head. "Do you remember, May, I said to you once: 'Still waters run deep'? Only of course she wasn't still. She was never still really. She was always jumping up and...."

"Oh, for heaven's sake, Edith, don't babble on like that!" Sir Hector interrupted. "Eighty pounds for these robes, my dear. That's a nice sum to pay for a morning's masquerade."

"Little beast," said Pamela loudly. "I detested her from the first. By the way, I saw the Vibart youth at the Grave-Smiths' dance last night. I didn't say anything about it at the time, because I was afraid that Lettice might be upset."

"Me upset?" Lettice exclaimed angrily. "Why should I have been upset?"

"Now, please, darlings, don't quarrel," their mother begged. "This is not the moment to quarrel among ourselves."

"I say, I've got rather a notion," Pamela announced. "Why shouldn't we ask the Vibart youth here and tell him where dear Cousin Jasmine is to be found? *That* would annoy Uncle Matthew."

"What would annoy Uncle Matthew?" asked Lettice scornfully.

"Sorry you still can't bear the thought of your beloved's treachery," said Pamela with a malicious affectation of sympathy. "But if you could calm your beating heart for the sake of the family, you'd see what I meant."

"If Pamela thinks she can say what she likes to me just because...."

"Now hush, darling. Don't lose your temper, my pet. I see what Pamela means," interposed Lady Grant soothingly.

"You always take Pamela's side."

"Now, my darling, I must entreat you not to argue so absurdly."

"I should have thought it would have been obvious to the meanest intelligence," said Pamela with lofty sarcasm.

"Oh, would you, cleversticks?" her sister sneered.

"Obvious to anybody that if the Vibart youth hangs round Uncle Matthew's, Uncle Matthew will think twice of being so fond of our sweet cousin."

"Pamela, you're a genius," her mother declared proudly.

"Oh, she is, she is!" cried Cousin Edith, clapping her hands with excitement, for the scheme appealed to the innate procuress within her. "I should never have thought of anything half as clever. She's a...."

"Edith," her own rich cousin interposed, "I wish you wouldn't be quite so enthusiastic."

"I'm so sorry," Edith murmured humbly. "Shall I go and give Spottles his bath? Poor old boy, he's been rolling again, Cook says." And by the way in which she washed her own hands as she went out of the room Cousin Edith managed to suggest with suitable regret that she too had been rolling.

Within three days of this conversation Harry Vibart called on Jasmine at Rouncivell Lodge.

"Look here," he said reproachfully, "why didn't you ever write?"

"You never wrote to me." Jasmine tried to be cold and dignified, but she was so glad to see him again that it was not a successful attempt.

"I wrote you six letters."

"I never got them. I expect my aunt wouldn't allow them to be forwarded."

Vibart was sure that Jasmine was misjudging her. No one could have been more anxious to help him find Jasmine. Why, she had taken the trouble to write to Mrs. Grave-Smith for his address, had asked him to lunch and then volunteered Jasmine's address, and, what is more, advised him to go and call on her.

The Italian half of Jasmine was capable of being suspicious; it warned her that people like Aunt May did not so abruptly change their point of view. Why should she have sent him here? Why?... Why?... It must be that Lettice and Pamela had a chance of being married at last and that in a spasm of generosity she wished to help her niece ... or was it that she was afraid of having her on her hands, and hoped to palm her off on Harry Vibart? Such an idea froze her, and the young man, taken aback by her change of expression, asked what was the matter.

"I'm afraid you must have found it a very long way up to Muswell Hill," she said stiffly.

"Longish. Longish," he agreed. "But I took a taxi."

At this moment the window of the room in which they were sitting was darkened by a shadow, and there was Uncle Matthew with his face pressed against the pane and wearing an expression of malevolence, ferocity, and alarm. When they looked up, he waved his sticks above his head and snarled at them.

"It's a lunatic," exclaimed Harry Vibart.

"No, no, it's my uncle."

"I say, I'm awfully sorry. Perhaps he's ill."

Uncle Matthew was still waving his sticks so oddly and making such strange faces that Jasmine was alarmed and ran out to see what was upsetting him.

"Are you ill?" she asked.

"Ill? Ill? No. But I shall be ill in a moment. Listen!"

From the direction of the gates of Rouncivell Lodge the engine of a taxi throbbed upon the warm June air.

"He thinks it's an aeroplane," Vibart whispered. "Poor old chap, he's probably afraid it's going to fall on the house. Old people who haven't seen many of them do often get worried like that. It's all right, sir," he added in a louder voice, "it's only my taxi running up the twopences."

"Take it away," the old gentleman screamed. "Take it away, and take yourself away with it. Who are you? What do you mean by coming here and visiting my niece and keeping a taxi buzzing outside the gate? Do you realize that it's costing a penny a minute? Take it away!"

Harry looked at Jasmine, and she signed to him that it would be right to humour her uncle. She really was afraid that he was going to have a fit.

"Perhaps I may call another day?" the young man suggested in a despondent tone of voice.

"Certainly not. You'll be driving up next in a golden coach. If you want to squander your money, squander it some other way."

It was useless to argue with the infuriated old gentleman, and Vibart took himself off.

"That's the last I shall see of him," thought Jasmine, turning sadly to follow her uncle into the house. Later on, however, when Uncle Matthew had recovered from the shock to his parsimony, he enquired who her visitor was, and she thought that she was able to reassure him.

"Well," said the old gentleman, "perhaps I was a little hasty. Yes, I think I was. Does he smoke?"

"Not cigars," said Jasmine quickly. "At least I've never seen him smoking a cigar."

"He can come and see you twice a week. Once in the morning and once in the afternoon. And then perhaps later on we'll ask him to lunch. But don't count on that. And now come and sit with me in the smoking-room. Because I must smoke a cigar to calm my nerves after that shock."

They passed out into the hall, and on his way through Uncle Matthew cast a glance, as his custom was, at the numerous walking-sticks.

"Whose is this?" he asked, picking a malacca from the stand. "H. V." he read. "This is your friend's. You see, my dear, he's careless through and through. I never left a walking-stick in somebody else's house. Never in all my life."

"I think you made him rather nervous," Jasmine explained apologetically. But the old gentleman paid no attention: he was searching for something he missed.

"Where is it?"

"Where's what?"

"Clara's silver-handled cane."

"I don't see it," Jasmine stammered apprehensively.

"It's gone. That villain must have stolen it."

"If Mr. Vibart has taken one of your sticks, Uncle Matthew, he must have done so by mistake."

"The young scoundrel! The young blackguard!" He became incoherent with rage.

"But, Uncle Matthew, if he has taken one of your sticks he'll bring it back."

"Hers! Hers!" the old gentleman was gasping.

"Oh, dear Uncle Matthew, I'm so dreadfully sorry."

"My poor little wife's! He's taken my poor little wife's silver-handled cane. And she was so fond of it. Her favourite. The ruffian! The—the—tramp! He might have taken any other but that. Oh dear! Oh damn! Why do you bring these people here, you abominable girl?"

That afternoon Jasmine arrived in Harley Street, and had to explain that Uncle Matthew would not have her to stay with him any longer. The Hector Grants welcomed her with something like friendliness, but the next day, when Vibart brought back the missing stick, it was Pamela who claimed the privilege of returning it to Uncle Matthew, and a few days later it was thought advisable for Jasmine to pay her promised visit to Aunt Ellen and Uncle Arnold at Silchester.

Chapter Seven

JASMINE had protested against the visit to Silchester; and this protest was in the opinion of the Hector Grants conclusive evidence of a thwarted intention to corrupt poor old Uncle Matthew. Her resentment of the humiliating unconcern for her own dignity that was being displayed in thus sending her round from one group of relatives to another was brushed aside as no more than the expression of a natural chagrin at finding that her schemes had miscarried. They did not, of course, accuse her in so many words of being crafty; but Jasmine understood well enough at what they were hinting, and the consciousness that she had allowed Selina to discuss her prospects in the old gentleman's will, coupled with the memory of her own dreams of what she should do if he did leave his money to her, gave Jasmine a sufficiently acute sense of guilt to cut short any further opposition to the Silchester visit.

"I simply cannot understand your prejudice against the Deanery," Aunt May avowed. "There must be something else which you are trying to conceal." One of Aunt May's foibles was to regard as potential jackdaws everybody not situated so advantageously as herself. "It can't merely be that you don't want to greet your Aunt Ellen. There must be some other reason. I'm sorry your friend Mr. Vibart should have made such an unfortunate impression on poor old Uncle Matthew. But that is not our fault, is it?"

"I never said that anything was your fault, Aunt May," Jasmine responded. "I know perfectly well that everything is my fault, and that's why I don't want to upset any more of my relations by this behaviour of mine that they seem to find so dreadful."

"Nobody has found your behaviour dreadful," Aunt May gently contradicted. "Try not to exaggerate. I don't think I have ever called you anything worse than inconsiderate."

"Well, but you hate having me on your hands," Jasmine burst out. "You hate it. Why don't you let me go back to Sirene?"

"I've already explained to you," continued Aunt May more gently than ever, "I've already explained to you that your uncle could not accept such a responsibility. What would people say if a man in his position allowed his niece aged nineteen to set up an establishment on her own in a place like Italy?"

"People wouldn't say anything at all," Jasmine argued. "People are not so violently interested in me as all that."

"No, dear, that may be. But they are interested in your uncle, and we have to think of him, have we not? Besides, I should have supposed that you would have been glad to meet your poor father's only sister. She is the kindest of women, and Uncle Arnold is the kindest of men. I cannot say how painful it is for me to feel that *I* have not succeeded in rousing the least little bit of affection. I was ready to make all kinds of excuses for you last year when you first arrived. I realized that excuses had to be made then. But now you have been nearly a year in England, and it is surely not unreasonable to expect you to begin to show a little self-control. I'm afraid your visit to Uncle Matthew has done you no good. I was strongly opposed to it from the beginning and told Aunt Cuckoo as much quite plainly. But Aunt Cuckoo gets Ideas into her head. This turning Roman Catholic, this adopting a baby, this packing you off to poor old Uncle Matthew. Ideas! However, it is not our business to discuss Aunt Cuckoo.... You say you don't believe your relations in Silchester want you. I contend they have shown quite clearly that they do. And I should also like to point out that, if you decline to go, you will grievously wound your Aunt Ellen, who is not...."

"Very well, I'll go, I'll go! I'll do anything you want if you'll only stop lecturing me!" Jasmine could almost have flung herself on her knees before Aunt May if by doing so she could have stopped this conversation. There had been a sweet-shop on the way to the School of Swedish Culture, with an apparatus that went on winding endlessly round and round a skein of fondant that apparently always remained of the same size and consistency. Jasmine used to avert her head at last as she went by, so depressing became the sight of that sweet and sticky mess being wound round and round and round ... her aunt's little talks reminded her of it.

Aunt May confided in Cousin Edith after this outburst that she had wondered for a minute or two if Jasmine was really human. Cousin Edith tried to look as though she still wondered if Jasmine was really human, and all she got for her desire to be agreeable was to be asked if she had a stiff neck.

It was quarter day by now, and Jasmine was advised to spend her allowance on suitable summer frocks; she was also advised not to buy too many, because next quarter day she would be requiring suitable autumn frocks, and she was to bear in mind that clothes for autumn and winter were more expensive. Jasmine longed to refuse her allowance, but her vanity was too strong for her pride; unable to contemplate appearing before her six boy cousins in the dowdy remains of last year's wardrobe, she accepted the money, and despising herself for being so weak, she bought a flowered muslin frock and a white linen coat and skirt, the latter of which was condemned as an extravagance by Aunt May, who had no belief in the English climate. Jasmine might have spared herself the humiliation of accepting Uncle Hector's allowance, because a day or two later Aunt Cuckoo, in a rapture over some alleged conversational triumph of Baboose, sent her a present of five pounds, over which Cousin Edith sizzled but a little less appetizingly than if it had been a present from Aunt May herself.

"Well, I declare," she exhaled. "If you aren't a lucky girl!"

And as the lucky possessor of five pounds all her own, Jasmine set out next day to meet another set of rich relatives.

The journey to Silchester in glowing blue midsummer weather through the fat pasture lands of Berkshire and Hampshire gave Jasmine such a new and such a pleasurable aspect of England that she began to wonder if she had been suffering all this year from a jaundiced point of view, if indeed Aunt May's assumption of martyrdom had any justification from her own behaviour. This landscape through which the train was passing with such an effect of deliberate and conscious enjoyment, with such an air of luxuriousness really, soothed her mind, warmed her heart, put her soul to bed and tucked it comfortably and safely in for some time to come. She determined to meet her new uncle and aunt in the same spirit as the train's; they were to be the natural products of such a landscape, and whether they placidly accepted her arrival like those rotund sheep or whether they threw their legs in the air and swished their tails like those lean and spotted cows pretending to be frightened of the train, she would survey them as amiably and as philosophically. Jasmine was smiling at herself for using such a long word when they ran into a tunnel, one of those long smelly tunnels in which the train seems to bang itself from side to side in despair of ever getting out. Yes, thought Jasmine, even if Uncle Arnold and Aunt Ellen were as stiff as this window, as unreceptive and unsympathetic as this strap and as ungenerous as the blue electric bulb in the roof of the compartment, she would still be philosophical, oh yes, and very very amiable, she vowed as the train escaped from the tunnel, and the air odorous with sun and grass deliciously fanned her. As for Harry Vibart, it was absurd to go on thinking of him. She might as well fall in love with a jack-in-the-box. Fall in love? She detected a faster heart-beat, a suggestion of creeping gooseflesh. Fall in love? Jasmine would have liked to lecture her own self now; she felt as censorious of her involuntary self as Aunt May. But it was no fun to lecture one's involuntary self unless it were done *viva voce*, and if she did that the woman on the other side of the carriage, who ever since Waterloo had been fecklessly trying to separate the green gooseberries in her string bag from the cracknel biscuits and French beans, might be alarmed. But how could she have ... of course it wasn't really his fault about the stick; in fact, he probably considered himself badly treated in the matter. But he must not come down to Silchester and create another scene there. Besides, what right or reason had she to let him come down there? He had never given her the slightest justification for supposing that he was anything more than mildly interested in her. To be sure, he had insisted that he had written to her half a dozen times. But had he? The proper course of action for herself, the dignified and in the circumstances the easiest attitude for her to adopt, was one of kindly discouragement. Yes, she would write to him from the Deanery and tell him plainly that she hoped he would not think of coming down to visit her there. She had just reached this decision when the train steamed into Silchester station.

Jasmine was waiting on the platform in the expectation of being presently accosted by any one of the several dowdy women round her when both her arms were roughly grabbed and she found herself apparently in the custody of two boy scouts.

"I say, are you Cousin Jasmine?" asked the smaller of the two in a squeaky voice.

Simple and obvious though the question seemed, it had an extraordinary effect on the other boy, who instantly let go of her arm in order to engage in what to Jasmine's alarmed vision looked to be a life-and-death struggle with his companion, which did not end until the smaller boy had cried in his squeaky voice 'Pax, Edred,' several times. Edred, however, was for prolonging the agonies of the requested armistice by twisting his brother's arm—for the ferocity with which they had fought was surely a sign that they were as intimately related—and making numerous conditions before he agreed to grant a cessation of hostilities.

"Will you swear not to chisel again if I let go your arm?"

"Yes, I swear."

"Will you swear not to be a rotten little chiseller, and when I say 'bags I asking' next time not go and ask yourself straight off?"

"Yes, I swear. Oh, shut up, Edred. You're hurting my arm most frightfully. You are a dirty cad!"

"What did you call me?" Edred fiercely enquired with a repetition of the torture.

"I said you were a frightfully decent chap. Ouch! You devil! The decentest chap in all the world."

"Well, kneel down and lick my boot," Edred commanded loftily, "and you can have pax."

"No, I say, don't be an ass," protested the younger. "Ouch! Shut up! You'll break my wrist if you don't look out, you foul brute!"

And then, in despair at the severity of the armistice conditions, he wrenched himself free and returned with fury to the attack. The fresh struggle continued until an old gentleman was knocked backward over a luggage truck, after which Edred told his brother to shut up fighting, because people were beginning to stare at them.

"Sorry to keep you waiting, Cousin Jasmine," he said genially, "but I had to give young Ethelred a lamming for being such a beastly little cheat. He's too jolly fond of it."

"Speak for yourself," Ethelred retorted. "You know mother said I'd got to come with you this time." And then he turned in explanation to Jasmine. "The last time Edred bagged going to see Canon Donkin off from the station he stood on the step outside the carriage door all the way along the platform until the train was going too fast for him to jump off, the consequence of which was he got carried on to Basingstoke. Father was sick as muck about it."

"It was rather a wheeze," said Edred simply but proudly. "I very nearly fell off. I would have, if old Donkin hadn't got hold of my collar. And I had an ice at Basingstoke," he added tauntingly to his brother.

"Well, so could I have had an ice too if I'd done the same, greedy guts," replied the brother.

"No, you couldn't."

"Yes, I could."

And the fight would have begun all over again if Jasmine had not entreated them to find her luggage. As this process involved making a nuisance of themselves in every direction they accepted the job with alacrity. When the trunk was found, Edred suggested as rather a wheeze that Ethelred should have it put on his back like a porter, and Ethelred, in high approval of such a course, accepted the position with zest. He was swaying about on the platform to the exquisite enjoyment of his brother when an old lady, who was evidently a stranger to Silchester, asked Jasmine if she was not ashamed to let a little boy like that carry such a heavy trunk. At that moment Ethelred was carried forward by the impetus of the trunk, which slid over his shoulders, and cannoned into the stream of people passing through the ticket barrier. The odd thing was that none of the station officials seemed to interfere with the behaviour of her cousins until the ticket collector, from having had most of his tickets knocked out of his hand, lost his temper momentarily and aimed a blow at Ethelred with his clip.

"How are we going to the Deanery?" Jasmine enquired when at last to her relief she found herself on the edge of the kerb outside the station.

"Edwy's going to drive us in the governess-cart," they informed her. Jasmine had not the slightest idea what a governess-cart was; but it sounded a fairly safe kind of vehicle.

"Edwy's rather bucked at driving you," said Edred. "He's going to pretend it's a Roman chariot. You'll be awfully bucked too," he added confidently to his cousin. "It's rather hard cheese we've got your luggage, because it will make a squash. I say, why shouldn't we leave it here?"

"Oh no, please," Jasmine protested.

"Right-o," said Edred. "But it would be quite safe here on the kerb. You see, Ethel and I wanted to drive, and if you left your luggage here we could come back and fetch it."

Jasmine, however, was firm in her objection to this plan, and at that moment a fat boy of about fifteen, whose voice was at its breaking stage, was seen standing up in a governess-cart shouting what Jasmine recognized as the correct language of a Roman charioteer from *The Last Days of Pompeii*. She asked the other two which cousin this was.

"I say, don't you know?" Edred exclaimed in incredulous surprise. "That's old Edwy, only we call him Why, and we call me Because, and we call Ethelred Ethel."

"No we don't, so shut up," contradicted Ethelred.

"Well, he looks like a girl, doesn't he, Cousin Jasmine?"

Jasmine was spared the embarrassment of a reply by Edwy's pulling up with the governess-cart.

"Did you win?" both the younger brothers asked eagerly.

Edwy nodded absently; his whip had coiled itself round a lamp-post. Greetings between herself and this third cousin over, Jasmine was invited to get in and recommended to sit well forward and not get tangled up with the reins. Her box was placed opposite her, and the younger boys mounted.

"Good Gum," Edwy exclaimed with contempt. "We can't race anything with this load, can we?"

Jasmine, perceiving the narrow High Street of Silchester winding before her, was thankful for the news.

"I tell you what we could do," Edred suggested. "We could pretend that it was three chariots, and that we were all three driving one against the other."

Edwy considered this offer for a moment, then "Right-o" he agreed calmly, and off they went. It might have been less dangerous if Edwy had raced another cart as originally intended, because with the convention they were then following both his younger brothers had to have a hand on the reins. They also had to have a turn with the whip. The extraordinary thing to Jasmine was that this reeling progress down the High Street did not seem to attract a single glance. She commented on the public indifference, and the boys explained that the natives were used to them.

"Monday and Tuesday were much worse than we are," said Edred.

"Monday and Tuesday?"

"Edmund and Edgar. The pater was only a Canon Residentiary in those days. He's been Dean for six years now. He's the youngest Dean that ever lived. Or the youngest Dean alive; I forget which. Then he was Regius Professor of Anglo-Saxon at Oxford."

"The youngest Dean that ever lived in Silchester, you ass," interposed Edwy with a gruff squeak.

"Oh well, it's all the same, and ass yourself!"

Jasmine, who feared the effect of another fight in the cart, changed the subject with an enquiry about Oxford.

"I can't remember being there," said Ethelred proudly. And his elder brothers appeared quite jealous of what was evidently a family distinction.

"Last lap!" Edwy shouted. "Don't go on jabbering about Oxford."

They were driving along a quiet road of decorous Georgian houses, at the end of which was a castellated gateway.

"Here's the Close," Edred cried as they passed under the arch into a green and grey world. "Blue leads! Blue leads!"

"Shut up, you fool, I'm Blue!" yelled the youngest.

While the rival charioteers punched each other behind their brother's back, Purple in the personification of Edwy pulled up at the Deanery and claimed to be the victor. The serenity of the Close after that break-neck drive from the station was complete. The voices of the charioteers arguing about their race blended with the chatter of the jackdaws speckling the great west front of the Cathedral in a pleasant enough discordancy of sound that only accentuated the surrounding peacefulness. Upon the steps that led up to the west door the figures of tourists or worshippers appeared against the legended background no larger than birds. At no point did the world intrude, for the houses of the dignitaries round their quadrangle of grass had nothing to do with the world, and if a town of Silchester existed, it was hidden as completely by the massed elm trees that rose up behind the low houses of the Dean and Chapter as the ancient Roman city was hidden in the grass that now waved above its buried pavements and long lost porticoes.

"It really is glorious here, isn't it?" Jasmine exclaimed.

"Yes, it's rather decent," Edred allowed. "We've got a swannery at the back of our garden, and that's rather decent too. They get awfully waxy sometimes. The swans, I mean," he supplemented. And in such surroundings, Jasmine felt, even swans had no business to lose their tempers.

The Deanery itself was externally the gravest and most impressive of the many grave and impressive houses round the Close. Beheld thus it presented such an imperturbable perfection of appearance that before he knocked upon its door or rang its bright brass bell, the most self-satisfied visitor would always accord it the respect of a momentary pause. But when the door was opened—and it was opened by a butler with all the outward and visible signs of what a decanal butler ought to be—that air of prosperous comfort, of dignity and solid charm, vanished. It was not that the entrance-hall was ill-equipped. Everything was there that one could have expected to find in a Dean's hall; but everything had an indescribably battered look, the irreverent mark that an invading army passing through Silchester might have left upon the Deanery, had some of the soldiers been billeted there. It was haunted by a sense of everything's having served some other purpose from that for which it was originally intended, and the farther one penetrated into the house the more evident were the ravages of whatever ruinous influence had been at work. Even Jasmine with her slight experience of English houses was taken aback by the contradiction between the exterior and the interior of the Deanery. She was used to entering Italian palaces and finding interiors as bare and comfortless as a barrack; but in them the discomfort and bareness had always been due to the inadequate means of their owners. It was certainly not poverty that caused the contradiction at the Deanery. The solution of the puzzle burst upon her when with a simultaneous onrush her cousins, each shouting at the top of his voice 'Bags I telling the mater Jasmine is here,' stormed the staircase like troops. The butler, listening to their yells dying away along the landing above, paused for a moment from the gracious pomp of his ministrations and observed to Jasmine: "Very high-spirited young gentlemen."

"But is the pony quite safe?" she asked, looking back to where the governess-cart with her trunk still inside was waiting driverless outside the door.

"Yes, miss, she's not a very high-spirited animal, and she's usually very quiet after the young gentlemen have driven her."

Again the yells resounded, this time with increasing volume as the three boys drew nearer, leaping, sliding, rolling, and cannoning down the staircase abreast. Jasmine received a thump from Edred, who was the first to reach her, a thump that was evidently the sign of victory, because the other two immediately resigned her to his escort for the necessary presentation to her aunt, while they went out to attend to the pony.

Aunt Ellen's room had escaped the pillaged appearance which upstairs at the Deanery was even more conspicuous than below; it was crowded with religious pictures in religious Oxford frames, religious Gothic furniture, and religious books. Apart from the fruit of her own religious tastes, Aunt Ellen had directly inherited from the Bishop of Clapham his religious equipment (accoutrements would be too highly coloured a word for the relics of that broad-minded prelate); and perhaps because she was fond of her episcopal father she had hesitated to sacrifice his memory, together with her husband and the rest of the household, upon the common altar of those six household gods, her sons. At any rate, when she carefully explained to her niece that the room was a sanctuary not so much for her own use as for old time's sake, Jasmine accepted its survival as due to some sentimental reason. But if Aunt Ellen's room had escaped, Aunt Ellen herself had certainly not. The weather-beaten gauntness of Uncle Eneas and Uncle Hector was in Aunt Ellen much exaggerated, although an aquiline nose preserved her from being what she otherwise certainly would have been, a grotesque of English womanhood, or rather, what English people would like to consider a grotesque of English womanhood; Jasmine, however, with many years' experience of English tourists landing at Sirene after a rough voyage across the Bay of Naples, considered Aunt Ellen to be typically English. She had acquired that masculine look which falls to so many women who have produced a number of sons. When Jasmine knew her better she found that her religious views and emotions resembled the religious views and emotions that are so widely spread among men of action, such as sea captains and Indian colonels. Her ignorance of anything except the gentlemanly religion of the professional classes was unlimited; her prejudice was unbounded. Jasmine soon discovered that the main reason why she had not been invited to the Deanery before was her aunt's fear of introducing a papist into the household. It was this, apparently, that weighed much more with her than the accounts she had received from Lady Grant of their niece's behaviour. True, she informed Jasmine that she had been anxious to correct the looseness of her moral tone. But how could she compete with priest-craft? She actually asked her niece this! Her religious apprehensions were only overcome by the menace of waking up one morning to find Jasmine the sole heiress of Uncle Matthew's fortune, which, as she wrote to her sister-in-law, without presuming to impugn the disposition of God, would be entirely unjust. It was not that she dreaded a direct competition with her own boys, because, proud though she was of them and of herself for having produced them, she never deceived herself into supposing that a personal encounter between them and their uncle would be anything but fatal, not merely to their chances of ultimate wealth, but also to her own. On her own chances she did build. She could not believe that her uncle (painfully without belief in a future state as he was) would ignore the rights of a niece married to the Dean of Silchester. After all, a Dean was something more than a religious figure; he was a worldly figure. Aunt Ellen was sharply aware of the might of a Dean, because that might was mainly exercised by her, the Dean himself by now taking not the least interest in anything except the history of England before the Conquest. Jasmine had derived an entirely false impression of her aunt from her letters, which, filled as they were with religious sentimentality, suggested that Aunt Ellen was softer than the rest of the family, that perhaps she was even like her own beloved father. She found, however, that except where her sons were concerned Aunt Ellen was hard, fierce, martial, and domineering. All her affection she had kept for her sons, all her duty for God. Jasmine was not so much discouraged as she might have been by her aunt's personality, because she found at any rate her three youngest cousins a great improvement on Lettice and Pamela, and if the three eldest ones turned out to be only half as amusing, she felt that she should not dislike her visit to the Deanery. Besides, she had the satisfaction of knowing that this was quite definitely only a visit, and that there was no proposal pending to attach her permanently to the household as a poor relation.

Jasmine did not discover all this about her aunt at their first meeting; the conversation then was crammed with the commonplace of family news; and how Aunt Ellen would have resented the notion that any news about the Grants could be described as commonplace! She might have gone on talking until tea-time if Edred's continuous kicking of the leg of her father's favourite table had not suggested a diversion in the form of Jasmine's long-delayed introduction to the Dean. She had hesitated to interfere directly with her son's harmless if rather irritating little pleasure; but the varnish was beginning to show signs of Edred's boots, and she announced that, although Uncle Arnold was working, he would no doubt in the circumstances forgive them for disturbing him.

Jasmine smiled pleasantly at the implied compliment, not realizing that the circumstances were the table's, not hers.

"I say, need I go?" asked Edred. He dreaded these visits to the study, because they sometimes ended in his being detained to copy out notes for his father.

"No, dear, you need not go."

Edred dashed off with a whoop of delight, turning round in the doorway to shout to Jasmine that he would be in the garden with Why and Ethel should she wish presently to be shown the swans.

"Poor boy," sighed Aunt Ellen when he was gone, and upon Jasmine's asking what was the matter with him, she told her that he had just failed for Osborne.

"It's such a blow to him," she murmured in a plaintive voice that was ridiculously out of keeping with her rockbound appearance. "If he had passed, he had made up his mind to become an admiral, and now I suppose we must send him back to school in September. Poor little boy, he's quite heartbroken. I've had to be very gentle with him lately."

Jasmine supposed it might be tactless to observe that Edred showed no signs of heartbreak, and instead of commenting she enquired sympathetically what Ethelred was going to do.

"Ah, poor Ethelred's a great problem. He wants to be an engineer, and really he is very clever with his fingers; but his father is quite opposed to anything in the nature of technical education until he's had an ordinary education. I think myself it is a pity, but Uncle Arnold is quite firm on that point. Ethelred was at Mr. Arkwright's school until Easter, but the school doctor wrote and told us that he thought the air on the east coast was too bracing for him. In fact, he insisted on his leaving for the dear boy's own sake."

"And Edwy?"

"Ah, poor Edwy! His heart is weak, and we can only hope that with care he will become strong enough for the Army by the time he goes to Sandhurst."

"Is his heart very weak?" Jasmine asked.

"Oh, very weak," her aunt replied, "and he has set it—his heart, I mean—on being a soldier, and so he is working with Canon Bompas, one of the minor canons. A great enthusiast of the Boy Scout movement. A delightful man who was in the Army before he took Orders, and who, as he often says jokingly, though of course quite reverently, still belongs to the artillery. He is a bachelor, though of course," added Aunt Ellen, "not from conviction. As you perhaps know, the Church of England is opposed to celibacy of the clergy. Yes, poor Edwy! He had such a lovely voice. I wish it hadn't broken just before you arrived."

It was hard to believe that Edwy's voice, which now alternated between the high notes of a cockatoo and the low notes of a bear, had ever been beautiful, and Jasmine was inclined to ascribe its alleged beauty to maternal fondness.

"Edmund and Edgar won't be back from Marlborough until the end of the month; but Edward is coming in a fortnight. He delighted us all by winning a scholarship at Trinity. He's so happy at Cambridge, dear boy; though I think everybody is happy at Cambridge, don't you?"

Jasmine agreed, though she really had no opinion on the subject.

"Well, come along," said her aunt, "and we'll go and find your uncle. Quite a walk," she added, "for his study is at the far end of the top storey. His library is downstairs, of course, but he found that it didn't suit him for work, and though it's rather inconvenient having to carry books backwards and forwards up and downstairs, we all realize how important it is that he should be quiet, and nobody minds fetching any book he wants."

This was said with so much meaning that Jasmine immediately visualized herself carrying books up and down the Deanery stairs day in day out through the whole of the summer.

"I told you about the difficulty he had with his typewriting, and how anxious he was that Ethelred should learn, but the dear boy's mind was so bent on mechanics that he was always taking the machine to pieces. Very cleverly, I'm bound to say. But of course it occupied a good deal of his time. So now he practises the piano again instead. People tell me he's very musical."

While Aunt Ellen was talking, they were walking up and down short irregular flights of stairs and along narrow corridors, the floors of which were billowy with age, until at last they came to a corridor at the head of which was a large placard marked SILENCE.

"The boys are not allowed along here," said their mother with a sigh, as if by not being allowed along here they were being deprived of the main pleasure of their existence.

"Uncle Arnold does not like us to knock," she explained when they came to the door at the end of the corridor, on which was another label DO NOT KNOCK. She opened the door, and Jasmine was aware of a long, low, sunny room under a groined ceiling, the gabled windows of which were shaded with lucent green. The floor was littered with docketed papers and heaped high with books from which cardboard slips protruded. From the fact that the windows looked out on the Close instead of on the garden, Jasmine divined that the Cathedral Close was considerably quieter than the Deanery garden. Seated at a large table at the far end of the room was her uncle, or rather what she supposed to be her uncle, for her first impression was that somebody had left a large ostrich egg on the table.

"Jasmine," her aunt announced.

The ostrich egg remained motionless; but the scratching of a pen and the slow regular movement of a very plump white hand across a double sheet of foolscap indicated that the room contained human life. At the end of a minute the egg lifted itself from the table, and Jasmine found herself confronted by a very bright pair of eyes and offered that very plump white hand. After meeting so many tall, gaunt relatives, it was a great pleasure to meet one who was actually shorter than herself. It was not merely that the Dean was shorter than herself which attracted her. He was regarding her with an expression that, had she not been assured of his entire attention's being concentrated upon Anglo-Saxon history, she would have supposed to be friendly, even affectionate; at any rate it was an unusually pleasant expression for a relative. It was probably that first impression of the Dean's head as an ostrich egg which led her to compare him to a bird; but the longer she looked at him—and she had to look quite a long time because her uncle said nothing at all—the more she thought he resembled a bird. His eyes were like a bird's, small, bright, hard, and round; he put his head on one side like a bird; and his thin legs, encased in gaiters beneath that distinct paunch, completed the resemblance.

"Not finished yet, my dear?" his wife asked in the way in which one asks an invalid if he should like to sit up for an hour or two while the sun was shining.

"No, my dear, not quite," the Dean replied; and his voice had a trill at the back of it like a bird's. "About six more volumes."

Mrs. Lightbody sighed. "The way he works! But don't forget, my dear, that the Archdeacon is coming to dinner."

In some odd way Jasmine divined that the Dean thought 'Damn.' She felt like somebody in a fairy tale who is granted the gift of understanding the speech of animals and the tongues of birds. What he actually said was: "Delightful! Don't open the '58 port. Foljambe has no palate."

He had put his head more than ever on one side by now, so that with one eye he was able to read over what he had just been writing, looking at the foolscap as a thrush contemplates a snail before he attacks it.

"I'm afraid that we—I mean that I've disturbed your work," Jasmine murmured.

"Yes," agreed the Dean, and so rapidly did he sit down that his niece was scarcely conscious of the movement until she saw the ostrich egg lying on the table again.

"Now I must take Jasmine to her room," proceeded Aunt Ellen, and she managed to convey in her tone that it was the Dean who had interrupted her and not she the Dean. He did not reply vocally; but as his hand travelled along the paper, a short white forefinger raised itself for a moment in acknowledgement of her remark, and then quickly drooped down to the penholder again.

Jasmine did not suppose that she had made any impression on her uncle, and she felt rather sad about this, because she was sure that if he would only give her an opportunity of being her natural self he would find her sympathetic. She was surprised, therefore, when he and Archdeacon Foljambe arrived in the drawing-room that evening after dinner, to perceive her uncle making straight for herself, exactly like a water wagtail with his funny little strut and funny little way of putting his hands behind his coat and flirting his tail.

"Can you type?" he asked.

And the twinkle in his eyes seemed to endow his question with a suggestion of daring naughtiness, so that when Jasmine told him that she did type, she felt that she was admitting the presence of a lighter side to her nature.

"Come up to my study to-morrow morning about half-past nine. I'll have a chair cleared for you by then."

And thus it was that Jasmine found herself booked to help Uncle Arnold every morning of the week. Yet in helping him she was not in the least aware of being made use of; on the contrary the work had a delicious flavour of impropriety. The machine itself was a good one, so good that it had survived Ethelred's attempted dissection of it; and Uncle Arnold, who when a difficult Anglo-Saxon problem required solution used to tap upon the table with his fingers, did not seem to mind the noise the typewriter made any more than a nuthatch on one branch might object to the pecking of a yaffle at another. Jasmine, remembering that her aunt had alluded in her first letter to the Dean's dislike of constantly changing typists, asked him one day on their way down to lunch why he had had so much trouble with his secretaries.

"One used a particularly vicious kind of scent. Another was continually scratching at her garter. One used to breathe over my head when she came across to give me what she had been doing. Another thought she knew how to punctuate. And one who had studied history at Lady Margaret's quoted Freeman against me! My clerical position forbade me to swear at them. My brain in consequence became surcharged with blood. So I used to work them to death, and when one of them who refused to be worked to death and refused to give notice ... Jasmine! this must never go beyond you and me...."

"No, Uncle Arnold," she promised eagerly. "But do tell me how you got rid of her."

"I used to put drawing pins on her chair. Not a word to a soul! My wife would suspect me of being a papist like yourself if she found out, and the Bishop, who now thinks I'm mad, would then be sure of it. Never let a bishop be sure of anything. He thrives on ambiguity."

Apart from her work with the Dean, Jasmine enjoyed herself immensely in garden games with the three youngest boys. The Deanery garden was a wonderful place, and to Jasmine it afforded a complete explanation of the affection that English people had for England. She had been so unhappy all this past year that she had come to think of Italy as having the monopoly of earth's beauty. But this garden was as beautiful as anything in Italy, this garden with wide green lawns, bird-haunted when she looked out of her window in the lucid air of the morning, bird-haunted when at dusk she would gaze at them from the candle-lit dining-room. The shrubberies here were glossy and thick, not at all like the shrubbery at Rouncivell Lodge. A high wall bright with snapdragon bounded the garden on the side of the Cathedral, and beyond it loomed the south transept and a grove of mighty elms. There was a lake in which floated half a dozen swans that puffed themselves out with esteem of their own white grace, while in the water they regarded those mirrored images of themselves, the high-sailing clouds of summer, or perhaps more proudly their own splendid ghosts. There was an enclosed garden where fat vegetables were girdled with familiar flowers, blue and yellow and red, an aromatic garden loud with bees. Finally there was an ancient tower, the resort of owls and bats, which the Dean sometimes spoke of restoring. But he never did; and the mouldering traceries, the lattices long empty of glass, and the worm-eaten corbels of oak grey with age went on decaying all that fine July. It would have been a pity to restore the tower, Jasmine thought, and replace with sharp modern edges that dim and immaterial building in its glade of larches. The dead lower branches of the trees wove a mist for the paths, on the pallid grass of which grew clusters of orange and vermilion toadstools; it would be a pity to intrude on such a place with the tramp of restoring workmen.

Jasmine's zest in the middle ages, her absorption in pre-Norman days, her surrender to the essential England were at first faintly troubled by having to attend mass at a little Catholic mission chapel built of corrugated iron. But from being pestered by Aunt Ellen to compare the facilities for worship in Silchester Cathedral with those in the church of the Immaculate Conception, Bog Lane, she began to wonder if the externals of history could effect as much as she had supposed. If the Cathedral was spacious, the mind of Aunt Ellen was not; if the church of the Immaculate Conception was tawdry ... but why make comparisons? She had never noticed in Sirene how ugly sham flowers looked upon the altar; when she made this discovery in Silchester, she was instantly ashamed of herself; and when she looked again, it seemed as if the gilt daisies in their tarnished vases were alive, as if they were nosegays gathered in Italy. If the church of the Immaculate Conception, Bog Lane, was hideous, what about the English church at Sirene? That was a poky enough affair. But again, why make comparisons? There were rich relatives and poor relations in churches just as much as in everything else.

Jasmine was fighting loyally against her inclination to criticize, when one blazing day at the end of July the Dean proposed a visit to the remains of Roman Silchester, at which his three sons expressed horror and dismay.

"Why, what's the matter with Old Silchester?" she asked.

"Oh, it's a most stinking bore! A most frightful fag!" groaned Edred.

"Father makes us sweat ourselves to death digging in the sun," croaked Edwy.

"And last time when I chivied a Holly Blue, or it may have been only a Chalk Hill Blue, he cursed me like anything," lamented Ethelred.

The boys groaned again in unison.

"There's nothing to see."

"There's nothing to do."

"It's absolutely foul."

"Father jaws all the time about history, which I hate," said Edred. "I say, can't you put him off taking us?"

But Jasmine declared that they were horribly unappreciative, and declined to intervene.

"Well, anyway," said Ethelred hopefully, "Lord George Sanger's Circus is coming the second week in August."

The thought of that sustained the boys to face a long summer's day among the ruins of the ancient city.

In the end the day was delightful. The Dean preferred his niece as a listener to his sons, and as Mrs. Lightbody had been unable to come, he was not driven by her irritating crusade on behalf of the boys' amusement to insisting upon their attention. The result was that they vanished soon after lunch to hunt butterflies, while the Dean expounded his theory of Old Silchester. Jasmine sat back enjoying the perfume of hot grass, the murmurous air, the gentle fluting of a faint wind, while the Dean proved conclusively that the Saxon invasion utterly swept away every trace of Roman civilization in Britain. The Dean's shadow while he wandered backward and forward among the scanty remains grew longer, and beneath his exposition the Roman Empire, so far as its effect on England was concerned, went down like the sun. Jasmine had been asleep, and she woke up suddenly in the fresh airs of sunset. Half a mile away the boys were coming back over the expanse of grey-green grass to display their captures.

"And how pathetic it is," the Dean was saying, "to think of this outpost of a mighty empire succumbing so easily to those invaders from over the German ocean. The last time they excavated here at all systematically, they turned over some of the rubbish heaps of the camp. Curiously enough they actually found the skins of the nutty portion of the pine-cone from *Pinus Pinea*, which is eaten to this day in southern Italy."

"*Pinocchi!*" cried Jasmine, leaping to her feet in excitement.

"Yes, *pinocchi*," the Dean confirmed. "The soldiers must have had packets of them sent from Rome by their sweethearts and wives and mothers. And that is one more proof that they remained strangers, whereas the Saxons bred themselves into the soul of the country."

While they jogged back in the waggonette through the twilight, Jasmine dreamed of those dead Roman soldiers, and herself longed for freshly roasted *pinocchi*. The boys jabbered about butterflies. The Dean went to sleep.

"I'm enjoying myself here comparatively," said Jasmine to herself that night. "But only comparatively. I still love Italy best."

But she was enjoying herself, and she hoped that she should not have to leave Silchester yet awhile.

Chapter Eight

EDWARD had written from Cambridge at the end of the term to say that his friend Lord Gresham was urging him to explore Brittany in an extended walking tour, and he had wondered in postscript if it would seem very rude should he not arrive home until the beginning of August; in view of the fact that the walking tour was to be in the company of Lord Gresham, his mother had been positive that it would be much more rude if he did arrive home, and she had telegraphed to him accordingly. Edmund and Edgar came home from Marlborough at the end of July. It was Edmund's last term at school, and he was going up to Cambridge in October with an exhibition at Pembroke and a reputation as a good man in the scrimmage. Edgar, who was seventeen, had another year of school before him. Jasmine knew from the youngest boys that 'Monday' and 'Tuesday' in their day had terrorized the inhabitants of Silchester much more ruthlessly and extensively than their juniors. Golf, however, had of late attracted their superfluous energy, and they spent the first fortnight of their holidays in trying to make what they described as a 'sporting' four-hole course in the Deanery garden. From their point of view the epithet was a happy one, for during the first match they broke a window of the dining-room and several cucumber frames, while in searching for lost balls they spoiled the gardener's chance of a prize at the horticultural show that year. The younger boys, jealous of such competent destruction, filled a ginger-beer bottle with gunpowder and blew a hole in the bottom of the lake. Jasmine, who was still working with her uncle, only heard of these events as nuns hear a vague rumour of the outside world. The proofs of the fifth volume were absorbing the Dean's attention; and even when Edred shot a guinea-pig belonging to the Senior Canon's youngest daughter he declined to interfere, much to the satisfaction of his wife, who considered that the Senior Canon should be ashamed to own a daughter young enough to take an interest in guinea-pigs. In fact it was not until a model aeroplane, subscribed for unitedly by the three youngest boys and flown by Ethelred from the ancient oak in the middle of the Close, maintained a steady course in the direction of the Dean's window, and to his sons' pride and pleasure flew right in to land on his table, scatter his notes with the propeller, and upset the ink over his manuscript, that he was moved to direct action. He then banished them to work in an allotment garden attached to the Deanery, where on the outskirts of Silchester for six hours a day they gathered what their father called the fruits of a chastened spirit. The punishment was ingenious and severe, because their enemy the head gardener benefited directly by their labour, and because the allotment afforded no kind of diversion except futile attempts to hit with catapults the bending forms of labourers out of range in the surrounding allotments.

The Dean worked harder than ever when his youngest sons were removed; and Jasmine, finding that she was being useful enough to be able to shake off the thought that she was an infliction, and that there was no hint of a wish for her departure from the Deanery, was anxious to prevent anything's happening to upset what so far were the jolliest weeks she had passed since she left Sirene. Although she had thought a certain amount about Harry Vibart, she had not allowed herself to grow sentimental over him, and after this sojourn at the Deanery, she had quite convinced herself that it would be wiser not to see him again. She had, of course, no reason to suppose that he wanted to see her again; at the same time she had had no reason to suppose as much at Rouncivell Lodge before he suddenly turned up with such disastrous results. His interruption had not mattered so much there, because she was only negatively happy at the time. Here she was something like positively happy, and it seemed from every point of view prudent to write him a letter and as sympathetically as possible to ask him not to disturb the present situation. She wondered whether if she sent it to him in the care of his uncle at Spaborough it would ultimately reach him. By a series of roundabout questions she arrived at the discovery that by looking up Sir John Vibart in Burke she could ascertain his address. When she had found that Sir John Vibart lived at Whiteladies, near Long Escombe in the North Riding of Yorkshire, she devoted herself to the composition of the following letter:—

The Deanery,
Silchester,
August 6th.

Dear Harry,

She had been tempted to go back to *Mr. Vibart*, but inasmuch as she was writing to ask him not to see her again, the formal address seemed to lend a gratuitous and unnecessary coldness to her request, and even to give him the idea that she was offended with him.

I am staying down here with my uncle the Dean, who is very nice and is writing a history of England before the Norman Conquest. I went with him to see the remains of the Roman city of something or other, a very long name, but it is quite near here, and fancy, in the rubbish heaps of the old Roman camp, they have actually found the skins—husks, I mean—of pinocchi. In case you do not know what a pinocchio is, I must tell you that they are the nutty part of the pinecombs from the big umbrella pines that grow all round Naples and Rome. It made tears come into my eyes to think of those Roman soldiers having those boxes of pinocchi sent to them by their mothers and friends all the way to England.

She had written *sweethearts* at the first draft, but the word looked wrong somehow in a letter that was meant to be discouraging.

I work quite hard at typewriting, and this is a very good machine. The only thing is that it won't do dipthongs, which is a pity, because Uncle Arnold gets very angry if Saxon names are not spelt with dipthongs. There are six cousins here who are called after the six boy kings. Uncle Arnold calls them Eadward, Eadmund, Eadgar, Eadwig, Ædred and Æthelred; but other people call them Eddy, Monday, Tuesday, Why, Because, and Ethel. Edward, who is the eldest, I haven't seen yet. He is at Cambridge. I hope you are enjoying yourself wherever you are, and that you haven't been taking any more people's walking-sticks!

Kindest regards,
Yours sincerely,
Jasmine Grant.

P.S. I think it would be better if you didn't come down here and try to see me.

Jasmine was very proud of this postscript; it did not strike her that the bee's sting is in its tail. She would have been astonished if anybody had told her that it was unkind to end up with such an afterthought, did she seriously mean to forbid Harry Vibart to see her again. And she would have been still more astonished and a good deal horrified if anybody had suggested that the prohibition put like that might actually have the air of an invitation, should the recipient of the letter choose to regard it cynically.

However, she did not receive so much as a bare acknowledgment of her letter, and she convinced herself, perhaps a little regretfully, that Harry Vibart, offended by her request, had decided not to bother any more about her.

Meanwhile Edward had arrived. Edward was one of those young men of whom it can be postulated immediately that he could never have been called anything else except Edward. He was a tall and awkward, an extremely industrious, a clever and an immensely conceited young man, who hid the natural gloom established by years of nervous dyspepsia, or more bluntly by chronic indigestion, under a pretentious solemnity of manner. His arrival at Silchester coincided with a change of weather, and the rainy days that attended in his wake created in Jasmine's mind an impression that he was even more of a wet blanket than she might otherwise have thought. For the first few days he hung about the rooms like a low cloud, telling long stories about his tour in Brittany with Lord Gresham, stories that for the most part were about taking the wrong road and putting up at the wrong inn. When he had bored his family so successfully that every member of it had reached the point of regarding life from the standpoint of a nervous dyspeptic, he grew more cheerful and aired his latest discoveries in modern literature. Then he decided to keep a journal, with the intention, it was understood, of immortalizing his spleen. Like most people who keep journals, he was usually a day or two in arrears, and when people saw him pompously entering the room with a notebook under his arm, they used to hasten anywhere to escape being asked what he had done on Thursday morning between eleven and one. At last the sun appeared again, and Edward, looking at Jasmine—by the intensity of his regard it might have been the first time he had seen her—divined, as if the sun had possessed the power of X-rays, that she lacked education. Edward, whose success in life had been the success of his education, considered that he owed it to his cousin to remedy her deficiencies; keeping in view his principle of never offering to give something for nothing, he suggested that, in exchange for his teaching her Latin, she should teach him Italian. Jasmine would have willingly taught him Italian without the advantage of learning Latin; but she did not wish to appear ungracious, and the bargain was made. Edward advanced much more rapidly in Italian than she advanced in Latin, partly because he was better accustomed to study than she was, and partly because of the four hours a day they devoted to mutual instruction, three and a half hours were devoted to Italian and only half an hour to Latin. The result of this was that by the end of September he was reading Petrarch with fluency, while she had only reached the first conjugation of verbs and the second declension of nouns.

"You're very slow," Edward reproved her. "I can't understand why. It ought to be just as easy for you to learn Latin as it is for me to learn Italian. It's absolutely useless to go on to the third declension until you remember the genitive plural of *dominus. Dominorum*, not *dominurum*."

"I said *dominorum*."

"Yes, but you mustn't pronounce it like Italian."

"I'm not," Jasmine argued. "I think the trouble is that I've got a slight Neapolitan accent, and you think I'm saying *urum* when I'm really saying *orum*. You forget that I've got to unlearn my pronunciation to suit yours."

"Well, that applies equally to me," Edward argued.

The result of these difficulties was that Edward gave up trying to teach Jasmine Latin and confined himself entirely to learning Italian from her. About this time he read somewhere that the only way to master a language was to fall in love with somebody who speaks it. Such an observation struck him as a useful tip, in the same way as when he was at school he would remember the useful tip:

Tolle me, mi, mu, mis,
Si declinare domus vis.

He therefore proceeded to fall in love with Jasmine in the same earnest acquisitive way in which he would have proceeded to buy a highly recommended new type of notebook. Edward's notion of falling in love was that he should be able to introduce into an ordinary conversation phrases that otherwise and outside his study of Petrarch would have sounded extravagant. He made up his mind that if Jasmine showed the least sign of taking him seriously—and he realized that he had to bear in mind that cousins are marriageable—he would explain that it was merely practice. At the same time he found her personable, even charming, and if without involving himself or committing himself too far he could for the rest of the summer establish between himself and her a mildly sentimental relationship, which at the same time would be of great benefit to his Italian, he should be able to go up to Cambridge next term with the satisfactory thought that during the Long Vacation he had improved his French, strengthened his friendship with Lord Gresham, effected an excellent beginning with Italian, amused himself incidentally, and made sufficient progress with his reading for the first part of the Classical Tripos not to feel that he had neglected the main current of his academic career.

Unfortunately for Edward's plans he found that Jasmine was inclined to laugh at him when in the middle of rehearsing a dialogue from the *Italian Traveller's Vade Mecum* between himself and a laundress he indulged in Petrarchan apostrophes. Now Edward was not inclined to laughter either at his own expense or at the expense of life in general, because his conception of the universe only allowed laughter to depend upon minor mistakes in behaviour or scansion. Therefore in order to cure Jasmine of her frivolity he was driven into being more serious and less academic than he had intended. In other words, Edward, even if he was already a perfectly formed prig, was not yet twenty-one, and to put the matter shortly, he really did fall in love with Jasmine; so much so indeed that he ceased to make love to her in Italian and began to make love to her in English. Jasmine, apprehensive of all the trouble such a state of affairs would stir up and knowing what an additional grievance it would create against her in the minds of her relatives, begged him not to be foolish. The more she begged him not to be foolish, the more foolish Edward became, so foolish indeed that he began to let his infatuation be suspected by his brothers, the result of which was that he lost the authority hitherto maintained for him by his attitude of discouraging gloom. In a weak moment he even allowed himself to bribe Ethelred to leave him alone with Jasmine in the dusky garden one evening after dinner, and Ethelred, realizing that Edwy and Edred would soon discover for themselves such a source of profit from their eldest brother, it might be to his own disadvantage, resolved to enter into a formal compact of blackmail with both of them.

Thenceforth Edward found himself being gradually deprived of various little possessions that however valueless in themselves had for him the sentimental importance he attached to everything connected with himself. In order to secure twilit walks with his cousin that she, poor girl, with one eye on a jealous mother, did her best to avoid, Edward parted with his choicest cricket bat, presented for the highest score in a junior match in the days before dyspepsia cramped his style; with a collection of birds' eggs made at the age of fourteen; in fact with everything that, should he die now, would have led anybody to suppose that he was once human. Finally he was reduced to forking out small sums of money to purchase the good will of his three youngest brothers. Their demands grew more exorbitant, and Edward, who had already decided to become a Government servant after that triumphant university career which was to crown his triumphant school career, tried to be firm. Indeed he smacked Edwy's head, and when he had done so felt that he had been firm. Unfortunately it was the worst moment he could have chosen to be firm—yes, he was certainly intended to be a Government servant—because the blackmailers had something up their sleeves, and of what that was Jasmine received the first intimation in the shape of a letter from Edwy.

Dear Jasmine,

If you will meet the undersigned by the blasted elm at the corner of the heath to-night at half-past eight, you will hear of something to your advantage. I mean the elm that was struck by lightening last spring at the corner of the paddock. But in future I shall not call it the paddock. The enclosed token will tell you what.

(signed)
A friend and well-wisher.

The enclosed token was a lock of hair tied up with the end of a bootlace. Jasmine supposed that the three youngest cousins had discovered a new kind of game in the pleasure and excitement of which they wished her to share; glad of an excuse to escape Edward's attentions after dinner, she presented herself at the blasted elm and tried to appear as mysterious as the requirements of the game demanded.

She had not been waiting more than a minute when three cloaked figures stealthily approached the trysting-place. They were all wearing what Jasmine hoped were only discarded hats of the Dean, and when they drew nearer she perceived that they were also wearing gaiters of the Dean. She wondered if the Dean had so many gaiters to spare for his sons' pranks, and she began to fear that some of his present wardrobe had been requisitioned. Edwy's voice, in trying to assume the appropriate bass of a conspirator, ran up to a high treble at the third word he uttered, which set his brothers off laughing so unrestrainedly that in order to conceal such an intrusion of their own modern personalities, they had to pommel each other until Edwy at last rescued his voice from the heights and called upon Jasmine to follow his lead. She, still supposing that some game of buried treasure or capture by brigands was afoot followed with appropriate caution along the winding paths of the shrubbery to that favourite haunt of mystery, the ruined tower.

"Fair maiden," the eldest conspirator growled, "your betrothed awaitest you within."

"You've surely never persuaded Edward to hide himself up there?" she laughed.

"Edward avaunt!" he hissed. "The doom of Edward is sealed."

"Sealed!" echoed Edred, more successfully hoarse than his brother.

Ethelred was unable to take up his cue, being choked by laughter.

"I say, do you think she ought to climb up by the rope-ladder?" Edred asked, falling back into his ordinary voice for the moment.

"Shut up, you ass," replied Edwy in the same commonplace accents. "Maiden," he continued in a bass that was now truly diabolic, "the ladder of knotted sheets for thy fell purpose awaitest thee."

"A terribly appropriate adjective," Jasmine observed with a smile. "I'm not really to climb up that, am I?"

"No," said Edwy reluctantly. "An thou wilt, thou cannest enter by the door."

"Poor Edward!" murmured Jasmine. "How he must be hating this!"

"Foolish maiden," Edwy reproached her. "It is not Edward who you seekest, but one more near, no, I mean more dear, but one more dear to thee. My trusty followers and me will watch without whilst thou speaketh with him."

The air of Bartelmytide was moist and chill, and Jasmine, with regretful thoughts of the Deanery fires which had just begun, hurried into the tower to finish off her part of the performance. She was not to be let off until she had mounted to the upper room, and though in the darkness the ladder felt more than usually wobbly and the stones on either side more than usually covered with cobwebs, she went boldly on, and had no sooner reached the upper room than she was aware that there was somebody there, somebody who did not greet her with the flash of a dark lantern, but with the flicker of a cigar-lighter.

"Well, this is a rum way to meet you again," Harry Vibart exclaimed genially.

"But...." Jasmine stammered, "I thought I told you not to come down here."

Vibart was too tactful to say that he had supposed the forbidding postscript was at least a suggestion if not an invitation that he should come down, and looking as suitably penitent as he could by the wavering beams of the cigar-lighter, he explained that he had only done so with great caution, and added a hope that she would forgive him.

"Yes, but supposing my uncle and aunt find out that you have arranged to meet me like this?"

"Oh, I didn't arrange to meet you like this," Vibart explained. "Those three young sportsmen downstairs arranged that. The only thing I did was to make enquiries beforehand where you were living, and somehow they got it into their heads—of course you'll think it ridiculous, I know—but ... well, to put it shortly, they imagined ... that I was ... rather keen on you."

"I suppose you realize that I am very angry indeed?" said Jasmine.

"Oh yes, I realize that," Vibart admitted. "I can see you're very angry. But don't you think that to-morrow I might call in the ordinary way? That's the main object of this interview. I've really rather enjoyed sitting up here thinking about you. I should have enjoyed it even more if something that was either a small bat or a large spider hadn't fallen on my head. But what about to-morrow?"

"Oh no, please," she expostulated. "No, no, no, you really mustn't. I'm quite enjoying myself here. I'm quite happy, and I know that if you arrive on the scene, something's bound to happen to make everything go wrong."

"That's very discouraging of you."

"I don't mean to be discouraging."

"You may not mean to be, but you certainly are. Look here, Jasmine, I've been thinking a tremendous lot lately about you, and if you'll risk it, I'll risk it."

"Risk what?"

"Well, you see ... confound this patent lighter; it's gone out."

The upper room of the tower was in complete darkness, and Jasmine was inclined to hope that it would remain in darkness; she felt that even the mild illumination of the cigar-lighter gave too intimate a revelation of her countenance for any promise to be made. Harry was gaining time for his reply by devoting himself to the cigar-lighter, and Jasmine felt that if this tension was continued, she should presently begin to emit white sparks herself.

"Risk what?" she repeated.

"Risk being cut off by my uncle and not having a penny to bless ourselves with, and getting married on what I made this August. I've had a topping August. I'm £84 10s. up on the bookies. And though of course it's not much for two, it would give us enough for an economical honeymoon, and I've got a friend who would give me a job in a teak forest in Burmah. It's a very useful wood, you know. They make boats of it and the better kind of packing-cases."

"Stop! Stop!" she exclaimed.

"What's the matter? Have you got a spider on you? Show me where it is and I'll brush it off. I'm frightfully afraid of spiders, but I'm so fond of you, you darling little girl, that I'll...."

"Oh, you mustn't call me that," Jasmine interrupted.

"Don't you like being called a darling little girl?" he asked with a sigh of relief. "Well, I promise you I won't ever call you that again. I assure you that it took a lot to work myself up to the scratch and get off that term of endearment. But, Jasmine, I love you. Look here, murmur something pleasant for goodness' sake. I'm feeling an awful ass now I've said it."

But Jasmine could not murmur anything at all. By what she had read of love and of the way people declared their love, she would have supposed that Harry Vibart was making fun of her. And yet something in the tone of his voice forbade her to think that. Moreover, the way her own heart was beating prevented her wanting to think that. So she stayed silent, while he occupied himself with the cigar-lighter in case her eyes should tell him what her tongue refused to speak. He managed at last to kindle the wick, and holding the little instrument of revelation above his head so that from the vastness of the gloom around he could conjure her beloved countenance, he stood waiting for the answer. In the few seconds that had fluttered past, Jasmine felt that she had grown up, and now when she looked at the freckled young man, so obviously fearful of having made a fool of himself, she felt several years older than he, so much older that she was able to speak to him with what it seemed was a weight of worldly knowledge behind her.

"I'm afraid you've been rather impetuous," she said austerely. "I could never dream of asking you to give up anything on my account." Jasmine gained eloquence from not meaning a word of what she said, and unaware that she was trying to persuade herself rather than Harry of the imprudence of his project, she grew more eloquent with every word she uttered. "You must remember that I have not a penny in the world, and that you cannot afford to marry a girl without a dowry. I know that in England men do marry even quite ordinary girls without a dowry, but I should never feel happy if I were married like that."

"What on earth have dowries got to do with being in love? Do you love me? Do you think you could get to love me?"

"You've no right to ask me that," said Jasmine, "unless you are able to marry me."

"Well, I told you I was £84 10s. up on the bookies this August. I should have proposed in July, but I had rather a rotten Goodwood, and...."

"Yes, but you can't afford a wife with only that. Why, even if my uncle went on allowing me £10 a quarter...."

"I told you there was a risk. I asked you if you would risk it," he interrupted in an aggrieved voice. "Anyway, the point I want to get at is this: do you or do you not care for me?"

"I like you very much," Jasmine admitted politely.

"Yes, well, that sounds rather as if I was a mutton chop. Look here, you know, you're driving me into making a scene. When I first saw you at York, I fell in love with you. I didn't mean to tell you that, because it sounds ridiculous. But I did. Then when you were such a little sport on that mackerel hunt, I loved you more than ever. And then you were whisked off. I felt desperate, and I tried to kill my love. Please don't laugh. I know it's almost impossible not to laugh if a chap talks like this, and I should have laughed myself a year ago. But do you realize that you've driven me into reading books? That's a pretty desperate state of affairs. I can't pass a railway book-stall now without buying armfuls of the most atrocious rot. And the worse it is, the more I enjoy it. About fifty darlings a page is my style now. Where was I? Oh yes, I tried to kill my love. You know, playing golf, and all that sort of thing. But as soon as I heard where you were, I came to see you. Well, it was bad luck to drop that brick over the old boy's malacca, and I felt desperate. And then when I got your letter on top of the worst Goodwood anybody ever had, I said to myself that, unless I was fifty pounds up by the end of August, I'd go out to the Colonies and work myself to death. Well, I made more than that fifty pounds, and here I am. I'd got a lot of jolly things all ready to say to you, but now I'm here I can't say anything. Jasmine, I'm as keen as mustard on you. There!"

He had spoken with such vehemence that the cigar-lighter had long ago been puffed out; in the darkness Jasmine felt her hand grasped.

"What a topping little hand," he murmured. "It's as soft as a puppy's paw. Topping!"

Jasmine had an impulse to let herself sigh out her happiness upon his shoulder; she knew somehow that his arms were open, and that the touch of his tweeds would be as refreshing to her tired spirit as if she were to fling herself into the sunburnt scented grass of a remote meadow; she could not summon to her aid a single argument against letting herself be folded in his embrace. Then, just as she was surrendering to the moment, a clod of earth was flung through the ruined oriel of the tower, and from down below came hoarse cries of "Cavé! Cavé! Edward's coming down the path! You'd better bunk!"

"What's up?" asked Vibart, making fresh efforts to kindle his cigar-lighter. "Who's Edward?"

"Oh, I knew this would happen! I knew this would happen!" Jasmine exclaimed distractedly. "I told you not to come down here."

"But who's Edward?" Vibart persisted.

"It's my cousin. He's dreadfully in earnest, and he thinks he's in love with me."

"Well, I'm not particularly afraid of Edward; but if it's the fashion here to be afraid of him, I'll pretend to be afraid of him too, and the best way of showing our terror is to sit here holding each other's hands until the dangerous fellow passes on. The closer we keep together, the less frightened we shall be."

"It's nothing to joke about," she said. "He's evidently suspicious about something, or he would never have come out into the garden to look for me in the tower."

Jasmine was sure that the conspirators, in their desire for a more dramatic climax than they might otherwise have secured, had conveyed a mysterious warning to Edward, who, when she was nowhere to be found in the house had, preserving his own dignity as far as possible, set out upon a voyage of discovery.

Whatever the conspirators had done in the way of precipitating this climax, they were now doing their best to deflect Edward from the path. The methods they chose, however, were not sufficiently subtle, and they only had the effect of putting their eldest brother in a very bad temper, as was evident from the threats that were audible outside.

"Look here, young Edred, I'll give you the biggest thrashing you ever had in your life if you fling any more of those toadstools at me. All right, Edwy, I can recognize you, and you'll find out when you go indoors again that you can't wear the pater's gaiters without trouble. Where's Jasmine?"

And then, like the croak of a night-bird, Edwy's response was heard.

"Recreant knight, the maiden whom thou seekest is safe from thy lustful arm. Beware of advancing another step."

"You young swine, I'll give you the biggest licking you ever had in your life!" retorted Edward, still advancing in the direction of the door.

"Look here," Vibart whispered to Jasmine, "I think I ought to go out and help those sportsmen."

At this moment Ethelred, who had retreated into the tower, came up the ladder and told them not to worry, because he had invented something that was going to put Edward out of action the moment he attempted to advance beyond the first rung.

"No, please, Ethelred," Jasmine begged. "Don't make matters worse than they are."

"No, really it's all right, I swear," Ethelred promised. "Don't get excited. And if you want to elope to-night, Edwy's made all the necessary arrangements. He's got the ladder hidden by the stable, and the pony's harnessed, and if you're pursued, he's going to put people off the scent by saying the house is on fire; or he may be trying to set it on fire really, I can't remember; and he's only told Wilson"—Wilson was one of the under-gardeners—"so you needn't be in a funk of being found out. And look here," he added to Vibart, "you won't forget that man-lifting kite, will you? Because Edwy's awfully keen to go up with it."

"That's all right," Vibart promised. "You stave off Edward, and I'll send you a kite that will lift an elephant."

"Don't encourage him," said Jasmine. "You don't understand how dreadful all this is going to be for me."

By this time Edward, undeterred by the missiles of Edwy or Edred, had reached the foot of the ladder, and was asking Jasmine in that academic voice she so much disliked if she was in the tower.

"If those young brutes have been playing practical jokes on you, *carissima*, just let me know and I'll give them a lesson they won't forget."

"Will you, you stinking pig?" muttered Ethelred, bending over and releasing a heavy weight on his brother's head.

"Heavens! What have you done?" Jasmine cried in apprehension.

"It's all right. It's only a bag of flour," Ethelred explained. "And I think it hit him absolutely plum."

However it hit Edward, it had the effect of rousing him to fury; without pausing to consider that the steps of the ladder were broken and that the floor of the tower contained several holes and that his sense of direction was considerably impeded by the flour in his eyes, he came charging up the ladder. Just as he reached the top there was a crack of giving wood, followed by a crash, a cry, a thud, and several groans.

"Great Scott! He's really damaged himself this time," said Vibart.

"I say, I didn't work that," Ethelred protested a little tremulously.

Edred and Edwy, who had followed in their brother's wake, were calling up that he had broken his leg. Vibart's cigar-lighter refused to shed even a momentary flicker on the scene, and there was nothing for it but to send one of the boys below back to the house for help. Jasmine begged Harry Vibart to escape if he could, but when he tried the floor with a view to letting himself down, the rotten planking began to break off, so that he had to draw back lest the whole floor of the room should collapse and precipitate himself and Jasmine upon the prostrate and groaning form of Edward underneath. He then attempted in response to Jasmine's entreaties to escape from the oriel window, but no sooner had he put himself into a position to make the drop than she begged him with equal urgency to come back.

"You might break your leg too, and it would be so dreadfully embarrassing to have you and Edward both in bed. My aunt would hate looking after you, and I should never be allowed to look after you."

"Are you sure of that?" he asked.

"Sure, sure. But why do you ask?"

"Because, if I thought there was a chance of getting you as my nurse, I'd break every bone in my body with the greatest pleasure."

The only one who escaped without damage moral or physical from that evening was Ethelred. When the Dean and Mrs. Lightbody with Edgar and Edmund, gardeners and lanterns and ladders, and an improvised stretcher, arrived at the tower, Ethelred managed somehow to get back to the house unperceived, and was able to claim, relying upon the loyalty of his fellow-conspirators, that he had gone to bed immediately after dinner with a bad headache. The rest of the family suffered in various degrees. Edwy suffered from being caught wearing his father's best gaiters, Edred from being caught wearing his father's best hat. The Dean suffered in his character as owner of the gaiters and the hat. Mrs. Lightbody suffered in her deepest feelings as a mother, as the wife of the Dean of Silchester, and as an aunt. Harry Vibart suffered from the ridiculous situation in which he found himself, and from the unpleasant situation in which his imprudence had placed Jasmine. Edward suffered from a broken leg, but derived some pleasure from the effort he had made to be noble. His nobility of behaviour consisted in abstaining from any comment on Vibart's presence in the tower, and the consciousness of his nobility was so sharp that the pain of his fractured limb was dull in comparison. Yet Jasmine was so unreasonable as to think him lacking in generosity because he did not explain away Vibart's presence, explain away his own accident, explain away the whole situation, in fact. She even blamed him for what had occurred, ascribing the disaster to his vanity in supposing that she would send him a message by the boys to meet her in the tower. But then Jasmine had suffered most of anybody; and it was she who was to discover that Aunt May at her worst was angelic beside Aunt Ellen.

"I'm bound to say, Jasmine, that I did not imagine the existence of such depravity. A servant would not behave like that. And what is so lamentable is that the boys knew that you were up in the tower with that young man. It seems to me almost criminal to put such ideas into their little heads. I've been so strict with them. I've even wondered sometimes if I could let them read the Bible to themselves. Your poor uncle has aged twenty years in the last twenty-four hours."

What really had happened to Uncle Arnold was a bad cold from going out in his slippers without a hat. But Aunt Ellen was enjoying herself too much for accuracy. She was in the raptures of a grand improvisation. Presently her fancy soared; she indulged in Gothic similes.

"It was like a witches' sabbath. And poor Edward! Not a word has he said in blame of you. He lies there as patient as a martyr. And then I suppose you'll go off this afternoon and confess to your priest down in Bog Lane, and come back under the impression that you're as white as driven snow. To me such a pretence of religion is disgusting."

"Perhaps you don't realize, Aunt Ellen," said Jasmine, "that Edward has been making love to me for weeks, and that I've had to laugh at him to prevent his doing something silly."

"What do you mean, doing something silly, you wicked and vulgar girl? I cannot think where you got such a mind. A servant would not get such disgusting ideas into her head. I suppose we must put it down to your mother."

"Stop!" said Jasmine, white with anger. "Stop, will you? Or I shall throw this inkpot at you." And when Aunt Ellen did stop, she was half sorry, because she was hating her so much that she was really wanting to throw the inkpot at her. However, she put it back on the table, rushed from her aunt's presence up to her own room, where, after weeping for an hour, she sat down and wrote to Harry Vibart.

Dear Mr. Vibart,

I hope you realize by now that you acted abominably in coming down here after what I said in my letter. I never want to see you again. Please understand that I mean it this time. However, I'm going back to Italy almost at once where people know how to behave themselves. I hate England. I've been miserable here, and you've made me more miserable than anybody.

Then she signed herself *Jasmine Grant* and fiercely blotted him out of her life.

Chapter Nine

AFTER the scene with her aunt, Jasmine longed to leave the Deanery at once, for she suffered torments of humiliation in having to stay on there in a disgrace that was being published all over Silchester. The Dean himself was kind, and perhaps it was because he understood the difficulty of her position that he asked her to come and work with him. But such an easy way out for Jasmine did not please his wife, who was continually coming up to the study and worrying him with her fears about the progress of Edward's fracture in order to impress both him and Jasmine with their heartless conduct in thus working away regardless of the martyr downstairs. The Dean was a kind-hearted man, but he considered his work on pre-Norman Britain the most important thing in life; finding it impossible to proceed under the stress of these continual interruptions, he presently announced that he must go to Oxford for a week or two and do some work in the Bodleian.

As soon as he had gone, Aunt Ellen's treatment of her niece became something like a persecution. She forbade the youngest boys to play with her; she took a delight in making the most cruel remarks to her before Edmund and Edgar; she was rude to her in front of the servants. Jasmine was on the verge of a nervous breakdown, and she was by now so passionately anxious to leave Silchester that she was actually on the verge of writing to Aunt May to ask if she could not come back to London. She did write to Aunt Cuckoo, who wrote back a pleasant little letter iced over with conventional expressions of affection like the pink mottoes on a white birthday cake. She was sorry to hear that Jasmine was unable to appreciate Aunt Ellen. She realized that the atmosphere in the higher circles of the Church of England was unsympathetic, *but* Baboose had shown symptoms of croup. She hoped that later in the autumn Jasmine could come and spend a week or two at The Cedars, *but* just now it was advisable to keep Baboose at Torquay. Uncle Eneas sent his love, *but* he was not very well, and Jasmine would understand how difficult it was to fit an extra person in seaside lodgings. She was sorry that Jasmine was unhappy, "*but* our wonderful religion will console you better than my poor self," she wound up.

"But! But!" Jasmine cried aloud. "Butter would be the right word."

Such was the state of affairs at the Deanery when one morning about a fortnight after Edward broke his leg, Cherrill the butler announced a visitor to see Jasmine. After what she had suffered from that ill-timed visit of Harry Vibart, her heart sank, particularly as Cherrill did not announce the visitor in a way that would have led anybody to suppose that his news would be welcome.

"For me?" Jasmine repeated. "Are you sure?"

"Yes, miss," said Cherrill firmly. "This, er...." he hesitated for a moment, "...elderly person wishes to speak with you for a moment on behalf of Miss Butt."

"Miss Butt?" Jasmine repeated. "Who's she?" For a moment she thought that her nervous condition was developing insanity and that the name was something to do with her outburst against the 'buts' of Aunt Cuckoo.

"Perhaps if you would come down, miss," suggested Cherrill, "to ascertain from the ... person more in full what exactly she does require, you could enquire from her who Miss Butt is."

Jasmine asked if the visitor had given her own name, and when Cherrill said that she had given the name of Mrs. Vokins she remembered that Mrs. Vokins was Selina's friend at Catford. It was all very odd, and without more ado she went downstairs.

In the dining-room a small thin woman with a long red nose came forward to shake hands with Jasmine in the serious way in which people who are not accustomed to shaking hands very often do.

"You've been sent here by Selina?" asked Jasmine impulsively. The question seemed to take Mrs. Vokins aback; she had evidently been primed with a good deal of formality to undertake her mission.

"I am Miss Butt's lady friend from Catford," she explained with an assumption of tremendous dignity.

"I remember her talking about you very often."

"Yes, miss," sighed Mrs. Vokins, taking out her handkerchief and dabbing the corners of her eyes. She evidently supposed that any reference to her in conversation must have included the sorrows of her past life, and she now put on the air of one to whom a response to sympathy is the most familiar emotion.

"And you have a message for me from Selina?"

"No, not a message, a letter. Miss Butt was unwilling to put it in the pillar-box for fear your aunt should look at it."

"My aunt?"

"That was how Miss Butt came to send me in place of the pillar-box. She wanted me to put the letter in my stocking for safety, but suffering as I do from vericlose veins, I asked Miss Butt to kindly permit of it being put in my handbag. You must excuse it smelling slightly of salts, but I'm very subject to headaches ever since my trouble."

Jasmine opened the letter, which was strongly perfumed with gin. The negotiations being conducted in such a ladylike polite spirit, Jasmine was not surprised to find Selina's letter couched in the same style.

Dear Miss Grant,

This is to inform you that poor old Mr. Rouncivell has been took very bad with inflammation of the bowls screaming and yelling himself hoarse fit to frighten anybody. I don't want to say more than I ought in a letter, but knowing what I know, I tell you you ought to come back with my lady friend Mrs. Vokins at once and not knowing if you have the money for your fare I take the liberty of enclosing a postal order for two pounds. Mrs. Vokins has a brother-in-law who is a fourwheeler and will drive you back to Muswell Hill as per arrangement.

"This is all very mysterious," Jasmine commented.

"Yes, miss, so it is, I'm sure," Mrs. Vokins agreed. "But then, as my friend Miss Butt says, life's very mysterious. And I said, answering her, 'Yes, Miss Butt, and death's very mysterious.' And she said, 'You're right, Mrs. Vokins, it is.' Miss Butt's very worried. Oh yes, I can tell you she's very worried, because she's given up the kitchen which I was using for her three times a week. If I might presume to give advice as a married woman, which I was before my poor husband died, I'd advise you to pack up your box and come along with me by the afternoon train, which my brother-in-law will meet with his cab. You need have no fear of familiarity, miss, because he was a coachman before he was a cabman, and was hounded out of his job by one of these motor-cars. Inventions of the Devil, as I call them."

"But does Selina want me to help her look after my poor uncle?"

"I'm sorry, miss, to appear stand-offish, and it's through no wish of mine, I'm sure, but Miss Butt's last words to me was: 'Keep your mouth shut, Mrs. Vokins.'"

Jasmine was too deeply moved by the thought of the poor old gentleman lying in pain at Rouncivell Lodge, and too much touched by Selina's kindly thought in enclosing her fare, to delay a moment in answering her request. In any case it was obvious that she would have to leave the Deanery almost at once, and it seemed an interposition of providence that she should have such a splendid excuse to escape from the ridiculous and humiliating position in which Edward's folly and Harry Vibart's thoughtlessness had placed her.

It was dark when the cab pulled up a hundred yards away from the gates of Rouncivell Lodge, and Jasmine hoped that the necessity for all this caution would soon be finished, because she was finding the gin-scented hushes of Mrs. Vokins that filled the interior of the dank old cab trying to her fatigued and hungry condition. However, there was not long to wait before Selina's voice, which always sounded to Jasmine as if the housekeeper had been eating a lot of stale biscuits without being able to obtain a drink of water after them, greeted her.

"Such goings on!" she snapped, and then turning to the cabman went on in her dry voice: "Perhaps, Mr. Vokins, you'll have the goodness to carry Miss Grant's trunk round to the back entrance without ringing."

"I suppose the horse will stand all right?" said the cabman doubtfully.

"Of course the horse will stand all right," said Selina. "My father was a coachman before you knew the difference between a horse and a donkey, Mr. Vokins."

"William," supplemented his sister-in-law, "remember what I told you on your doorstep first thing this morning."

Mr. Vokins without another word went off to leave Jasmine's trunk where he had been told to leave it. While he was gone, the conversation was kept strictly to the minor incidents of Mrs. Vokins' mission.

"You got off then quite comfortably, Mrs. Vokins?" Selina enquired.

"Yes, Miss Butt, thank you. I had no trouble. Or I should say none but what come from me being so silly as to break my smelling salts in my bag by not noticing I had put my bag *under* me on the seat instead of *beside* me as I had the intention of. Oh yes, when anyone makes up their mind to it, you can get about nowadays and no mistake."

"And you gave Miss Grant the postal order all right, Mrs. Vokins?" enquired Selina sharply.

"We haven't known each other all these years, Miss Butt," replied her friend with elaborate haughtiness, "for you to have any need to ask me *sech* a question *now*."

"It was so kind of you, Selina, to think of that," said Jasmine, putting out her hand to touch the yellow-faced housekeeper's arm. Selina blew her nose violently, and then observed that a little quietness from everybody would not come amiss.

It was not until the two Vokins had disappeared into the December night and Selina had conducted Jasmine with the most elaborate caution along the gloomy path known as the Tradesmen's Entrance and had seen her safely seated by the kitchen fire that she allowed herself the luxury of a complete explanation; and even then she broke off just when she had gathered her skirts together before sitting down to observe that Jasmine was looking very pale, and to ask if she was hungry.

"I haven't had any dinner," Jasmine explained.

"Well, there's nothing but muffins; but I suppose you wouldn't object to muffins. If a Frenchman who isn't hungry can eat frogs and snails, you can eat muffins when you are."

"I should love some muffins," said Jasmine, and she ate four while Selina sat back and stared hard at her all the time. As soon as she had finished, the narrative opened.

"Well, it's best to begin at the beginning, as they say, and when you got into trouble over Her walking-stick, that there Pamela planted herself down here. And now perhaps you'll understand why I said nothing in front of Mrs. Vokins?"

Jasmine looked bewildered.

"Well, of course, she poisoned him. Oh, undoubtedly she poisoned him. Well, I mean to say, people don't fall ill for nothing, do they?"

"Selina!" Jasmine gasped. "You're making the most dreadful accusation. You really ought to be careful."

"That's what I am being. Careful. If I wasn't careful, I should have gone and hollered it out in the streets, shouldn't I? But I know better. Before I'd hollered it out once or twice I should have been asked to eat my words, if you'll excuse the vulgar expression. And then where should I have been?"

"Yes, but I don't think you ought to say things like that even to me. After all...." Jasmine hesitated; she was debating indeed whether to say 'Miss Pamela' or 'Pamela.' If she used the former, she should seem to be dissociating herself too much from Selina, which in view of having accepted the loan of that money would be snobbish; and yet if she called her simply 'Pamela' she should seem to be associating herself too intimately with Selina, even perhaps to be endorsing the terrible accusation, which was only one of Selina's ridiculous exaggerations, on the level of her theory that the human race was without exception damned. "After all," she had found the way to put it, "my cousin, you see she *is* my cousin."

"Well," Selina granted unwillingly, "if she didn't poison him with arsenic, she poisoned his mind. The things she used to say at the dinner-table! Well, I give you my word, I was in two twos once or twice whether I wouldn't bang her on the head with the cover of the potato dish. I give you my word, it was itching in my hand. Nasty sneering way of talking! I don't know where people who calls theirselves ladies learn such manners. And no sooner had that there Pamela gone than that there Lettice appeared. Lettice, indeed! There's not much green about her. Anyone more cunning I've never seen. Nasty insinuendos, enough to make anyone sick! Small wonder the poor old gentleman had no appetite for his food! And of course she attempted to set him against me. Well, on one occasion he akcherly used language to me which I give you my word if he'd of been a day younger I wouldn't have stood it. Language I should be sorry to use to a convick myself. Well, there have been times when I've wondered if the Lord wasn't a little bit too particular. You know what I mean, a little too dictatorial and old-fashioned. But I give you my word since I've had two months of them I sympathize with Him. Yes, I sympathize with Him! And if I was Him, I'd do the same thing. Well, I never expected to enjoy looking down out of Heaven at a lot of poor souls burning; but if this goes on much longer, I shall begin to think that it's one of the glories of Paradise. I could watch the whole lot of them burning by the hour. And that's not the worst I've told you. Even if they didn't akcherly poison him, they're glad he's ill, and I wouldn't mind who heard me say that. I'd go and shout out that this very moment in Piccadilly Circus. And their mother! Nosey, nasty, stuck-up—well, it's no use sitting here and talking about what they are. What we've got to do is to spoil their little game. If I go up to see if he wants anything, I get ordered out of the room like the dirt beneath their feet. 'We've got to be very careful,' says that smarmy doctor they've got in to annoy me. 'Very careful.' says I, looking at him very meaning. 'Terrible to hear anyone suffer like that,' he says. 'Yes, it is terrible,' says I. 'And the terrible thing is,' he says, 'that however much one wants to alleviate the pain, we daren't do it. And whyever won't he come out of that dreadful little room,' he says, 'when there's all those nice bedrooms lying empty?' 'You let him be where he is,' I said, 'it's his house, isn't it?' And then, before I could stop them, they started lifting the box mattress and trying to move him out of the bathroom. And the way he screamed and carried on, it was something shocking to hear him! And I know the reason perfectly well. Underneath the mattress in the bath he keeps his coffin. Many's the time he's congratulated himself to me on getting that coffin so cheap. 'It's oak, Selina,' he used to say, 'and I got it cheap for a misfit, and it fills up the bath a treat.' Well, it stands to reason, doesn't it, that now of all times he wants to keep it handy? 'No deal coffins for me, Selina,' he used to say. Besides, it's my belief he's got his will inside of that coffin. Depend upon it, he's got his own reasons for not wishing to be moved. So I stood in the doorway, and I said very fierce: 'If you want to move him, you'll have to move me first.' And then it came over me all of a sudden that if I got you back here to help we might be able to do something both together."

In spite of Selina's marvels and exaggerations and absurd misconstructions, her tale convinced Jasmine of Uncle Matthew's hatred of being taken charge of by the Hector Grants. Naturally she sympathized with his point of view on this matter. To be helpless in the hands of the Hector Grants struck her as a punishment far in excess of anything that the old gentleman deserved. She did not feel that it was her duty to interfere in the slightest degree with the normal process of his will, but she did feel that she had a right if he were not comfortable to protest her own anxiety to look after him, even more, to insist upon looking after him. She supposed that her Aunt May would attribute the lowest motives to this intention; Aunt May, however, always attributed low motives to everybody, and the lowest motives of all to her niece.

"Well?" asked Selina sharply when Jasmine did not offer any remarks upon her tale.

"I'm sorry," said Jasmine, pulling herself together. "I was wondering what excuse I should be able to give my aunt for seeming to interfere."

"Excuse?" Selina repeated angrily. "No excuse is needed, I assure you, for putting yourself forward on his behalf, as you might say. What he requires is looking after. What he's getting is nothing of the kind."

At that moment a scream rang through the house. Jasmine looked at Selina in horror.

"What did I tell you?" the housekeeper demanded triumphantly. "I told you he carried on something awful, and you wouldn't believe me. It's a wonder he hasn't started in screaming before. I've never known him quiet for so long at a stretch. Bloodcurdling, I call it. You often read of bloodcurdling screams. Now you can hear them for yourself. There he goes again."

And it really was bloodcurdling to hear from that old man's room what sounded like the shrieks of a passionate, frightened, tortured child. It had the effect of rousing Jasmine to an immediate encounter with her aunt, an encounter to brace herself up to which, until she had heard Uncle Matthew scream, had been growing more and more difficult with every moment of delay. Now she sprang out of her chair and hurried up the wide central staircase, past the countless figures in the pictures that stared at her when she passed like a frightened crowd. She ran too quickly for Selina to keep up with her, and when she turned down into the passage at the end of which was her uncle's little room, she beheld what, without the real agony and pain at the back of it, would have been a merely grotesque sight. The box-mattress on which Uncle Matthew was lying was half-way through the door of his bedroom, carried by two men of respectful and sober appearance whom she recognized as two male nurses that she had once seen on the steps of Sir Hector's house in Harley Street arming an old man with a shaven head into a brougham. The old man's eyes had been wild and tragic, and their wildness and tragedy had been rendered more conspicuous to Jasmine by the very respect with which the attendants treated him and the very sobriety of their manner and appearance; to such an extent indeed that the personalities of the two men, if two such colourless individuals could be allowed to possess

71

personality, had been tinged, or rather not so much tinged as glazed over, with a sinister aura. So now when she saw them for the second time, struggling in the doorway while her uncle held fast to the frame and tried to prevent the bed's being carried out, she had a swift and sickening sensation of horror. She was hurrying down the passage to protest against the old gentleman's being moved against his will, when her aunt emerged from one of the nearer bedrooms and stood before her.

"What are you doing to Uncle Matthew?" demanded Jasmine furiously, not pausing to explain her own presence. She had a moment's satisfaction in perceiving that Lady Grant was obviously taken aback at seeing her there; but her aunt soon recovered herself sufficiently to reply with her wonted coldness:

"It scarcely seems to concern you, my dear; and may I enquire in my turn what *you* are doing *here*?"

"Oh, you needn't think you can put me off like that," Jasmine went on apace. "I've left Silchester, and I'm going to stay here until Uncle Matthew is better, and I'll answer no questions until he is better."

"Indeed? That will be for your uncle and me to decide."

"Oh no, it won't. You're not my guardians. You weren't appointed my guardians, and you've got no say in the matter at all. If Uncle Matthew doesn't want to be taken out of his own room, why should he be, when he's ill?"

Another person now appeared, a sleek, pale, old young man, whom Jasmine recognized from Selina's allusion as the 'smarmy' doctor. She took advantage of his presence to run past her aunt and speak to the old gentleman, who was so much occupied in holding on to the frame of the door that he was apparently unconscious of his niece's arrival.

"If you please, miss," said one of the nurses, "you'd better not excite the patient just now."

Jasmine paid no attention to this advice, but knelt down and with all the force she could achieve kept on calling out to know what Uncle Matthew wanted, until at last the old gentleman was induced to recognize her. He was evidently pleased at her arrival, so much pleased that he offered her his hand in greeting, a gesture which cost him his hold on the frame of the door. The male nurses were quick to take advantage of this, and while Jasmine was still on her knees, they hurried him along the passage and vanished through the door from which Lady Grant had just emerged. Jasmine realized that her interference had only succeeded in helping the other side, and in a mist of mortification and self-reproach she followed the bed into the room prepared to receive the sick man. She was bound to admit to herself that the room was well chosen and admirably prepared. Yet she knew that the more careful the preparations, the more acutely would they aggravate her uncle's discomfort. The fire burning lavishly in the grate, the flowers blooming wastefully on the table, the sick room's glittering equipment, they would seem to him detestable extravagances which in his feeble condition he was powerless to prevent. As soon as Uncle Matthew was safely out of his little bath-bedroom, Lady Grant locked the door and put the key in her bag; but Selina arrived on the scene in time for this action by her ladyship, to whom she proceeded to give, or rather at whom she proceeded to throw a piece of her mind. When the housekeeper paused for breath, her ladyship merely said coldly that if she did not behave herself, she would find herself and her boxes in the street.

"This kind of thing has been going on long enough," Lady Grant proclaimed to the world. "It was time for his relations to interfere."

Jasmine, when she made an effort to consider the situation calmly, could not help acknowledging that by that world to which she had appealed all the right and all the reason would be awarded to her aunt. An abusive housekeeper trying to interfere between doctor and patient would stand little chance of obtaining even a hearing for her point of view, especially when that doctor was Sir Hector Grant. Moreover, she began to ask herself, might not Selina have merely got a bee buzzing in her bonnet about interference for the sake of interference? Had not her own judgment been wrought up by Selina's mysterious way of summoning her to Rouncivell Lodge and by the stifling atmosphere that enwrapped it to imagining what was, after all, looked at sanely, a melodramatic and improbable situation? One thing she was determined to do, however, and that was to stay in the house herself, not for any purpose connected with wills concealed in coffins under beds, but simply in order to be able to devote herself to Uncle Matthew's comfort. If her aunt really was trying to manipulate the old gentleman's end—and of course the idea was absurd—but if she were, she would find her niece's presence an obstacle to the success of her schemes, and if her wicked intentions were nothing more than the creation of Selina's highflown fancy.... Jasmine broke off her thoughts and went back to her uncle's new room, where, pulling up a chair beside his bed, she took his hand and asked if he did not feel a little better. The effort he had made to resist removal had exhausted him, and he was lying on the box-mattress breathing so faintly and looking so pale that she rose again in alarm to call the doctor, who was talking to Lady Grant outside. She had not moved a step from the bed before Uncle Matthew called to her in a weak voice, a voice, however, that still retained the accent of command, and bade her sit down again. It was at least a satisfaction to feel that he had grasped the fact of her presence and that he was evidently anxious to keep her by his side. Presently, when the respectful and sober male nurses had respectfully and soberly left the house, like two plumbers who had accomplished their job, the doctor came back to ask softly if Mr. Rouncivell could not bring himself to change his bed as well as his room. The old gentleman made no further opposition, but allowed himself to be lifted down from the box-mattress and tucked up in the big four-poster, after which the box-mattress, upon which he had slept for so many years in his bath, was carried away. Jasmine was now alone with him, and he beckoned her to lean over to catch what she feared might be his last whisper.

She was unnecessarily nervous.

"They think I'm going to die," he chuckled. "But I'm not. Ha! Ha!"

Five minutes afterward he was peacefully sleeping.

Downstairs Jasmine was allowed the pleasure of thoroughly and extensively defying her aunt. Nothing that Lady Grant said could make her flinch from her avowed determination not to leave Rouncivell Lodge until her uncle was definitely better. Only when she was satisfied on this point would she agree to go wherever she was sent. She even took a delight in drawing such a heightened picture of the affair with Edward and Harry Vibart at the Deanery as to call down upon her the epithet 'shameless.' She announced that if after she had visited Uncle Alec and Aunt Mildred she found that she did not get on better with them than with the rest of her relations, she should somehow borrow the money to return to Sirene, whence nothing should induce her ever to return to England.

"It occurs to me," said Lady Grant, "that you are trying to be impertinent."

"I don't care what occurs to you," Jasmine retorted. "I am simply telling you what I intend to do. I've got a kind of fondness for Uncle Matthew—not a very deep fondness, but a kind of fondness—and although you think me so heartless, I really am anxious about him, and I really should like to stay here until he's better."

It must have been difficult for Lady Grant to refrain from giving expression to the implication that was on the tip of her tongue; but she did refrain, and Jasmine could not help admiring her for doing so. However, she was determined to provoke a discussion about that very implication, and of her own accord she assured her aunt that she need be under no apprehension over Uncle Matthew's money, because she had no intention of trying to influence him in any way whatever.

"Impudent little wretch!" Aunt May gasped. And Jasmine gloried in her ability to have wrung from that cold and well-mannered woman such a betrayal of her radical femininity.

Jasmine did not expect to have the house to herself; nevertheless, in spite of continual visits from Lettice and Pamela, from Aunt Cuckoo and Aunt Ellen—the last-named greeting Jasmine as an abbess might greet a runaway nun—most of Uncle Matthew's entertainment fell upon her shoulders. This was not that the others did not take their turn at the bedside, but when they did, the old gentleman always pretended to be asleep, whereas with Jasmine he was conversational, much more conversational, indeed, than he had ever been when he was well. One day she felt that she really was forgiven when he asked her to go down to the hall and bring up his collection of sticks, all of which in turn he looked at and stroked and fondled; after this he made Jasmine put down in pencil the cost of each one, add up the sum, divide it by the number of sticks, and establish the average cost of each. When he had established the average cost, all the sticks that had cost more he made her put on one side, and all the sticks that had cost less on the other. After the sticks were classified, she was told to fetch various pieces of bric-à-brac on which he was anxious to gloat, as a convalescent child gloats over his long-neglected toys; finally one afternoon the musical-box was brought up, and the whole of its twelve tunes played through twice over.

Next morning he announced that he should get up.

"Oh no, I'm not dead yet," he said. "And, after all, why should I be? I'm only seventy-six. I've got a lot more years to live before I die."

Since the old gentleman had been out of danger, Selina had ceased to worry; but she still insisted that his will was in the coffin, and that time would prove her words true one of these days.

"Depend upon it," she told Jasmine, "they meant him to die without leaving any will at all. They meant him to die untested. Oh yes, that's what they meant him to do, and her ladyship—though why she should call herself a ladyship any more than Mrs. Vokins is beyond me, and I've known many real ladyships in my time—oh yes, her ladyship had worked it all out. She knew she couldn't expect to get it all, the cunning Isaacs. So she thought she'd have it divided amongst the lot, thinking as half a loaf's better than no bread. You'd have been a loser and I'd have been a loser by that game. And depend upon it the old gentleman saw through her, and made up his mind he would not die. Oh dear, if he'd only make up his mind to get salvation, there's no reason why he should worry about anything at all. No reason whatever. Think how nice it would be if we could all meet in Heaven one day and talk over all this. Oh, wouldn't it be nice? Think of the lovely weather they must always get in Heaven. I suppose we should be sitting about out of doors half the time. Or that's my notion anyway. But you and he won't be there, so what's the use in making plans to meet?"

Chapter Ten

JASMINE was not even yet cynical enough to keep herself from feeling hurt when Uncle Matthew on his recovery did not press her to stay on with him at Rouncivell Lodge, and, what was even more pointed, did not suggest that she might accompany him to Bournemouth, where in accordance with the prescription of Sir Hector Grant he was to regain all the vigour possible for a man of his age to enjoy. The Hector Grants, in their eagerness to help the old gentleman's convalescence, had taken a furnished house among the pines, the superb situation of which, with a great show of deference and affection, he had been invited to enjoy. Perhaps the old gentleman, who had been for several weeks the unwilling host of so many anxious relations, wanted to get back some of the expenses of hospitality. Jasmine thought that he owed as much to her devotion as to insist on her company; Uncle Matthew, however, did not appear sensible of any obligation, and he accepted Lettice and Pamela as his companions for alternate weeks without a murmur on behalf of Jasmine. Lettice and Pamela themselves were furious. They would have much preferred to sacrifice any prospects in Uncle Matthew's will to the dances of the autumn season; nor were they appeased by their mother's suggestion that separation from each other for a time might lead to many offers of marriage from young men who had hitherto been perplexed by the difficulty of choosing between them.

"I suppose you want me to go and stay with Uncle Alec and Aunt Mildred?" Jasmine asked one day when Lady Grant was demanding from the world at large what was the wisest thing to do with Jasmine and when Cousin Edith was apparently sunk in too profound an abyss of incertitude to be able to reply for the world at large.

"Why should you suppose that?" Lady Grant enquired gently.

"Well, they're the only relatives left to whom I haven't been passed on," said Jasmine. She was still able to hold her own against Aunt May in the bandying of words; but the failure of Uncle Matthew to appreciate her services had been fatal to any advance toward a real independence, and she was already beginning to wonder if it was worth while being rude to Aunt May, and if she might not be more profitably occupied in ousting Cousin Edith and securing for herself Cousin Edith's humiliating but superficially comfortable position in the household at Harley Street.

"What curious expressions you do employ, Jasmine. When I was your age, I should never have dreamed of employing such expressions. But then in my young days we were taught manners."

"And deportment," Cousin Edith added. "Don't you remember, Cousin May, how strict about that the Miss Watneys used to be in the dear old days at school?"

But Lady Grant did not wish to remember that she was once at school with Cousin Edith, and in order to snub Cousin Edith she had to forgo the pleasure of lecturing Jasmine upon her curious use of verbs.

"It is quite a coincidence," she went on, "that you should mention Uncle Alec and Aunt Mildred, because only this morning I received an invitation for you to go and stay with them at Curtain Wells. The trouble is that since the unfortunate affair at your Aunt Ellen's I feel some responsibility for your behaviour. Uncle Alec and Aunt Mildred are very strict about the Prince. They have to be. And inasmuch as one of the reasons for entrusting him to them was the advantage of being given Uncle Hector's particular attention, really I don't know...."

At this moment Sir Hector himself came into the room, and his wife broke off to ask him what he thought.

"What do you think, my dear, about this proposed visit to Alec and Mildred? Could you recommend Jasmine in the circumstances? I know that in many ways she might make herself very useful. You must learn ludo, Jasmine, if we let you go. The Prince is very fond of ludo. But——" Lady Grant paused, and Jasmine, who did not at all want to entertain the royal lunatic, hurriedly suggested that she should go and live with Selina at Rouncivell Lodge while Uncle Matthew was recuperating at Bournemouth.

"What extraordinary notions you do get hold of," her aunt declared.

"Extraordinary!" Cousin Edith echoed.

Both ladies looked at Sir Hector as if they supposed that he would at once certify his niece insane after such a remark. He did not seem to find the notion so extraordinary, and his wife went on hurriedly, for she was realizing that Jasmine's suggestion of living with Selina attracted her husband.

"I'm inclined to think that Selina will not stay long at Rouncivell Lodge," she said. "After her behaviour during poor old Uncle Matthew's illness you may be sure that she will receive no help from me. Frankly, I shall do my best to persuade Uncle Matthew that she is an unsuitable person."

How glad Jasmine would have been to retort with a sarcastic remark about Aunt May's behaviour! But she could not; she was falling back into complete dependency; she would soon begin to wither, and she gazed at Cousin Edith as if she were a Memento Mori, a skeleton whose fingers pointed warningly at the future.

"Anyway," said Jasmine to herself when she took her seat in the train at Paddington, "this is the last lot. And if they're worse than the others it won't be so bad to come back to Harley Street."

Colonel Alexander Grant was and always had been outwardly the most distinguished of the Grants. He had escaped the excessive angularity of his elder brothers, and although he was much better looking than Sholto, Jasmine's father, there was between them a family likeness, by which Jasmine was less moved than she felt she ought to be. In fact, the amount she had lately had to endure of family duties, family influence, family sensibilities, had made her chary of seeming to ascribe any importance at all even to her own father so far as he was a relation. The Colonel, in addition to being an outwardly distinguished officer in a Highland regiment of repute, had married one of the daughters of old Sir Frederick Willoughby, who was Minister at the Court of the Grand Duke of Pomerania at the time when Captain Grant, as he then was, found himself in Pomerania on matters connected with his profession. He had not been married long when the Boer War broke out, his success in which as an intelligence officer put into his head the idea of becoming a military attaché, an ambition that with the help of his father-in-law, then Ambassador at Rome, he was able to achieve.

His wife may not have brought him as much money as the wives of Hector and Eneas, but she brought him quite enough to sustain without financial worries the semi-political, semi-military positions that he found so congenial, and through his success in which, coupled with his double relationship to Sir Frederick Willoughby and Sir Hector Grant, he was given the guardianship of the lunatic Prince Adalbert of Pomerania.

Enough pretence of state was kept up at 23, The Crescent, Curtain Wells, to make the Colonel and his wife feel their own importance. He had the Distinguished Service Order, could still reasonably turn the pages of the *London Gazette* two or three times a year with a good chance of finding himself with the C.M.G., and had not yet quite given up hope of the Bath. He had picked up in Rome the Crown of Italy, in Madrid the Order of Isabella the Catholic, while from Pomerania he had received the cordon of St. Wenceslaus, and the third class of the Order of the Black Griffin (with Claws). His responsibility for the younger son of a royal house gave him in Curtain Wells, after the Mayor, the Member, and the Master of Ceremonies at the Pump Room, the most conspicuous position among his fellow-townsmen, and when the barouche which by the terms of the guardianship had to be maintained for His Serene Highness made a splendid progress past the arcades and along the dignified streets of the old watering-place, Colonel Grant, observing the respectful glances of the citizens, felt that his career had been a success.

Aunt Mildred, even as a girl, had been considered eccentric for a Willoughby; her marriage with a soldier of fortune had done nothing to cure this reputation; association with Prince Adalbert had done a great deal to develop it. To this eccentricity was added a strong squint.

Military attachés are notorious for the cynical way in which they sacrifice everybody to their careers, and it might be argued in favour of Colonel Grant that he had sacrificed himself as cynically as any of his friends.

Jasmine's visit opened inauspiciously, because by mistake she travelled down to Curtain Wells by an earlier train than the one to which she had been recommended by her aunt; she therefore arrived at The Crescent about two o'clock without having been met at the station. When her aunt came to greet her in the drawing-room, Jasmine had an impression that she was still eating, and apologized for interrupting her lunch.

"Lunch?" repeated Aunt Mildred, still making these curious sounds of eating. "We finished lunch at twelve, and we dine at four." The sound of eating continued, and made Jasmine so shy that she was speechless until she suddenly realized that what she had mistaken for incomplete mastication was merely the automatic play of Aunt Mildred's muscles on a loosely fitting set of false teeth. Mrs. Alexander Grant, unaware that she was making this noise, did not pay any attention to her niece's want of tact; but Jasmine was so much embarrassed that she evidently did not make a favourable first impression.

The spacious Georgian proportions of the drawing-room at 23, The Crescent, were destroyed by a mass of marquetry furniture, antimacassars, and photographs in plush and silver frames of royal personages, the last of which gave the room an unreal and uninhabited appearance like the private parlour of a public-house where respectable groups of excursionists take tea on Sunday afternoon; for these people with ridiculous coiffures and costumes, signing themselves Albertina or Frederica or Adolphus, were as little credible as a publican's relatives.

However, Jasmine was too anxious about her presentation to His Serene Highness to notice anything very much, and if she had offended her aunt by arriving too soon or by not knowing the time for dinner, she made up for it by asking how she was to address the Prince. This was a topic on which her aunt obviously liked to expatiate, and she was delighted to be asked to instruct Jasmine how to curtsey, and to inform her that he was always addressed as 'Sir' in the English manner, because his mother, the Grand Duchess, had expressed a wish that the more formal German mode of salutation should be dispensed with in order to provide a suitable atmosphere of simplicity for the simple soul of her youngest son.

"Is he very mad?" asked Jasmine.

"Good heavens, child," her aunt gasped, "I beg you will not use that word here. Mad? He's not mad at all."

At that moment the door opened to admit a diminutive figure in livery. Jasmine was just going to curtsey under the impression that it was the Prince, when she heard her aunt say, "What is it now, Snelson?" in time to realize that it was the butler.

"His Serene Highness is being rather troublesome, madam," said Snelson.

"Oh? What is the matter?"

"Well, madam, when he got up this morning he would put on his evening dress, and now he wants to go for a drive in evening dress."

"Why, Snelson?"

"I think he wants to go to the theatre again. He enjoyed himself very much last night. Quite a pleasure to hear him chuckling when he got home. I told him if he was a good boy he should go again next week, but he went and lost his temper, and now he's gone and thrown all his lounge suits into the area. The maids are picking them up as fast as they can. Perhaps you could come up and speak to him, madam? He's got it into his head I'm trying to keep him from the theatre."

"Such a boy!" sighed Aunt Mildred, and her intense squint gave Jasmine a momentary illusion that she was referring to Snelson. "Such a boy! You see what a boy he is. He's as interested in life as a sparrow. *You're* going to be devoted to him, of course. You'll rave about him."

Jasmine was wondering why this was so certain, when one of the maids came in to say that it was not a bit of good her collecting His Serene Highness's clothes, because as fast as they were collected, he was throwing them out of the window again.

"And he's started screaming," added the maid.

"Snelson, you ought never to have left him," Aunt Mildred said severely. "You ought to have known he would start screaming. You should have sent for me to come up."

"I've locked him in his room, madam."

"Yes, and you know that always makes him scream. He hates being locked in his room."

Aunt Mildred went away with Snelson, and Jasmine was left to herself, until Uncle Alexander came in and got over the awkwardness of avuncular greetings by asking her what all the fuss was about. She told him about the Prince's throwing his clothes out of the window, which her uncle attributed to excitement over her visit.

"No, I don't think it's that," said Jasmine. "I think he wants to go to the theatre again."

"Oh no, he's excited about your visit. You must humour him. Very nice fellow really. Very nice chap. And as sane as you or me if you take him the right way. I think Snelson irritates him. If he wants to put on evening dress, why shouldn't he put on evening dress? So silly to thwart him about a little thing like that. I can always manage him perfectly well. I spoke to my brother Hector about it, and he agreed with me that there are only two ways to deal with lunatics ... with patients, I mean ... either to give way to them in everything or to give way to them in nothing."

Jasmine thought this sounded excellent if ambiguous advice.

"Now I humour him," said the Colonel. "The other day he heard some tactless people talking about electric shocks, and he got it into his head that he couldn't touch anything without getting an electric shock. Well, you can imagine what a nuisance that was to everybody. What did I do? I humoured him. I put a saucer on his head and told him he was insulated, and he went about carrying that saucer on his head for a week as happy as he could be. He's forgotten all about electricity now. Take my advice: humour him." At this point Snelson came down again.

"If you please, sir, Mrs. Grant says His Highness insists on wearing his evening dress."

"Well, let him wear his evening dress, damme, let him wear it," the Colonel shouted. "Let him wear it. Let him wear his pyjamas if he wants to wear his pyjamas."

"Very good, sir," said Snelson in an injured voice as he retired.

A few minutes later the subject of all this discussion appeared in the drawing-room.

Prince Adalbert Victor Augustus of Pomerania was a tall and very thin young man, though on account of his habit of walking with a furtive crouch he did not give an impression of height. He had a sparse beard, the hairs of which seemed to wave about upon his chin like weeds in the stream of a river. This beard did not add the least dignity to his countenance, but he was allowed to keep it because it was considered unsafe to trust him with a razor, and he would never allow Snelson to shave him. He walked round an ordinary room as if he were crossing a narrow and dangerous Alpine pass, and he would never let go his hold of any piece of furniture until he was able to grasp the next piece along the route of his progress. Owing to this way of moving about, Jasmine, when he first came into the room, thought he was going to attack her. She supposed that it would be discourteous to watch him all the way round the room, and she could not help feeling nervous when she heard him behind her. Mrs. Grant, perhaps because she was nearly as idiotic as the Prince himself, assumed the airs of a mother with him, and always addressed him as Bertie.

"Now, Bertie, be a good boy," she said, "and come and shake hands with my niece. You've heard all about her. This is little Miss Jasmine."

The Prince suddenly released the piece of furniture he was holding, and just as some child makes up its mind to venture upon a crucial dash in a game like Puss-in-the-corner, he rushed up to Jasmine, and after muttering "I like you very much, thank you, little Miss Jasmine," he at once rushed back to his piece of furniture so rapidly that Jasmine had no time to curtsey. She was not yet used to the direction of her aunt's eyes, and now observing that they were apparently fixed upon herself in disapproval, she began her obeisance. The Prince evidently liked her curtsey, for he began curtseying too, until the Colonel said in a sharp whisper: "For goodness' sake don't excite him. The one thing we try to avoid is exciting him with unnecessary ceremony." So evidently her aunt had not been looking at her, and this was presently obvious, because while she was telling Snelson to order the barouche, her eyes were still fixed on Jasmine.

"Are you coming for a drive, dear?" she asked her husband. "It was quite sunny this morning when I woke up."

The Colonel shook his head.

"And now, Bertie," she went on, "be a good boy and put on your other suit."

"I want to go to the theatre," the Prince argued.

"Well, you shall go to the theatre to-night."

"I want to go now," the Prince persisted.

"Now come along, your Serene Highness," said Snelson. "Try and not give so much trouble, there's a good chap. You can go to the theatre to-night."

However, the Prince did not go to the theatre that night, for after a stately drive through Curtain Wells, from which Jasmine on the grounds of untidiness after a journey excused herself, they sat down to play bridge after dinner. Jasmine did not know how to play bridge. Her uncle told her that her ignorance of the game did not matter, because she could always be dummy, the Prince also being perpetual dummy. Even as a dummy, the Prince wasted a good deal of time, because he had to be allowed to play the cards that were called for, and it took him a long time to distinguish between suits, let alone between court cards and common cards. He had a habit, too, of suddenly throwing all his cards up into the air, so that Snelson was kept in the room to spend much of his time in routing about on the floor for the cards that his royal master had flung down. The Prince had other obstructive habits, like suddenly getting up in order to shake hands with everybody in turn, which, as Mrs. Grant said, expressed his delightful nature, although it rather interfered with the progress of the game.

When the Colonel, with Jasmine as his dummy partner, had beaten his wife and the Prince, he became jovial, and there being still half an hour before the Prince had to compose his excitement prior to going to bed, a game of ludo was suggested. This would have been a better game if Prince Adalbert had not wanted to change the colour of his counters all the time, which made it difficult to know who was winning, and impossible to say who had really won. The Colonel, after humouring him in the first game, grew interested in a big lead he had established with Red in the second game and objected to the Prince's desire to change him into Green. It was in vain that Jasmine and her aunt offered him Yellow or Blue: he was determined to have Red, and when the Colonel declined to surrender his lead, the Prince decided that the game was tiddly-winks, which caused it to break up in confusion.

Prince Adalbert was really too idiotic to be bearable for long. Living in the same house with him was like living on terms of equality with a spoilt monkey. There were times, of course, when his intelligence approximated to human intelligence, one expression of which was a passion for collecting. It began by his going down to the kitchen when the servants were occupied elsewhere and collecting the material and utensils for the preparation of dinner. Not much damage was done on this occasion, except that the unbaked portion of a Yorkshire pudding was concealed in the piano. On another occasion he collected all Jasmine's clothes and hid them under his bed. Aunt Mildred evinced a tendency to blame Jasmine for this, even going so far as to suggest that she had encouraged him to collect her clothes, though in what way this encouragement was deduced except from Jasmine's usual untidiness was not made clear. Snelson was ordered to keep a sharper look out on his master, as it was feared that from collecting inside the house, he might begin to collect outside the house, which, as the Colonel said, would be an intolerable bore. The passion for collecting was soon after this exchanged for a desire to cohabit with owls, the Prince having observed on one of his drives a tame owl in a wicker cage outside a small fruiterer's shop. The owner of the bird was persuaded to part with it at a price, and the Prince drove home in a state of perfect bliss with his pet on the opposite seat.

"It's really lovely to watch him," said Aunt Mildred.

"Never known him so mad about anything as His Serene Highness is now about owls," said Snelson. "He'll sit and talk to that owl by the hour together."

The Prince's devotion to the bird occupied his mind so completely that it was thought prudent to import two more owls in case anything should happen to the particular one upon which he was lavishing such love. The first owl remained his favourite, however, and it really did seem to return his affection, in a negative kind of way, by never actually biting the Prince, although it bit everybody else in the house. Jasmine had no hesitation about encouraging him in this passion, because it kept him so well occupied that bridge, ludo, and tiddly-winks were put on one side, and the Prince himself no longer screamed when he had to go to bed. In fact, he was only too anxious after dinner to get back to his room in order to pass the evening saying, 'Tu-whit, tu-whoo!' to his owls. Unfortunately there was begotten from this association an ambition in the Prince's mind to become an owl himself, and when one evening the Colonel found him with six feathers stuck in his hair, perched on the rail of the bed and trying to eat a mouse he had caught, the owls were banished. The Prince's desire to be an owl was not so easily disposed of. For some time after his pets had disappeared he replied to all questions with 'Tu-whit, tu-whoo!' and once when the Colonel impatiently told him to behave himself like a human being, he rushed at him and bit his finger.

"Who started him off in this ridiculous owl idea?" the Colonel demanded of his wife irritably. "Nice thing if the Baron comes over to find out how he's getting on, and finds that he believes himself to be an owl. You know perfectly well that they don't really approve of his being looked after in England, and I can't understand why Jasmine doesn't make herself more pleasant to him. We all thought before she came that she would be a recreation for him. It seems to me that he's much madder now than he's ever been yet."

"Oh, hush, dear!" Aunt Mildred begged her husband, having vainly tried with signs to fend off the threatened admission of the Prince's state of mind.

But the Colonel's finger was hurting him acutely, and he would not agree to keep up the pretence of the Prince's sanity.

"You can't expect me to go about pretending he's not mad. Why, the people come out of the shops now in order to hear him calling out 'Tu-whit, tu-whoo!' as he drives past. Supposing he starts biting people in the street? I really do think," he added, turning to Jasmine, "that you might put yourself out a little bit to entertain him. Of course, if he bites you, we shall have to do something about it, but I don't think he will bite you."

Luckily the Prince's memory was not a strong one, and a week after the owls had been banished, he had forgotten that such birds existed.

From envying the life and habits of an owl His Serene Highness passed on to imitating Mrs. Alexander Grant's squint. This was an embarrassing business, because evidently neither the Colonel nor Snelson liked to correct him too obviously for fear of hurting Mrs. Grant's feelings. As for her, either she did not notice that he was manipulating his eyes in an unusual manner, or she supposed that he was paying her a compliment. She was such a conceited and idiotic woman that she would have been flattered even by such imitation. When he first began to squint across the table at Jasmine, she supposed that it was an old habit of his temporarily revived; but in the passage the next day Snelson came up to her and asked if she had noticed anything wrong about His Serene Highness's eyes. Jasmine suggested that he was squinting a little bit, and Snelson replied: "It's those owls."

"I thought he had forgotten all about them."

"He's for ever now trying to make his eyes look like an owl's."

"Oh," said Jasmine doubtfully, "I hadn't realized that. I thought that perhaps...." and then she stopped, for it could not be her place to comment to the butler on his mistress's squint.

"You think he's trying to imitate the old lady?" asked Snelson in that hoarse whisper that clung to his ordinary method of speech from his manner of asking people at dinner what wine they would take. "Oh no, he wouldn't ever imitate her. He might imitate you, though!"

"In what way?" asked Jasmine, rather alarmed.

"Oh, you never can tell," said Snelson. "He's that ingenious, he'd imitate anybody. He started off imitating me once, and, of course, through me not being very tall, I didn't quite like it. The Colonel thought he was imitating a frog when he came into the room like me, and if I hadn't been here so long, I should have left. I wish you'd take him up a bit—you know, encourage him a bit, and all that. Time hangs very heavy on his hands, poor chap. I got the cook's little nephew once to come in and amuse him of an afternoon, but it was stopped. Etiquette you know, and all that. Of course, etiquette's all very well in its way, and I'm not going to say etiquette isn't necessary within bounds; but he wants amusing. If you can bring him in a toy now and again when you go out for a walk. I don't mean anything as looks as if it could be eaten, because he'll start in right off on anything as looks as if it could be eaten. But any little nice toy, not that small as he can get it right into his mouth, and not that big as he can hurt himself with it."

Jasmine supposed that Snelson knew what he was talking about, and next day she bought the Prince a small clockwork engine. He enjoyed this for about two minutes; then he got angry with it and stamped on it; and when Snelson told him to behave himself, he pulled Snelson's hair, upon which the Colonel intervened and reproved Jasmine for exciting His Serene Highness. The atmosphere at 23, The Crescent, began to get on Jasmine's nerves. It seemed to her pitiable that for the sake of the honour of being guardians of a royal imbecile her uncle and aunt should abandon themselves to a mode of life that in her eyes was degrading. The long dinners dragged themselves out in the November twilights, and though the Prince ate so fast that if only he had been concerned dinner would have been over in ten minutes, a pretence of ceremony was maintained, and the endless courses must have put a strain on the china of the establishment, for there used to be long waits, during which the Colonel had a theory that His Serene Highness's moral stability would be increased by twiddling his thumbs.

"You may have noticed," he used to say to Jasmine, "how much I insist on his using his thumbs. You no doubt realize that the main difference between men and monkeys is that we can use our thumbs. The Prince has a tendency always to carry his thumbs inside his fingers. I'm sure that if I could only get him to twiddle them long enough every day, it would be of great benefit to his development."

After dinner the old round of double dummy bridge followed by ludo had begun again, and though an attempt was made to vary the games by the introduction of halma, halma had to be given up, because once when the Colonel had succeeded in establishing an impregnable position, His Serene Highness without any warning popped into his mouth the four pieces that were holding that position.

Nor were the drives on fine mornings in the royal barouche much of a diversion. Jasmine could not help feeling ashamed to be sitting opposite His Serene Highness when he made one of his glibbering progresses through Curtain Wells. It seemed to her that by accepting a seat which marked her social inferiority she was endorsing the detestable servility of the tradesmen who came out and fawned upon what was after all no better than a royal ape. She felt that presently she should have to break out—exactly in what way she did not know, but somehow, she was sure. Otherwise she felt that the only alternative would be to become as mad as the Prince himself. Indeed, so much did he get on her nerves that she found herself imitating him once or twice in front of her glass, and she began to realize that the proverbial danger of associating with lunatics was not less great than it was reputed to be.

Then came the news that the mother of Prince Adalbert, the Grand Duchess herself, proposed to pay a visit to England shortly, and, what was more, intended to honour The Crescent, Curtain Wells, by staying in it one whole night. This news carried Aunt Mildred to the zenith of self-congratulation, at which height the prospect of the world at her feet was suddenly obscured by a profound pessimism about the behaviour of her household during the royal visit.

"She is travelling strictly incognito, and is not even to bring a lady-in-waiting," she lamented.

"Incognita, my dear," corrected the Colonel, who had once added an extra hundred pounds a year to his pay by proficiency in one European language.

"I have it," cried Aunt Mildred, and in the pleasure of her inspiration she squinted so hard that Jasmine for a moment thought she had something far more serious than an inspiration. "I have it: you shall act as parlourmaid when the Grand Duchess comes!"

"Me?" echoed the Colonel, who in the vigour of her declaration had forgotten to allow for the squint. However much he owed to his wife for advancement in his profession, he could not quite stand this.

"Not you, silly," she said, "Jasmine."

"What on earth is that going to effect?" he asked.

"Now don't be so hasty, Alec. You've always tried to snub my little ideas. I am much more sensible than you think. And more sensible than anybody thinks," she added. "Ada is an excellent parlourmaid, but she is a nervous, highly strung girl, and I'm quite sure that the mere prospect of entertaining the Grand Duchess...."

"But *she's* not going to entertain the Grand Duchess," interrupted the Colonel.

"Now please don't muddle me up with petty little distinctions between one word and another," said Aunt Mildred. "You know perfectly well what I mean. 'Look after' if you prefer it. Ada has never been trained to look after royalty."

"Nor have I," Jasmine put in. "Snelson's the only person in this house who has been trained to look after royalty."

"Jasmine, I'd rather you were not vulgar," said Aunt Mildred reprovingly. "It's extraordinary the way girls nowadays don't respect anything. If you and Uncle Alec would only wait a moment and not be so ready both of you to pounce on me before I have finished what I was going to say, you might have understood that the suggestion was made partly because I appreciate your manners, partly because I have travelled a great deal and don't find your little foreign ways so irritating as your other relations did.... Where was I? If you and your uncle *will* argue with me, I can't be expected to plan things out as I should like. Where was I, Alec?"

"I really don't know," said the Colonel almost bitterly. "All I know is that Ada's a perfectly good parlourmaid fit to wait on anybody. If the Grand Duchess comes without a lady-in-waiting, she comes without a lady-in-waiting to please herself. Really, my dear, you give the impression that you are unused to royalty."

To what state the hitherto tranquil married life of Colonel and Mrs. Alexander Grant might have been reduced if the discussion about the fitness of Jasmine to act as temporary parlourmaid during the Grand Duchess's visit had gone on much longer, it would be hard to say. The problem was solved, for Jasmine at any rate, by two telegrams arriving within half an hour of one another, one from Aunt May to say that Lettice and Pamela were both ill with scarlet fever, and another from Aunt Cuckoo to say that her little son was ill without specifying the complaint. Both telegrams concluded with the suggestion that Jasmine should pack up at once and come to the rescue. Jasmine would have preferred to go straight away to Aunt Cuckoo; but aware as she was of Aunt Cuckoo's fickleness and knowing that, if she did go to Aunt Cuckoo in preference to Aunt May, Aunt May would never forgive her, a prospect that a short time ago she would not have minded, but which now she rather dreaded, for since her visit to Curtain Wells she was feeling afraid of the future, she tried to avoid making a decision for herself by consulting Uncle Alec and Aunt Mildred. Both of them were sure that she should go to Aunt May, and Aunt Mildred pointed out with what for her was excellent logic: "Lettice and Pamela are both ill and they are both her daughters, whereas this infant is not Aunt Cuckoo's son, and if Aunt Cuckoo deliberately adopts sons she ought to be able to look after them herself."

"In fact," the Colonel said, "I should not be surprised to receive a telegram from Eneas asking *me* to look after Aunt Cuckoo. Well, we shall miss you here," he added; but Jasmine could see that he was really very glad that she was going. Aunt Mildred too was evidently not sorry to escape from the argument about the parlourmaid. Now she could go on believing for the rest of her life that if Jasmine had stayed she would have had her way and turned her into a temporary parlourmaid for the benefit of the Grand Duchess.

The Prince, whose capacity for differentiating the various human emotions was most indefinite, danced up and down with delight at hearing that Jasmine was going away. Aunt Mildred tried to explain that he was really dancing with sorrow; but it appeared presently that the Prince had an idea that he was going away with her, and that he really had been dancing with delight, his capacity for differentiating the human emotions not being quite so indefinite as it was thought to be. When he found that Jasmine was going away without him, he could not be pacified until Snelson had got into a large clothes-basket, and pretended to be something that Jasmine never knew. Whatever it was, the Prince was reconciled to her departure, and the last she saw of him he was sitting cross-legged in front of the clothes-basket with an expression on his face of divine content. She thought to herself with a laugh as she drove off that Snelson would probably spend many hours in the clothes-basket during the next two or three weeks. In fact, he would probably spend most of his time in that clothes-basket, until the Prince found another pet upon which to lavish his admiration, or until he grew envious of Snelson's lot and decided to occupy the clothes-basket himself.

Chapter Eleven

THERE is no doubt that if Lady Grant could have found the smallest pretext for blaming her niece, she would have held her responsible for the scarlet fever which had attacked her daughters. As it was, she had to be content with dwelling upon the inconvenience of Jasmine's succumbing to the malady.

"You so easily might catch it," she pointed out, "that I do hope you'll bear in mind what a nuisance it would be for us all if you did catch it. Of course, those who understand about these things may decide it would be more prudent if you did not expose yourself to any risk by going to visit the poor girls." Lady Grant could never miss an opportunity to emphasize the mysterious and sacerdotal omniscience that belonged to the profession of medicine. "Those who understand about these things will tell us what we must do. But meanwhile, although I am only speaking as an ignoramus in these matters, I should say that if you always remembered to disinfect your clothes and all that sort of thing and were very careful to follow the doctor's directions, there would be no danger of your catching scarlet fever yourself. I need not tell you what a terrible blow it was to me when I had to give my consent to their being taken away from Harley Street to a nursing home. A terrible blow! But your uncle felt that it would not be fair to his patients if they stayed in the house. That's the worst of being a doctor. He has to think of everybody. Poor dear children, and there's so little one can do! In fact there's really nothing one can do except take the darlings grapes every day."

The rules of the nursing home were more strict than Lady Grant had expected, and, much to her indignation, permission to visit the patients was denied to Jasmine, who thereupon suggested that, since she could not be of any use in nursing her cousins, she ought to go and help Aunt Cuckoo with the illness of her adopted son.

"And what about me?" demanded her aunt. "You seem to forget, my dear child, and your Aunt Cuckoo seems to forget, that I have a slight claim to consideration. As if the girls' illness was not enough, Cousin Edith must needs go and carelessly visit some friend of hers at Enfield and bring back with her a violent cold, so that what with her sniffling and sneezing and snuffling it's quite impossible to stay in the same room with her. So, at this moment of all others, I am left entirely at the mercy of the servants, who after all have quite enough work of their own to run the house properly, and really I'm afraid I cannot see why you should go to Aunt Cuckoo."

It was thus that Jasmine found herself after what Aunt May now called her adventures of the last eighteen months in that very position which Aunt May had no doubt arranged in her mind when she first wrote and insisted on her niece's leaving Sirene and coming to England. Cousin Edith's cold, which Jasmine had to admit was one of the most aggressive, the most persistent, the most maddening colds she had ever listened to, was ascribed by Aunt May to the London climate in winter, and as soon as Jasmine was fairly at work on her aunt's correspondence, Cousin Edith was sent away to recuperate in Bognor, where it was generally understood at 317, Harley Street she would remain for the rest of her life. If anything more than the cold had been needed to confirm Aunt May in her resolve to get rid of Cousin Edith, it was the death of Spot.

"So long as poor old Spot was alive," she said to Jasmine, "I never liked to send poor Edith away. The poor old dog was very devoted to her, and I'm bound to say that poor Edith with all her faults was very devoted to dear old Spot. But Spot has gone now, and I don't feel inclined to form fresh ties by getting a puppy. Puppies have to be trained, and I very much doubt if Cousin Edith is capable of training a puppy nowadays. She seems to have gone all to pieces since she caught this cold. I told her at the time that I could not understand why she wanted to make that long journey to Enfield. She came back on the outside of the tram, you know. It's all so unnecessary."

Spot had died when the famous cold was at its worst, and the grief Cousin Edith had tried to express was not more effective than a puddle in a deluge. The body was sent to the Dogs' Cemetery, and through having to represent Cousin Edith at the funeral Jasmine nearly caught a cold herself. She did sneeze once or twice when she got home; but Aunt May talked at such length about colds that Jasmine made up her mind that she simply would not have a cold, and she actually succeeded in driving it away, for which her aunt took all the credit.

The night before Cousin Edith left to recuperate at Bognor she invited Jasmine up to her room, when Jasmine realized that the poor relation was perfectly aware what a long convalescence hers was going to be, and perfectly aware that her visit to the seaside would only be terminated by her death.

"In many ways, of course," she said, "I shall enjoy Bognor, and in many ways I shall probably be happier at Bognor than I have ever been here. I quite understand that Cousin May requires somebody more active than myself. She is a woman of immense energy, and when I look at her nose I sometimes think that there may after all be something in character reading by the face. I often meant to take it up seriously. I once bought a book on physiognomy when I was a girl and gave readings at a bazaar. I made quite a lot of money, I remember—sixteen shillings. It was for a new set of bells for my uncle's church at Market Addleby. As his curate said to me, very beautifully and poetically, I thought, when I handed him the sixteen shillings: 'You will always be able to think, Miss Crossfield'—my uncle never encouraged him to call us by our Christian names on account of the parish—'always able to think every time the new bells ring out for one of our great Church festivals, that your little labour of love this afternoon and this evening has contributed a melodious note to one of the most joyful chimes.' I remember my uncle, who was a very jocular man for a clergyman, observed when this was repeated to him that if I had only made a little more money it might have been called Edith's five-pound note. I remember we all laughed very much at this at the time. But as I was saying to you, my dear ... let me see, what was I saying to you?... oh yes, I remember now, I wanted to give you this little brooch which contains some of my grandmother's hair when she was a baby. I've often noticed that you've very few little mementoes; I noticed it because I haven't very many myself. Now with regard to this room, which you will probably occupy when I've gone, it really is a delightful room, in fact the only little fault it has is that the bell doesn't ring. In some respects that is not a bad fault, because no doubt the servants do not like answering bells all the time, and I think I have been rather tactful in never once suggesting that it should be mended. I'm only telling you this so that you shall not go on ringing and ringing and ringing and ringing under the impression that the bell is making the least sound. I remember it was quite a long time before I found out that it was broken, and I derived an impression at first that the servants were deliberately not answering this particular bell. I shall miss poor old Spot very much, but Hargreaves has a married sister whose cat has a very nice kitten which she wants to give away, and her little boy is meeting me with it in a basket at Victoria to-morrow. If you are ever down at Bognor at any time, of course I shall be very glad to see you and give you a cup of tea. My address will be 88, Seaview Terrace. You can see the sea from the corner of the road, so you won't forget the name of the road. But how will you remember the number? Of course, it's eleven times eight, but you might forget that too."

"I'll write it down," said Jasmine brightly.

Cousin Edith looked dubious. "Of course, yes, to be sure you can do that. But supposing you mislay the address?"

"Well, I don't think I shall ever forget eighty-eight," Jasmine affirmed with conviction.

Cousin Edith had worn black ever since it was settled that she was to leave Harley Street, or perhaps it was a tribute to the late Spot. Jasmine, looking at her, thought that she resembled a daddy-longlegs less nowadays and more one of those wintry flies that survive the first frosts of autumn and spend their time walking up and down window panes in an attempt to suggest that if the window were open they would be out and about, delighting in the brisk wintry weather.

"Well, good-bye," Cousin Edith was saying. "I shall be in such confusion to-morrow morning that I may not have time then to say good-bye to you properly. I won't kiss you on the mouth because of my cold. I wonder if you will be as sorry to leave 317, Harley Street as I am, when *you* have been here fifteen years."

Jasmine thought for a moment that Cousin Edith was being malicious and sarcastic; but apparently she meant exactly what she had said.

The next day Jasmine moved into the vacant room, and if Cousin Edith's mourning brooch had contained a lock of her own hair instead of a grandmother's she would not have thought it inappropriate, for the departure of the poor relation had impressed her mind like a death more than a visit to the seaside.

It is hardly possible to picture anybody who lives between Baker Street and Portland Road, however happy he may be, however much in love with life he may feel, as able to maintain an attitude toward life more vital than the exhibition of waxworks in the galleries of Madame Tussaud. There were moments when Jasmine felt that the waxworks were the real population of this district, and sometimes when in the late dusk or at night she was walking down Harley Street or any of the neighbouring streets she would receive a strong impression that all the houses were serving like stage scenery to give nothing but an illusion of reality. This morbid fancy might be justified by the fact that so many of the houses actually were unoccupied at night, and that in the daytime they were haunted not inhabited by figures in the world of medicine who by the uniformity and convention of their gestures and observations had no more life than waxworks. Moreover, passers-by in Harley Street and the neighbourhood had among them such a large proportion of sick men and women that even if one ignored the successive brass plates of the doctors, their presence alone would be enough to cast a gloom on any observer that happened to come into daily contact with such a procession of afflicted individuals.

Jasmine's window, high up in the front of the house, never contributed anything to the gaiety of her private meditations, and she used to think that if a famous prisoner, he of Chillon or any other, had been invited to change his outlook with her own, he would soon have begged to be put back in his dungeon. Many human beings, ailing, miserable, poverty-stricken, victims of misfortune or suppliants of fate, have found in a window their salvation. Jasmine was not one of these. She never seemed able to look out of her window without seeing some hunched-up man or wrapped-up woman who was being helped up a flight of steps, at the head of which the conventionally neat parlourmaid would admit them to their doom; and she used to picture these patients when the sleek doors closed behind them being greeted by the various doctors in attitudes like those of the poisoners in the Chamber of Horrors. There was one figure, that of Neil Cream, a gigantic man with a ragged beard and glasses, who stood for her behind every door in Harley Street. In fact, Jasmine was suffering now when she was twenty the kind of nervous distortions of imagination and apprehension through which most London children pass at about eight. And really, considering her experiences in England since she arrived from Italy, so many of them had to do with disease and death and madness that her morbid condition was excusable. When she was staying with Uncle Alec and Aunt Mildred she had been amused by Prince Adalbert, but now, looking back at that experience, she began to feel frightened, just as when one sees a ghost, one is more frightened when the ghost has vanished than when it is actually present. Looking back now on Uncle Matthew's illness she was again seized by a fear and repulsion which at the time had been merged in indignation. Looking back on her visit to Aunt Cuckoo and Uncle Eneas, the whole of it was now shrouded in an atmosphere of unhealthiness; and looking back further still to her last memory of Sirene, even that was blackened by the sorrow of her father's sudden death. As for the house she was living in at the moment, her sensitive mind could not fail to be affected by the thought that so many of the people who passed along that spacious hall and waited round that sombre table littered with old *Punches* and *Tatlers* and odd numbers of unusual magazines were either mad or moving in the direction of madness. Sir Hector Grant's waiting-room was probably one of the most oppressive in Harley Street, because it had no window, but was lighted from above by a green dome of glass, to Jasmine curiously symbolical of the kind of imprisonment to which madness subjects the human soul. The absence of Lettice and Pamela at the nursing home, although Jasmine had not the slightest desire to see them or hear them ever again, added in its own way to the general air of depression. When Lettice and Pamela were in the house the sense of contact with the ordinary frivolities of the world was never absent; but without them the house became nothing but a cul-de-sac, a kind of condemned cell, so deep did it lie under the spell of dreadful verdicts.

In addition to these influences that spoilt her leisure time, Jasmine's work with her aunt did not encourage her to look upon the brighter side of life. Those numerous charities were no doubt a pleasure and a pride to their originator, but Jasmine, who lacked the sustenance of the egotism that inspired them, was only impressed by the continuous reminder they gave her of the world's misery. The Club for Tired Sandwichmen was for Aunt May something upon which to congratulate herself, an idea that had occurred to no other prominent philanthropist. It was Jasmine's duty to harrow subscribers' feelings with details of the private lives of sandwichmen in order to extract from them as much as would help to maintain the three bleak rooms in a small street off Leicester Square, where these wrecks and ruins of human endeavour could take refuge from the rain and cold outside. Upon Lady Grant herself the individual made not the least impression unless he came into the Club drunk and broke one of the chairs, in which case she interested herself sufficiently in his future to banish him from the paradise she had created.

When Jasmine first again took up secretarial work for her aunt, she wrote all the letters.

"But really I think I shall have to find you another typewriter," said Aunt May after a week of this. "I always understood that convent-educated girls were taught to write well; but your handwriting resembles the marks made by a fly that has fallen into the ink-pot."

"I think I feel rather like a fly that has fallen into the ink-pot," said Jasmine.

Her aunt did not pay any attention to this retort; but a few days later the new typewriter arrived, and it was conferred upon her as if it was a motor-car for her own use.

"I really do think that with this beautiful new machine you might do some of Sir Hector's work too," suggested Aunt May. "That is, if he can be persuaded to send a typewritten letter."

Luckily for Jasmine Sir Hector's ideas of the courtesy owing from a medical baronet did not allow him to do this. He continued to employ a clerk with a copper-plate hand to send in his bills, so Jasmine was not called upon to help him in any way.

"You will have a lot of time on your hands," Aunt May regretfully sighed after her husband had declined the use of the typewriter for himself. "Don't I remember your once saying that you sewed very well? That, surely, they must have taught you at the convent. Cousin Edith used sometimes to sew for me, and there is always her machine standing idle."

Perhaps Cousin Edith's ingratiating touch had spoilt that machine for another. When Jasmine tried her hand on it, it behaved like an angry dog, gathering up the piece of work, the hem of which it was being invited to stitch, worrying it and pleating it and tearing pieces off it and chewing up these pieces, until first the needle snapped and then some of the mechanism made a noise like a half empty box of bricks. It was plain that nothing more could be done with it.

"Ruined," declared Aunt May when she came upstairs to see how Jasmine was getting on. "Well, I hope you'll take a little more trouble over the flowers for the dinner-table to-night."

The only mechanical device that Jasmine could think of in connection with flowers was a lawn-mower, so she felt safe in promising that the dinner-table should present an appearance of a little more trouble having been taken with it than with the piece of work in the sewing-machine. These dinner parties were by no means the least irritating products of her cousins' illness, which had struck Lady Grant as an excellent opportunity for inviting all their most ineligible acquaintances while her daughters were away; and Jasmine, who did not enjoy even the pleasure of being able to choose between more than two evening frocks, felt bored by these dreary men and women, for whose existence she could not imagine any possible reason, let alone discover a reason for asking them out to dinner. Two or three days before one of these occasions Aunt May's invariable formula was that Jasmine was going to be put next to a most interesting man, and always half an hour before the gong sounded she would decide that she must take Mrs. So-and-so's or Miss What's-her-name's place next to somebody who was not interesting at all. She was used, in fact, by her aunt very much as umbrellas are used to reserve seats in a train.

A month or five weeks passed thus, after which Lettice and Pamela emerged from hospital, unable to talk of anything for several days except the details of their peeling. It was now decided that they required change of air, and the question of Jasmine's ability to look after her uncle while his wife and daughters went to Mentone was debated at some length.

"It would be such an opportunity for you to learn housekeeping," said Aunt May. "And if you were a success, who knows, I might even let you take entire charge of the house when I come back. I wonder...." She hesitated, awe-struck by her vision of the future. "I don't want to move Cousin Edith from Bognor. Her cold is quite well now, and it would be such a pity to start her off with it again. And she's apt to irritate your uncle in little things. Of course, he likes people to be attentive to him; but he hates them to make a show of being attentive. And Cousin Edith was always rather apt to make a show of being attentive. You won't do that, will you, dear?"

Jasmine promised that she would not do that, and in the end she was left with her uncle in charge of the house. She decided at once that the only way to manage Hargreaves and Hopkins and the rest of the servants was to make friends of them and become as it were one of themselves. On the whole she rather liked this, and she found that down in the kitchen below the level of Harley Street even Cook became a human figure. As for Hopkins and Hargreaves, they were like butterflies emerging from those two pupæ that waited on the other side of the baize door separating the world below stairs from the world above.

Jasmine found that this communion with the servants was the only natural way in which she could still associate with humanity, and in consequence of it she found herself being more and more completely cut off every day from the family with which she was living. Lady Grant would unquestionably have condemned such society as degrading; but since nothing was offered her in its place, Jasmine continued to frequent the servants' company, and before many weeks had elapsed she had almost come to regard her cousins, her aunt, and her uncle from the point of view of the servants' hall, as eccentric beings living in a queer inaccessible world. She used to think that she might just as well have been left quietly in Sirene. Looking back on the motives for bringing her to England, it was now clear to Jasmine that no real consideration for her future had actuated any of her relatives. She did not mean to suggest to herself that they had consciously or deliberately thought out a plan by which she could be made useful to each in turn; but they all of them had tried to make her useful, and she supposed that such an attempt was like the instinct that leads a person to accept a useless ornament for a bad debt rather than be left with nothing. They had probably all been afraid that if she stayed in Sirene by herself, sooner or later some scandal would supervene which would necessitate more trouble in the future than they felt bound to exert in the present. Really, she thought to herself, she should be happier if she quite definitely ceased to be Miss Jasmine Grant, and became Jasmine, a parlourmaid. But, of course, Jasmine would be considered too flowery a name for service, and she should be known as Grant. Grant! A not unimpressive name for a parlourmaid. She once actually discussed the project with Hargreaves, Hopkins, and Cook; but they evidently thought she was mad to suggest such a thing; they evidently thought it would be better to go on serving in Heaven than begin to reign in Hell; not one of them had a trace of Lucifer in her temperament.

And so a dreary year passed away, a long dreary year during which Jasmine's most breathless and most daring ambition was to be a parlourmaid, her most poignant regret that she had not stayed long enough at Curtain Wells to have rehearsed the part.

"I cannot say how greatly I think you have improved, Jasmine," said Aunt May one day just a year after Jasmine had gone to Harley Street. "You were so wild at first, so heedless and impulsive. But I notice with pleasure that you are quite changed. I was speaking about it to your uncle to-day, and I suggested to him that as a token of our appreciation of the effort you have made to recognize what we have already done for you we should allow you an extra ten pounds a year. You are at present getting ten pounds a quarter, and we discussed for quite half an hour whether it would be better to allow you twelve pounds ten shillings a quarter or to present you with the extra ten pounds all at once, say on your birthday or at Christmas or on some such occasion. Of course, we did not want you to suppose that you are to regard this in any way as a substitute for a Christmas present. It is not. No, you are to regard it as an expression of our approval."

Ever since she had been in England, Jasmine had ceased to believe in the reality of anything talked about beforehand, so she thought no more about that extra ten pounds. But sure enough at Christmas she received it, and not only the ten pounds, but also a parrot-headed umbrella from Aunt May, a sachet of handkerchiefs from Lettice, the particular monstrosity in porcelain that was in vogue at the time from Pamela, and a kiss from Sir Hector.

Although Lettice and Pamela were not yet even engaged to be married, social life at 317, Harley Street was conducted on the principle that at any moment they might be. There could have been few young men about town who had escaped having tea there at least once. None of them interested Jasmine in the least, and it was perhaps just as well that she was not interested, because if she had been interested she would certainly have had no opportunity of displaying her interest owing to the fact that she always had to pour out tea. A woman pouring out tea for one man can make of the gesture a most alluring business; but a woman pouring out tea for twenty young men cannot escape disenchantment, however charming she may be at leisure. The fumes of the teapot, the steam from the kettle, the wrinkles provoked by her attempt to remember who said he did and who said he did not take sugar, all these combine to ravage the sweetest face. As for the dinner parties, although they belonged to another order of dinner parties compared with those given when Lettice and Pamela were away, there always seemed to be one person at least for whose presence of a dinner party, nay more, for whose very existence in the world no excuse could be found. This person invariably took in Jasmine. No doubt her relatives individually never intended to be positively unkind. Whatever unkindness came to the surface was inherent in her position as a poor relation. Besides, nowadays she seldom offered any occasion for people to be unkind to her. She sometimes would ask herself with a show of indignation how she had allowed herself to surrender to this extent; but she had to admit that from the moment she entered Strathspey House she had foreseen the possibility of such a life's being in store for herself, and looking back at her behaviour during the first eighteen months of her stay, she could not see that at any point she had made a really determined stand against this kind of life. To be sure, she had had a few quarrels and arguments; she had delivered a few retorts. But what ineffective self-assertion it had all been! She had had at any rate one opportunity of striking out for herself during Uncle Matthew's illness, and what a muddle she had made of it, because she had been too proud to force herself upon Uncle Matthew, and because with a foolish dignity that was in reality nothing but humility she had given way to his unwillingness to confess an obligation.

And another year passed; a year of writing letters for her aunt in the morning, of going downstairs to see Cook about this, and of going upstairs to talk to Hargreaves about that, of running round the corner to Debenham and Freebody's to see if they could match this for the girls, or of spending the whole morning at Marshall and Snelgrove's with her aunt to see if they could match that for her.

On Christmas morning Lady Grant took her niece aside and confided to her that, so heavy had been her own expenses and so heavy had been Sir Hector's expenses, she was sure Jasmine would understand if she did not receive the extra ten pounds as usual. To hear Aunt May, one might have supposed that the donation had been customary since her niece's birth.

"Our expenses are going to be even heavier this year," she announced. "There is so much entertaining to do nowadays."

When she first came to England Jasmine might have commented at this point on the fact that Lettice would be thirty next birthday and that Pamela was well in sight of being twenty-nine. But two complete years in Harley Street had taken away her desire to score visibly, and she was content nowadays with a faint smile to herself.

"What are you laughing at?" her aunt asked. "It is one of the few rather irritating little tricks you still have, that habit of smiling to yourself suddenly when I am talking to you. Some people might think you were laughing at me."

"Oh no, Aunt May," Jasmine protested.

"No, of course I know you are not laughing at me," her aunt allowed. "But I think it's a habit you should try to cure yourself of. It's apt to make you seem a little vapid sometimes."

"Yes, I often feel rather vapid," Jasmine admitted.

"Then all the more reason why you should not let other people notice it," said her aunt; and Jasmine did not argue the point further.

The loss of the ten pounds meant that Jasmine would not be able to have a new evening frock that winter. She was not yet sufficiently dulled by Harley Street not to feel disappointed at this. It has to be a very beautiful evening frock which does not look dowdy after being worn twice a week throughout the year, and the better of Jasmine's two evening frocks was nothing more than pretty and simple on the evening she put it on for the first time.

"Another long miserable year," she thought. "Nothing new till the twenty-fifth of March. All this quarter's allowance has gone in Christmas presents."

Jasmine's most conspicuous present that year was a sunshade that Aunt May had bought at the July sales.

"As if one wanted a sunshade in England," Jasmine said to herself.

Chapter Twelve

THE new year opened with such a blaze of entertaining that even Hargreaves, who was much more reticent than Hopkins, allowed herself to observe to Jasmine that it really seemed as if her ladyship was determined to find husbands for Miss Lettice and Miss Pamela at last. The atmosphere of the house was charged with that kind of accumulated energy which is the external characteristic of all great charitable efforts. If Lettice had been a new church tower that had to be paid for or if Pamela had been a new wing for a hospital, it would have been impossible to promote a fiercer intensity of desire to accomplish something at all costs no matter what or how. January twinkled like a Christmas tree with minor festivals; but on February 14th—the date was appropriate, although it was not chosen deliberately—Lady Grant was to give a large dance in the Empress Rooms.

"And if it's successful," she told Jasmine, "I daresay I shall give another dance in May."

Jasmine refrained from saying "If it's unsuccessful, you mean," and merely indulged in one of those irritating little smiles.

"Oh, and by the way," her aunt added, "did you see that your old friend Harry Vibart has succeeded to the title?"

She looked at her niece keenly when she made this announcement; but Jasmine was determined not to give her the gratification of a self-conscious blush. Nor was it very difficult to appear indifferent to the news, because, as she assured herself, Harry Vibart, by his readiness to acquiesce in her decree of banishment and by his complete silence for over two and a half years, was no longer of any emotional importance. At the same time, no girl who had been compelled to spend such an empty or rather such a drearily full two years as she had just spent could have helped letting her mind wander back for a moment, could have helped wondering whether if she had behaved differently, everything might not have been different.

"Of course, one does not want to say too much," said Lady Grant, "but one cannot help remembering what great friends he and the girls were some years ago, and really I think ... yes, really I think, Jasmine, it would be only polite if we sent him an invitation."

Jasmine's heart began to beat faster; not on account of the prospect of meeting Harry Vibart again, but with the effort of preventing herself from saying what she really thought of her aunt's impudent distortion of the true facts of the case.

The re-entry of one person from the past into her life was followed by the re-entry of another; for that very afternoon, a bleak January afternoon of brown fog, Hopkins came up to tell Jasmine that Miss Butt had called to see her and to ask where should she be shown? The only people who ever came to see Jasmine were dressmakers with whom she had been negotiating on behalf of her aunt and her cousins, and for whose misfits Jasmine was to be held responsible. These dressmakers were usually interviewed in the dining-room; but Hopkins informed Jasmine that Miss Butt had emphatically declined to be shown upstairs and had expressed a wish to interview her in the servants' hall. Such a request had affronted Hopkins' conception of etiquette, and she was anxious to know what Jasmine intended to do about it. Jasmine was on sufficiently intimate terms with the servants by now to explain at once that Miss Butt and her ladyship were never on any account to be allowed to meet face to face, and she asked Hopkins if she thought that Cook would mind if in the circumstances she made use of the servants' hall.

"No, Miss Jasmine, I don't think she would at all," said Hopkins. "In fact from what I could see of it when I come upstairs, they was getting on very well together. But I didn't think it right to say you'd come down and see her there, until I had found out from you whether you would "

"All right, Amanda, I'll come down at once." Nowadays Jasmine was allowed in her own room to call Hopkins Amanda.

Mrs. Curtis, the cook of 317, Harley Street, was a woman of some majesty, and when she was seated in her arm-chair on the right of the hearth in the servants' hall, she conveyed as much as anyone Jasmine had ever seen the aroma of a regal hospitality mingled with a regal condescension. When Jasmine beheld the scene in the servants' hall she could easily have imagined that she was watching a meeting between two queens. Selina, in a crimson blanket coat, wearing a ruby coloured hat much befurred, with a musquash stole thrown back from her shoulders, was evidently informing Mrs. Curtis of the state of her kingdom; Mrs. Curtis was nodding in august approval, and from time to time turning her head to invite a comment from Hargreaves, who like a lady-in-waiting, stood at the head of her chair, whispering from time to time: "Quite so, Mrs. Curtis." Grouped on the other side of the table and not venturing to sit down, the junior servants listened to the conversation like respectful and attentive courtiers.

As soon as Selina saw Jasmine, she jumped up from her chair and embraced her warmly.

"An old friend come to see you," said Cook with immense benignity.

"Dear Selina!" Jasmine exclaimed. "How nice to see you again!"

"The pleasure's on both sides," said Selina. "Mrs. Vokins is dead."

Jasmine looked at Selina in astonishment. Nothing in the style of her attire suggested such an announcement; in fact, she could not remember ever having seen Selina wear colours before, and that she should have chosen to break out into crimson on the occasion of her friend's death was incomprehensible.

"When did she die?"

"Six months ago," said Selina. "And I went into strict mourning for six months. Last night she appeared to me, as I've just been telling Mrs. Curtis here. She said she was very happy in heaven; told me to stop mourning for her, and pop round to see you."

"Wonderful, isn't it?" Mrs. Curtis demanded from her juniors, who murmured an unanimous and discreet echo of assent.

"Then Mrs. Vokins was saved after all?" said Jasmine. "I remember you used to think that she couldn't be saved."

"Some of us think wrong sometimes," said Selina.

"That's true, Miss Butt," put in Cook.

"Some of us think very wrong sometimes," Selina continued. "And it's perfectly clear Mrs. Vokins was sent down to me to say as I'd been thinking wrong."

"Wonderful, isn't it?" Cook demanded once more.

85

"'I'm very happy in heaven, Miss Butt,' was her words, and though I hadn't time to ask exackly which of my friends and relations was up there with her, I put it to myself it was unlikely Mrs. Vokins would call and tell me she was very happy unless she shortly expected me to join her. She was never a woman who cared to disappoint anybody. So I'm looking forward to seeing a lot of people I never expected to see again. In fact I've given up the Children of Zion and turned Church of England, which my poor mother always was, until a clergyman spoke to her in a way no clergyman ought to speak, telling her what to do and what not to do, until she turned round in his face and became a Primitive Methodist, where she always poured out the tea at the New Year's gathering. Yes, Mrs. Vokins has been a good friend to me, and she's been a good friend to you, because she put it into my head to come down here and ask you if you'd like to come and live in my rooms at Catford where she used to live, with the use of the kitchen three times a week as per arrangement."

"Dear Selina, it's very kind of you to invite me," said Jasmine, "but ..." she broke off with a sigh.

"Which means you won't come," said Selina. "That I expected; and if Mrs. Vokins hadn't of been in such a hurry, I should have told her as much before she went. She vanished in a moment before I even had time to say how well she was looking. 'Radiant as an angel,' they say; and Mrs. Vokins was looking radiant. 'You certainly are looking celestial,' was what I should like to have said."

"Why haven't you been to see me all these two years?" asked Jasmine.

At this point, Mrs. Curtis, realizing that Jasmine and her friend might have matters to discuss which it would be undignified for them to discuss before the servants, asked the scullery-maid sharply if she intended to get those greens ready, or if she expected herself, Mrs. Curtis, to get them ready. The reproof administered to the scullery-maid was accepted by her fellow-servants as a hint for them to leave Jasmine and her visitor together, and when they were gone Mrs. Curtis, rising from her arm-chair like Leviathan from the deep, supposed that after all she should have to go and look after that girl.

"For girls, Miss Butt, nowadays.... Well, I needn't tell you what girls are. You know."

"Yes, I know," said Selina. "A lot of rabbits."

"That's very true, Miss Butt; a lot of rabbits," echoed Cook solemnly as she sailed from the room.

"Well, why haven't you been to see me, Selina?" Jasmine persisted when they were alone.

"Why haven't you been to see *me*?"

"How could I? Uncle Matthew never invited me. Surely, Selina, you can understand I didn't want to force myself where I wasn't wanted. The last thing I wanted to do was to give him the impression that I wanted anything from him. He's had plenty of opportunities to ask for me if he wished to see me. My cousins have been over to see him lots of times."

"They have," agreed Selina, grimly.

"And they never brought me back any message."

"That doesn't say no message was sent," said Selina. "You know as well as I know Mr. Rouncivell never sends a letter of his own accord. He can't bring himself to it. I've seen him sit by the hour holding a stamp in his hand the same as I've seen boys holding butterflies between their fingers."

"Well, you could have written to me," Jasmine pointed out.

"I could have," Selina asserted. "And I ought to have; but I didn't. It's not a bit of good you going on talking about what people ought to have done. If we once get on that subject we shall go on talking here for ever. And it's no good being offended with me, even if you won't show a Christian spirit and go and live at Catford. I think you ought to have learnt to forgive by now. I've been forgiving people by the dozen these last two days. And although I don't think I shall, still you never know, and I may go so far as to forgive *her*," Selina declared pointing with her forefinger at the ceiling to indicate whom she meant.

Jasmine tried to explain that she no longer felt herself capable of taking such a drastic step as going to live in Catford. She found it hard to convince Selina how impossible it was to accept her charity, and she was quite sure that her relatives would not dream of continuing her allowance should she go to Catford.

"In fact, my dear Selina, I think you'd better let me alone. I think that some people in this world are meant to occupy the kind of position I occupy, and I've got hardened to it. I don't really care a bit any more. I have enjoyed seeing you very much, and I hope you will come and see me again. It really isn't worth while for me to make any effort to get away from this. It really isn't."

Selina lectured Jasmine for a while on her lack of Christian spirit—evidently Christian spirit to her mind conveyed something between willingness to forgive and courage to defy—and then rising abruptly she said she must be off. Jasmine heard nothing more from her for some time after this.

Ten days before the dance at the Empress Rooms Sir Hector, for what he insisted was the first time in his life, was taken ill. He was apparently not suffering from anything more serious than a slight bronchial cold, but he made such a fuss about it that Jasmine was ready to believe it really was the first time in his life he had ever been ill. In addition to his apprehensions about his own condition and the various maladies that might supervene, he seemed to think that his illness was something in the nature of a national disaster, like a coal strike or a great war.

"Dear me," said his wife. "I'm afraid it looks as if you won't be at the dance."

"Dance!" shouted Sir Hector as loudly as his cold would let him. "Of course I shan't be at the dance. Even if I'm well enough to be out of bed, which is very improbable, I certainly shan't be well enough to go out. And if I were well enough to go out, which is practically impossible, I certainly shouldn't be well enough to stand about in draughts. No, I shall stay at home. It's a fearful nuisance being ill like this. I can't think why I should get ill. I never *am* ill."

"It's dreadfully disappointing," said Aunt May soothingly. "We had such a particularly nice lot of young men coming. All dancing men, too, so you wouldn't have had to talk to them for more than a minute. I don't like to put it off. I never think things go so well after they've been put off."

"Oh, no, for goodness' sake don't put it off," said Sir Hector. "Quite enough things have been put off on account of my illness as it is. The Duchess of Shropshire is in despair because I can't go and see her. She can't stand Williamson." Dr. Williamson was Sir Hector's assistant. "Nothing serious, of course, but it creates such a bad impression if a man like me is ill. It shakes my confidence in myself. I can't think where I got this cold."

"People do get colds very often in January," said his wife.

"Other people get colds. I never do. Now what is that horrible mess that Jasmine is holding in her hand? It's no good just feeding me up on these messes and thinking that that is going to cure me: because it isn't."

Jasmine was expecting every minute to hear her aunt regretfully inform her that owing to Sir Hector's condition it would be impossible for her to go to the ball, because somebody would be required to stay at home and look after the invalid. To her surprise nothing was said about this, and she began to turn her attention to a new evening frock This was a moment when the extra ten pounds she failed to get at Christmas would have been useful. Notwithstanding the surrender of her pride, Jasmine still had a little vanity; and when she took out of her wardrobe the two evening dresses that had served her during the last year, and saw how worn and faded they were, she began to wonder if after all she should not be glad if her aunt settled things over her head by telling her that she could not go.

She was vexed, when she opened her aunt's correspondence that morning and read that Sir Harry Vibart accepted with pleasure Lady Grant's kind invitation for Wednesday, February 14th, to detect herself the prey of a sudden impulse to go to this dance at all costs. She debated with herself whether she should not ask Miss Hemmings, the little dressmaker in Marylebone High Street who made most of her things, to make her an evening frock on the understanding that she should be paid for it next quarter. At first Jasmine was rather timid about embarking upon such an adventure into extravagance; but she decided to do so, and when she had a moment to herself she slipped out of the house and hurried round to Miss Hemmings' little shop. Alas, Miss Hemmings; like Sir Hector, was also in bed with a bronchial cold; she was dreadfully sorry, but quite unable to oblige Miss Grant by the 14th.

"Oh, well, it's evidently not to be," Jasmine decided.

She got home in time to meet Selina coming up the area steps, dressed this time in a brilliant peacock blue blanket coat and an emerald green hat.

"Selina!" exclaimed Jasmine. "You seem to go in for nothing but clothes nowadays."

"You must dress a bit if you belong to the Church of England," said Selina sharply. "It's as different from the chapel as the stalls are from the pit. Don't forget that."

"Well, I've just been trying to get a frock for a dance on Wednesday, but my dressmaker's ill and...." Jasmine broke off; she did not wish to make Selina think that she was in need of money, for she felt that if she did, Selina would immediately offer to lend her some. And if she accepted Selina's charity it would be more than ever difficult to refuse to occupy those three rooms at Catford.

"Well, that's awkward," said Selina. "But I'll lend you anything you want."

"Oh, thank you very much, but it's an evening frock."

"Ah! That I don't go in for, and never shall. Low necks I shall never come to. Do you want to go to this party very much?"

"I do rather," Jasmine admitted.

"There's my bus," said Selina suddenly; and without a word of farewell she vanished round the corner shouting and waving her umbrella.

The next morning, which was Tuesday and the day before the dance, Jasmine received a postcard on which was printed the current price of coal. She thought at first that it had been put in her place by mistake; but looking at it again she saw written in a fine small hand between the Wallsends and the Silkstones *Come to Rouncivell Lodge to-morrow at eleven o'clock*; and between the Silkstones and the Cobbles the initials M. R.

Aunt May failed to understand how Uncle Matthew could be so inconsiderate as to invite Jasmine to Muswell Hill on the very day before she was giving a dance, and particularly when it would have been advisable in any case that Jasmine should be at home that morning in case her uncle wanted something.

"You must write and tell him you will go later on in the week."

Jasmine agreed to do so, but she added that she should have to give Uncle Matthew a reason for refusing to go and see him, and Aunt May, realizing that such a reason would involve herself with the old gentleman, gave a grudging assent to Jasmine's going that day. Jasmine had difficulty in escaping from Harley Street early enough to be punctual to her appointment with Uncle Matthew, but she managed it somehow, although at one time it seemed as if Sir Hector was wanting so many things which only Jasmine could provide that she should never get away. In the end when Lady Grant was calling 'Jasmine!' from the first landing, Hopkins replied 'Yes, my lady,' and before Lady Grant had time to explain that she did not want Hopkins, her niece was hurrying on her way north.

Jasmine wondered in what gay colours she should find Selina when she reached Rouncivell Lodge; but Selina met her at the gate in her customary black, and advised her sharply to make no allusions to her clothes in front of the old gentleman.

"Why haven't you been to see me before?" Uncle Matthew demanded as the clocks all over the house chimed eleven o'clock.

"I never go anywhere unless I'm asked."

"Well, don't put on your hoity-toity manners with me, miss. Do you expect me, at my age, to come trotting after you? I told your aunt several times I should like to see you."

"She never gave me your message."

"No, I suppose she didn't," said the old gentleman with a grim chuckle. "Now what's all this about wanting a dress for a ball? Do you expect me to provide you with dresses for balls?"

"Of course I don't," said Jasmine, looking angrily round to where Selina had been standing a moment ago. But the yellow-faced housekeeper had gone.

"Well, I've borrowed Eneas' carriage for the day, and I'll take you for a drive. I don't know how that fellow can afford to keep a carriage. I can't. At least, I can't afford to keep a carriage for other people to use, and that's what always happens. Oh, yes, they'd like me to have a carriage, I've no doubt. But I'm not going to have one."

"It's at the door, Mr. Rouncivell," said Selina, putting her head into the room.

Uncle Matthew was so voluminously wrapped up for this expedition that it seemed at first as if he would never be able to squeeze through the door of the brougham; but by unwinding himself from a plaid shawl he managed it.

"Where am I to drive to?" asked Uncle Eneas' gardener in an injured voice. He evidently disapproved of being lent to other people.

"Drive to London," said the old gentleman.

"Where?" the coachman repeated.

"To London, you idiot! Don't you know where London is?"

"London's a large place," said the coachman.

"I don't need you to tell me that. Drive to Regent Street."

The drive was spent in trying to accommodate Uncle Matthew's wraps to the temperature of the inside of the brougham, and in an attempt to calculate how much it cost Eneas to keep a horse, carriage, and coachman. This was a complicated calculation, because it involved deducting from the cost per week not merely the amount saved in artificial manures, but also the amount saved by growing bigger vegetables than would otherwise have been grown.

"But whatever way you look at it," said Uncle Matthew finally, "it's a dead loss!"

When they reached Regent Street, Uncle Matthew told Jasmine to stop the carriage at the first shop where women's clothes were sold.

"Women's clothes?" repeated Jasmine.

"Yes, women's clothes. I'm told you want a gown for a ball to-morrow. Well, I'm going to buy you one."

Jasmine could scarcely believe that it was Uncle Matthew who was talking, and her expression of amazement roused the old gentleman to ask her what she was staring at.

"Think I've never bought gowns for women before?" he asked. "I used to come shopping every day with my poor wife, fifty years ago."

The brougham had stopped at a famous and fashionable dressmaker's, and Jasmine wonderingly followed the old gentleman into the shop.

"I want a gown," said the old gentleman fiercely to the first lady who wriggled up to him and asked what he required.

They were accommodated with chairs in the showroom, and presently a young woman emerged from a glass grated door and walked past them in an Anglo-Saxon attitude.

"You needn't be shy of me," said Uncle Matthew. "I'm old enough to be your grandfather." The show-woman tittered politely at what she supposed was Uncle Matthew's joke.

"Do you like that model?" she said.

"Model?" echoed the old gentleman.

"That gown?" the show-woman enquired.

"Gown?" echoed Uncle Matthew. "What gown?"

"Miss Abels," the show-woman called, "would you mind walking past once more?"

"You don't mean to tell me that what she's wearing is an evening gown you propose to sell me?" asked Uncle Matthew, on whom an explanation of the young woman's behaviour was beginning to dawn. "Why, I never thought she was dressed at all."

The show-woman again tittered politely.

"We consider that one of our most becoming gowns," she said. "So simple, isn't it? Don't you like the lines? And it's quite a new shade. Angel's blush."

"It's very pretty," said Jasmine.

"Well," said Uncle Matthew, "I suppose you know what you want, and I daresay you're right to choose something simple. It's no good wasting money on a lot of frills. How much is that?"

"That gown," said the show-woman. "Let me see. That's a Paris model. Quite exclusive. Thirty-five guineas."

"What?" the old gentleman yelled. "Come out of the shop, come out of the shop!" he commanded Jasmine.

"I never heard of anything so monstrous in my life," he said indignantly to Jasmine on the pavement outside. "Thirty-five guineas! For a piece of stuff the size of three pocket-handkerchiefs! No wonder you can't afford to go to parties! Well, I made a mistake."

"But, Uncle Matthew," Jasmine explained, "I didn't want to go to a fashionable shop like this. There are lots of other shops where evening frocks don't cost so much."

"You can't have a dress made of less than that," he said.

"It isn't a question of amount. It's a question of cut and material."

But the old gentleman could not bring himself to go to another shop. He had suffered a severe shock, and he wished to be alone.

"I'll drive home by myself," he said. "You can get back to Harley Street quite easily from here. Thirty-five guineas! Why, poor Clara's bridal dress didn't cost that."

They were all very curious at Harley Street to know why Uncle Matthew had sent for Jasmine. She did not feel inclined to tell them the real reason, and she merely said that he wanted to see her. Aunt May, however, was feeling bitterly on the subject, and she was suspicious of Jasmine's reticence.

"It's a pity he should have fetched you all that way for nothing," she said. "You had better have done as I suggested and gone the day after the dance. We have all been so busy this morning that poor Uncle Hector has been rather neglected, and I've had to leave a great deal undone which will have to be done this afternoon, and I'm afraid he'll still feel a little neglected, so really, Jasmine, I don't know.... I suppose you'd be very disappointed if you didn't come to the dance, but really I don't know but that it may be necessary for you to stay at home to-morrow and look after Uncle Hector."

"I'll stay at home with pleasure," said Jasmine.

Her aunt looked at her. "Oh, you don't object to staying at home?"

"Why should I? I haven't got a frock fit to wear."

"Not got a frock fit to wear? Really, my dear, how you do exaggerate sometimes! That's a very becoming little yellow frock you wear. A very becoming little frock. You must be very anxious to impress somebody if you are not content to wear that."

Jasmine turned away without answering. She would not give her aunt the pleasure of seeing that the malicious allusion had touched her.

The following afternoon it was definitely decided that Sir Hector was too ill to be left in the hands of servants, and, very regretfully as she assured her, Lady Grant told her niece that she must ask her to stay at home.

"You mustn't be too disappointed, because perhaps I shall give another dance in April or May, and perhaps out of my own little private savings bank I may be able to add something to your March allowance that will enable you to get a frock which you do consider good enough to wear."

Jasmine thought that it would probably annoy her aunt if she looked as if she did not mind staying at home; so she very cheerfully announced her complete indifference to the prospect of going to the dance, and her intention of reading Sir Hector to sleep. Dinner was eaten in the feverish way in which dinners before balls are always eaten. Before starting Pamela called Jasmine into her room to admire her frock, and Jasmine took a good deal of pleasure in telling her that she was not sure, but she thought she liked Lettice's frock better; and to Lettice, whom she presently visited, she said after a suitable pause that she was afraid Pamela's frock suited *her* better than her own did. Hargreaves and Hopkins, who were both indignant at Jasmine's being left behind, took the cue from her and they both praised so enthusiastically the other's dress to each sister, that the two girls went off to the dance feeling thoroughly ill-tempered.

"What would you like me to read you, Uncle Hector?" asked Jasmine when the house was silent.

"Well, really, I don't know," he said. "I don't think there's anything nowadays worth reading. I don't care about these modern writers. I don't understand them. But if they came to me as patients, I should know how to prescribe for them."

"Shall I read you some Dickens?" Jasmine suggested.

"It's hardly worth while beginning a long novel at this time of the evening."

"I might read you *The Christmas Carol*."

"Oh, I know that by heart," said Sir Hector.

"Well, what shall I read you? Shall I read you something from Thackeray's *Book of Snobs*?"

"No, I know that by heart, too," said Sir Hector.

"If you don't like modern writers, and you know all the other writers by heart...."

"Well, if you want to read something," said Sir Hector at last, as if he were gratifying a spoilt child, "you had better read me Mr. Balfour's speech in the House last night."

It was lucky for Mr. Balfour that Sir Hector had not been present when he made the speech, for at every other line he ejaculated: "Rot! Unmitigated rot! Rubbish! The man doesn't know what he's talking about! What an absurd statement! Read that again, will you, my dear? I never heard such piffle!"

In spite of Sir Hector's interruptions, Jasmine stumbled through Mr. Balfour's speech, and she was just going to begin Mr. Asquith's reply when the door of the bedroom opened and Uncle Matthew walked in.

Sir Hector's first instinct when this apparition presented itself was to grab the thermometer and take his temperature; but perceiving that Jasmine was as much surprised as himself and that it was certainly not a feverish delusion, he stammered out a greeting.

"I don't advise you to come into the room, though," he said. "I've got a dreadful cold."

"I thought you were never ill," said Uncle Matthew.

"Well, I'm not. It's a most extraordinary thing. Where I got this cold I cannot imagine," Sir Hector was declaiming when Uncle Matthew cut him short. Jasmine always felt like giggling when Sir Hector was talking to his uncle, because she could not get used to the idea that both Sir Hector and herself should address him as Uncle Matthew. She was still young enough to conceive all people over fifty merged in contemporary senility.

"I thought you were going to a dance," said Uncle Matthew to Jasmine.

"Oh, Jasmine very kindly offered to stay behind and look after me," Sir Hector explained.

"Well, I'll look after you," said Uncle Matthew.

His nephew stared at him.

"Yes, I'll look after you," the old gentleman repeated. "What time do you take your medicine? *You* had better get along to the dance," he said to Jasmine.

"But Jasmine can't go off to a dance by herself," Sir Hector protested.

"Can't she?" said Uncle Matthew. "Well, then I'll go with her, and Selina shall look after you."

He went to the door and called downstairs to his housekeeper.

"I never heard anything so ridiculous," Sir Hector objected.

"Didn't you?" said the old gentleman sardonically. "I'm surprised to hear that. You've been listening to the sound of your own voice for a good many years now, haven't you?"

Perhaps Sir Hector's cold was worse than one was inclined to think, from his grumbling, for if he had not been feeling very ill the prospect of being left in charge of Selina must have cured him instantly.

"When do you take your medicine?" asked Uncle Matthew.

The old gentleman was evidently determined that whatever else was left undone for his nephew's comfort, he should have his full dose of medicine at the hands of the housekeeper. Selina came into the room and settled herself down by the bed with an air of determination that plainly showed the patient what he was in for. Selina's new and more optimistic creed would probably not tend so far as to include Sir Hector Grant among the saved, and what between the patient's pessimism about his state in this world and Selina's pessimism about his state in the world to come, Jasmine felt that if she was ever going to be appreciated by Uncle Hector she should be appreciated by him that night. Meanwhile Uncle Matthew, after settling his nephew, was hurrying her downstairs.

"I have found you a gown after all," he announced, "and a much prettier gown than anything you could find in London nowadays. If that gown yesterday cost thirty-five guineas, the one I have got for you would have cost a hundred and thirty-five guineas."

"Where is it?"

"Where is it?" her uncle repeated. "Why waiting upstairs in your bedroom, of course, for you to put it on. Now be quick, because I don't want to be kept up all night by this ball. I have not been out as late as this for thirty-one years. I'll give you a quarter of an hour to get ready."

Jasmine ran upstairs to her room, where she found Hargreaves and Hopkins standing in astonishment before the dress which Uncle Matthew had brought her. The fragrance of rosemary and lavender pervaded the air, and Jasmine realized that it came from the frock. Uncle Matthew was right when he said that it was unlike any frock that could be found nowadays.

"Wherever did he get it?" wondered Hargreaves.

"It's beautiful material," said Hopkins.

Jasmine was not well enough versed in the history of feminine costume to know how exactly to describe the frock; but she saw at once that it belonged to a bygone generation, and she divined in the same instant that it was a frock belonging to Uncle Matthew's dead wife, one of the frocks that all these years had been kept embalmed in a trunk that was never opened except when he was alone. It was an affair of many flounces and furbelows, the colour nankeen and ivory, the material very fine silk with a profusion of Mechlin lace.

"Whoever saw the like of it?" demanded Hargreaves.

"Whoever did?" Hopkins echoed.

"It would be all right if it had been a fancy dress ball," said Hargreaves.

"Of course, it would have been lovely if it had been fancy dress," Hopkins agreed.

"Well, though it isn't a fancy dress ball," said Jasmine, "I am going to wear it."

The maids held up their hands in astonishment. But Jasmine knew that the crisis of her life had arrived. If she failed in this crisis she saw before her nothing but fifteen dreary years stretching in a vista that ended in the sea front at Bognor. She realized that, if she rejected this dress and failed to recognize what was probably the first disinterested and kindly action of Uncle Matthew since his wife's death, she should forfeit all claims to consideration in the future. Along with her sharp sense of what her behaviour meant to her in the future, there was another reason for wearing the dress, a reason that was dictated only by motives of consideration for Uncle Matthew himself. It seemed to her that it would be wicked to reject what must have cost him so much emotion to provide. What embarrassment or self-consciousness was not worth while if it was going to repay the sympathy of an old man so long unaccustomed to show sympathy? What if everyone in the ballroom did turn round and stare at her? What if her aunt raged and her cousins decided that she had disgraced them by her eccentric attire? What if Harry Vibart muttered his thanks to Heaven for having escaped from a mad girl like herself? Nothing really mattered except that she should be brave, and that Uncle Matthew should be able to congratulate himself on his kindness.

While Jasmine was driving from Harley Street to the Empress Rooms, she felt like an actress before the first night that was to be the turning-point of her career. She was amused to find that Uncle Matthew had again borrowed the Eneas Grants' brougham, and she could almost have laughed aloud at the thought of Uncle Hector's being dosed by Selina; but presently the silent drive—Uncle Matthew was more voluminously muffled than ever—deprived her of any capacity for being amused, and the thought of her arrival at the dance now filled her with gloomy apprehension. The brougham was jogging along slowly enough, but to Jasmine it seemed to be moving like the fastest automobile, and the journey from Marylebone to Kensington seemed a hundred yards. When they pulled up outside the canopied entrance, Jasmine had a momentary impulse to run away; but the difficulty of extracting Uncle Matthew from the brougham and of unwrapping him sufficiently in the entrance hall to secure his admission as a human being occupied her attention; and almost before she knew what was happening, she had taken the old gentleman's arm and they were entering the ballroom, where the sound of music, the shuffle of dancing feet, the perfume and the heat, the brilliance and the motion, acted like a sedative drug.

And then the music stopped. The dancers turned from their dancing. A thousand eyes regarded her. Lady Grant's nose grew to monstrous size.

"Hullo!" cried a familiar voice. "I say, I've lost my programme, so you'll have to give me every dance to help me through the evening."

Jasmine had let go Uncle Matthew's arm and taken Harry Vibart's, and in a mist, while she was walking across the middle of the ballroom, she looked back a moment and saw Uncle Matthew, like some pachydermatous animal, moving slowly in the direction of her aunt's nose.

THE END

Made in the USA
Middletown, DE
05 May 2025